'Reading it was an immersive and absorbing experience. I found myself effortlessly drawn into the three characters' separate but connected inner conflicts, their pain hauntingly real and etched so subtly and believably against the powerful background of storm, sea and sky.'

JOANNA GLEN, author of *The Other Half of Augusta Hope*, shortlisted for the Costa First Novel Award

'In peeling back the veneer of rural Irish existence, so deftly and without flinching, to reveal the often terrible but also at times heartbreaking and utterly beautiful universality of the local, this is a novel that sings with refined truths. The characters who populate *Winter People* are those we glance at every day without realising that each of them is an entire world within the world, fully and truly existing and, occasionally, for better and for worse, colliding. Gráinne Murphy has crafted a stunning and profoundly moving piece of work, one that deserves a broad and enthusiastic readership. It's a book that won't be easily forgotten.'

BILLY O'CALLAGHAN, author of *The Boatman*, a Costa Short Story Award finalist

'Compassionate, contemplative, and absorbing. *Winter People* takes a quiet yet clear look at family, love and loss, and the ways in which people might heal.'

CLAIRE FULLER, bestselling author of *Unsettled Ground*, winner of the Costa Novel Award 2021

'A subtle, addictive, beautifully written story of intertwined lives.'

'*Winter People* is a beautifully written novel about three vulnerable, endearing characters whose lives intertwine in the bleak, alluring winter of West Cork. There is a gentleness and depth here that is engrossing.'

WINTER PEOPLE

Gráinne Murphy

Legend Press Ltd, 51 Gower Street, London, WC1E 6HJ
info@legendpress.co.uk | www.legendpress.co.uk

Contents © Gráinne Murphy 2022
The right of the above author to be identified as the author of this work has
been asserted in accordance with the Copyright, Designs and Patents Act
1988. British Library Cataloguing in Publication Data available.

Print ISBN 978-1-91505-435-7
Ebook ISBN 978-1-91505-436-4
Set in Times. Printing managed by Jellyfish Solutions Ltd
Cover design by Rose Cooper | www.rosecooper.com

Excerpt from Matthew Sweeney's *My Life as a Painter* (Bloodaxe Books,
2018) is reproduced with permission of Bloodaxe Books.
www.bloodaxebooks.com

Winter People received financial assistance from the Arts Council of Ireland

Gráinne Murphy grew up in rural West Cork, Ireland. At university she studied Applied Psychology and Forensic Research. In 2011 she moved with her family to Brussels for 5 years. She has now returned to West Cork, working as a self-employed language editor specialising in human rights and environmental issues.

Gráinne's debut novel *Where the Edge Is* was published by Legend Press in 2020 and *The Ghostlights* was published in 2021.

Visit Gráinne
www.grainnemurphy.ie

Follow her on Twitter
@GraMurphy

and Instagram
@gramurphywriter

*For Mum & Dad – for showing me that reading is the
closest thing to magic and then letting me read all the books*

Reality is only for
those who lack
imagination

'It's all there, you know. It's all in the sea.
The battle is there, the inevitability of it all,
the purpose.'

(Matthew Sweeney, *Dialogue with an Artist*)

STORM

SIS

They had a lie-in, herself and Laddy. A fat morning, the French called it, with their characteristic keen interest in size and shape. It would be more accurate to say she let the dog have a lie-in; Sis herself was awake before dawn. She woke with the birds. She could have stretched across the bed to turn on the clock radio that still sat on Frank's locker, but that risked waking Laddy, and the poor old creature needed his rest. She had pretended not to hear him when he heaved himself onto the bed during the night, too old anymore for stealth. He was a long way from the shivering pup intended for the rain barrel. When Tom Creed's bitch had yet another litter, Laddy was the last in line to be drowned, but one of the grandchildren came in before they could do the job. 'Such crying and carrying on,' Tom told her, leaning on the door frame, the little dog in a straw-filled cardboard box on the front step. 'You're under no obligation to say yes. She'll never know which or whether.' Frank reached past Sis and lifted him out of the box. 'Boys oh boys, aren't you a lucky little laddy all the same?' he said to the pup, and that was enough about it.

Sis didn't begrudge Laddy the rest today – couldn't she have the radio all the day long, and wasn't the sea better company? The wind had picked up overnight and was hurrying the waves a little faster than they would have liked. She could hear their resistance in the way they slapped off the rocks, their cross withdrawal. Beside her, Laddy whuffled in his sleep. Dreaming of a river or a run or a rabbit. She could give him another half an hour. He deserved it. She had the world to do and precious little time to do it, but no matter. Let the wind blow itself out before their morning walk. If they wanted a fat morning, a fat morning they would have. Whose business was it but their own?

Sis pulled the back door closed behind her and snapped the lead on to Laddy's collar. She stopped briefly at the gable wall, bracing herself for the wind waiting for them on the other side. Then she faced into it, planting her feet carefully and holding on to Laddy for ballast. They both knew the lead was for her more than him.

The blinds were still down on the Blue House as they passed. 'We're not the only lay-abeds this morning,' she told the dog, but his tail wag was half-hearted. He was more interested in the fox shit along the verge of the road.

They made their way to the concrete steps that led down onto the beach. When she was a girl, there were no steps here, just a grassy bank you had to scramble down and clamber up. For years she had mourned its loss, but wasn't she glad of the steps now? Much good the beach would be to her if she had to look at it from her window like an invalid.

At the top of the steps, she bent to the concrete base of the newel post and picked up the good-sized stone that lay there, placing it in her pocket before tackling the steps. She dropped the lead, even though there was little fear Laddy would pull ahead and trip her – he was as slow as she was – but if she were to fall, she wouldn't like him to think it was his fault.

Once she reached the sand, she turned right, towards Bunty's Cove. It meant walking into the wind, but it was as well to have it at her back on the return trip.

They progressed down towards the sea where the sand was

more compact. Laddy sniffed around the edges of the waves before squatting to do his business – not so near there was any danger of getting his arse wet but close enough that the sea would shortly tidy it away for her with no need for all the fumbling. Those little bags were nothing but a curse. What must dogs think of them at all, gathering up their shit as if to preserve it like treasure.

She gave Laddy his privacy, turning instead to look at her little house set into the shallow hollow scooped out of the landscape. There were just the two houses on this stretch, her own and the Blue House. If they walked in the opposite direction, away from Bunty's Cove, they would reach the hotel. Closed now for the season, it would open the week before Christmas for well-heeled weddings, then open fully after Christmas for the families worn out from the effort of being together.

Her own little house was looking well. Danny Creed had painted it a handsome dark green the spring before Frank died and it was holding nicely two years on. At the time, Frank had complained about the cost, but it was worth every penny.

Beside it, the Blue House was too big. Too blue. When the owners knocked the old cottage that stood there and began to build something new in its place, Frank watched its progress with keen interest, shaking his head over all their perceived missteps.

'They had right to renovate the cottage,' he said, every inch the armchair architect. 'A two-storey perpendicular extension would have been a far better job.'

'Don't go getting any ideas,' Sis told him, but it was just something to say, certain as she was that her own house would stay the way it was until they were both gone from it.

When she could no longer get him from the bed to the living room, she gave him updates on the progress of the Blue House. Even after work stopped, she made things up for him, describing the arrival of slates and paving slabs, a Belfast sink – 'back in favour,' he said approvingly – a claw-foot bath. One bad day, she gave them a delivery of the wrong size windows entirely and was gratified when Frank found the energy to comment, 'That'll set them back weeks.'

When he was gone, she was lonesome after the work herself and it gladdened her heart when the workmen reappeared at the end of the summer. They were all business and it was a pleasure to see the little changes day by day until they packed up for good a fortnight ago and lights began to come on at night.

Today, the blinds were still closed in the windows of the Blue House. Late rising was a sure sign of a summer woman. Whoever she was, she would find it a penance being this far west in a wet November if she wasn't prepared to get out and see the beauty in the wildness.

In front of Sis, a seagull pecked at the base of the dune. She could walk right up to it, she knew, and it would hold its ground. They were fearless little bullets on air or land, with their four foot of wingspan coiled like a whip around them. Spread wide, they were the length of a child. The length of seven-year-old Bunty, that last summer she was still well and growing, being buried in the sand by her sister, trying not to let the giggles curl and shorten her.

Sis reached into her pocket for the rind off yesterday's slice of ham. Laddy caught the movement of her hand and whimpered briefly.

'The gull is only getting your leavings,' she called to him and he turned back to his business.

Sis threw the rind onto the sand near the bird. 'You like it better when there are no people, I'd say,' she said to the seagull. 'When we're all asleep or afraid or otherwise or elsewhere. You prefer it then.'

The bird grabbed the rind and off he flew, as if to prove her point. An effortless lift, on the ground one second and in the air the next, unleashing a mournful screech that the wind flung to the four corners of the beach or so it seemed. What could be finer, Sis thought, than to call out and find the world has nothing to throw back but your own voice, amplified and grand.

Laddy finished and on they went, the wind tugging at the corners of Sis's woolly cap. Nearly fifteen years she'd had this cap and it hadn't let her down yet. The trick was to buy it a bit tight, the way the wind's fingers would find no purchase. 'There's a man whose hat fits his head,' Frank used to say whenever he met someone he approved of. Someone whose philosophy of life coincided with his own. Not that he would have described it like that.

With the wind at their backs, Sis and Laddy made better ground on the return leg, arriving back at the steps just as the first drops started to fall. 'Even if it buckets down, we can go no faster,' she told Laddy as they stopped to catch their breath halfway up the steps. Not that a bit of rain would make much difference, with the salt, windborne and deep, already in all her creases. At the top, Laddy rubbed his paws in the dampening grass at the side of the road to get rid of the grains of sand. He never liked the feel of it, even as a pup, when he used to run the length of the beach with the sand flying behind him. Sis held on to the newel post, steadying herself before reaching into her pocket for the stone and replacing it on the concrete base. 'There, now,' she said, as much to herself as to the dog. 'There's a mark made on the day.' A little addition and subtraction of their progress through the world. Weren't they entitled to it? Sure, if they didn't notice themselves, who would?

Sis opened the back door to let Laddy into the kitchen, then crossed the yard to the henhouse. It used to be she had to brace herself for the smell before going inside, but that was many years and many hens ago. There was Henny alone now, a cantankerous old bird as likely to peck the hand off her as give an egg.

But lo and behold, wasn't there an egg in the warmth of the straw, as brown and speckled as her palm. 'I was wronging you,' Sis told the hen, but the hen turned her backside to her. She was entitled to it, Sis supposed, after having her egg taken from her and nothing but an insult in return.

Inside, she made herself and Laddy a cut of toast and a mug of tea for their breakfast, humming along to the ads on the radio. She made sure to butter the toast right out to the edges. Anything less and a person felt cheated at the finish. She no longer bothered with the toaster. Wasn't it a waste with the fire already burning in the range? It was a matter of pride to lift the hatch and hold the bread on a long-handled fork, near the lick of flame yet out of danger.

The wind had died down and she heard a car coming along the road. From the living-room window, she saw an old Renault Clio driven by a young woman with a phone clamped to her ear. She called to the Blue House on Tuesdays and Thursdays for two hours. The cleaner, Sis assumed. She had nothing against cleaners or those who used them. Didn't she know as well as anyone – and better than most – that it was honest work? The woman in the Blue House was as entitled to her comforts as anyone. Still, Sis herself would have had three holiday apartments done in that length of time. Though that was when her back was strong, she reminded herself. When her arms and legs were all muscle rather than skin and veins.

Maybe the visitor was a home help. Sis had yet to see the woman, so for all she knew, she was one age with Sis herself, or had been sent to the Blue House for a cure. She would need to get outside if that was the case. The sea and air did a person no good from indoors.

More likely she wasn't ill at all. Several times Sis had

walked past the house and noticed a wine glass on the sill inside the picture window. That wasn't a thing that was ever seen inside this house. Frank wouldn't hear of it. A lifetime teetotaller, his pioneer pin was his pride and joy, moved carefully in the morning to the lapel of his shirt for the day. He would no sooner go out without his pin than without his underpants. When he got sick, she started pinning it to his pyjamas for him so he would feel more like himself.

There were two routes into the pioneers, he told her when they were first courting. Either you were overly fond of the drink or overly fond of God.

'And which are you?' she had asked, half-afraid of the answer.

'I'm the exception, Sis, and well you know it.'

How he made her laugh!

She was smiling as she picked up the black notebook that served as her diary. She used to wonder if it counted as a diary when she wrote it in the morning rather than at night, but sure she had no one to answer to only herself, so *diary* it was.

It started as a habit when the children were babies, when she had to write a list to keep her straight through the day or there was a danger she would take them to the beach and lose the day entirely until the sun was setting. She got into the habit of adding a line or two on her... what? Not so much her feelings – in those days, she used to stride out, her mood in her legs – but her thoughts. Whatever they were. Whatever was uppermost in her mind. Her state-of-the-nation, Frank used to call it and he wasn't wrong.

Well, her nation had held firm while her legs weakened and these days her striding was done on paper. In her old Pitman shorthand, a holdover from when she was poor in time and privacy.

Lonesome was the word that came to mind this morning. For the first while after Frank died, Laddy used to miss the rub of his rough hands. Sis had fashioned a replacement out of a pair of winter gloves stuffed with newspaper and tied them to the back of the chair the way Laddy could rub himself against them, but sure the dog took one sniff and ignored them ever after. He was no fool.

'Me and you, isn't that it?' she said to him then, with every intention of keeping her word.

Sis left the tea bag in the mug while she washed her few bits and hung them on the bars over the range to dry so they would be ready when she needed them. Good thick tights were hard to get her hands on now she didn't get the bus to the city anymore, but as long as she had one pair to wear and one to wash, what more did she need? A person had only the one pair of legs. She gave the tea bag a quick rinse under the tap and left it on the side to dry. She could get her lunchtime cup out of it as well, she took it so weak. Frank used to tease her about it. Whenever one of the children was making the tea, he would lean in and say, 'Mind you just show the cup the tea bag.' It never failed to raise a laugh.

'Didn't the day clear up lovely?' she asked Laddy as she opened the back door to tip the toast crumbs into the yard for the birds. The rain clouds had passed, leaving the sky the watery grey that always reminded her of Mike when he was sick as a child. He used to take to the bed with the smallest thing – a headache, a cold, a pain in his leg, a mean comment from one of his friends. The smallest thing laid him flat. Cathy would rush to bring him what he needed, of course, and stay to entertain him whether he wanted her or not. Doreen had little sympathy for him; she was forever hiding in corners thumbing pages of a book, entirely oblivious to the world around her. After Frank's funeral, she boxed up her treasured childhood books and took them away with her. It stung at the time, but Sis was glad that the care and keeping of Doreen's books was not on her list of things to do. Wasn't it a blessing in disguise when houses emptied themselves?

Even without the books to worry about, there was plenty

to do. The place could do with a good clean for a start. You wouldn't call it dirty – herself and Laddy weren't hard-wearing occupants – but neither would you call it spotless. Restlessness indoors meant Sis was an indifferent housekeeper. Frank learned fast not to bring anyone home unannounced. Not after the time he invited a work colleague for dinner and the pair of them arrived in the kitchen to find Sis waltzing in the door in her bra and pants after an impulse swim. 'The poor man could see everything,' he told her later. 'Could he, faith,' she said back. 'And what about yourself? Did you see anything you liked?' She was young then, and brazen with life.

Sis sighed. She had gone to sleep one night, it seemed, and woken up in an old lady's body. '"Rip Van Winkle" was no story,' she told Laddy. If she had time, she could have explained who Rip Van Winkle was, maybe gone to Doreen's room to take down the book – no, the book was gone – but the day was getting away from her and she had a house to clean and three letters to write and there would be no peace of mind until all that was done.

She could begin the letters now, but it might be better to start with cleaning the bathroom. Get the dirtiest job out of the way. '*Tús maith, leath na hoibre*,' she said aloud. A good start was half the work. She would have earned a bit of fresh air by lunchtime and with a little thought she might outline the first letter in her mind while her hands were busy. Cathy's letter would be the first, she decided. She was the eldest, so it was the right thing. Also the most difficult, of course, but that was neither here nor there. If Sis got Cathy's letter right, Doreen's and Mike's would surely flow easier.

Washing soda. White vinegar. Salt. One kettle of water, then a break to stand in the kitchen doorway and watch the clouds while she waited for the kettle to boil again. They were pale grey horses, darkening towards the west, their restless anger growing. Like her mother watching the clock for her father to stumble home. The first kettle of water went cold while Sis stood in the doorway with the sky for company. Oh well. If she had to scrub that bit harder, it was worth it for a few minutes of sky.

Back to the bathroom. Lower herself to the ground, one knee at a time, genuflecting to the bath. It was altar enough in its day. Saturday nights when the children were growing up, the walls had fairly echoed with whispered secrets. *Bless me, Father, for I have sinned.* Scour the ring all the way around, the edge of the bath hard against her ribcage. It left a bruise no one but herself would see. With Frank gone, she was the sole keeper of her body's map.

Lord but the lino was murder on her knees. She could feel the bumps in the concrete underneath. There was no time to smooth it out when they did the extension. Her mother was in a rush to have everything ready when Bunty came home from hospital and there wasn't time for fiddling and foostering, she said. Sis put her two hands on the side of the bath and raised one knee. A sharp twinge in her hip meant she got no further. She stopped and breathed into it, gentled it, the way you would an animal. At her age, when your body spoke, you listened.

The last time she was in the bath was after Frank's funeral, when Cathy stayed the night and it was safe to get in knowing there was someone to get her out should that awful need arise. Nothing would have pleased Cathy more than to see her mother helpless. It was that alone that heaved Sis up and out under her own steam, letting the water drain away and trying not to think of the sinful waste of all that lovely warmth leaking out of her bones. With the water gone, she was able to roll onto all fours – wouldn't it tickle Laddy to see her stretched the length of the bath! – rising slowly to her knees and to her feet and then, shaking lightly with cold or relief, into her clothes.

Now she tried a cautious movement and her hip twinged again, a bright flash that closed her eyes and drew her breath in sharply. Breathe into it, let it ease. Her gaps and joinings had given her a lifetime, she could give them a few minutes in exchange. There was nothing that couldn't wait.

Opening her eyes, the bright yellow of the rubber gloves blazed like furze, calming her. She always had great time for furze. For anything that gave its best in the winter when people needed it most. Sis lifted one hand off the bath, then the other, *careful careful*, and began to peel them off. Pinch the little finger, pull the glove an inch. Pinch the ring finger, pull an inch. Middle finger. Index finger. Thumb. Then grasp the loose flapping yellow and work it off. Her mother used to drag the cuff of the glove over her knuckles, turning it inside out to reveal the pink of her hand. Like skinning a rabbit. The easy option, right up until it came to turning it right-side out. Better in the long run to take the few minutes this way and leave them ready for the next time.

She chanced an experimental shimmy of her hips and all seemed well. Sis unfolded her leg again – this time the hip held, but don't think too much about it, don't jinx it – and hauled herself upright. A genuflection in reverse. How she didn't pull the bath from the wall, she would never know. Her knees creaked. There now, wasn't she standing just fine and no need for all the fuss and worry? With both confession and penance done.

She did the sink and the toilet. Might as well while she had everything dragged out. She slid the cracked mirrored door of the cabinet above the sink. It held little of hers besides the pot of Vaseline she rubbed into her cheeks and forehead before going out for a walk on bitter days. Frank's razor she put in the bin. The pill bottles were half-full. She would have to ask the chemist to get rid of them properly. In the meantime, they could wait on the kitchen sill. She would have done the lino as well, but only a fool would risk kneeling and rising again so soon.

In the doorway, she turned to look at her work, nodding with satisfaction at what she found. She had plenty of practice cleaning, after all. For money above in the hotel and for nothing here at home.

'They can inspect the bathroom all they like now. They

won't find Sis Cotter wanting,' she told Laddy, but he was already in the kitchen, pressing his old bones close to the heat of the range.

There was plenty eating in an egg if you added milk to the pan. Sis spooned it onto a piece of toast and took it outside to the back wall. Frank had built the wall himself, determined that the yard would be sheltered from the worst of the weather. Making his own mark on the place, Sis guessed. Bettering her father's time as man of the house. But work was scarce that year and the wall was up to waist height when the money ran out. Frank never finished it, even after things picked up. She no longer remembered why. Maybe he was spending his Saturdays in town by then.

Yet here was the selfsame half-wall, the perfect height in the end. At her feet, the chickweed and shepherd's purse were snug in its shelter. Pale and brave, they had always reminded her of Bunty. When she told Frank that, he went and planted her favourite wild pansies beside them, so that herself and Bunty could chat the seasons away, as he put it.

Sis set the plate carefully beside her so she could tip her face back to look up into the sky. At her age, to do the two things together could result in a mischief. She had made it this far on her own and she didn't intend to be helped out of the place now. Above her, the sky was a wintry blue, so pale it was almost glassy. As if you could see through into whatever was beyond if you were patient. 'Can you see me, Frank?' she asked. 'Didn't the wall work out grand?' Laddy snuffled at her feet, but he would have to be content with a small bite. Eggs didn't suit his system and he was too old to have to suffer the shame of not making it to the back door in time.

She was just thinking she could write her letters out there – what better place for it – when the landline rang in the hall. It had to be the solicitor. Cathy – when she phoned at all – insisted on calling her mother's mobile which was either dead or off and so had the unfortunate, and possibly deliberate, result of permanent one-way communication. She could phone Cathy, Sis reminded herself often, but it was held in her mind like an emergency option. More of a touchstone than something a person might really do.

Doreen sent postcards. Dark obscure things that she sketched herself. The back would contain a few brief words, suggesting that whatever it was Doreen was moved to say was really contained in the murky images, if a person had the wit to decipher it. Sis didn't, and Doreen knew it well, which begged several questions about the purpose of the postcards and the emotions they were intended to produce. Sis read them and then pushed them into the desk drawer and hoped her daughter at least was getting something from it all. As for Mike, well. To expect a boy to phone his mother was to swing for the moon. 'Swim for the moon' she used to think the expression was, and she still wished she was right.

Slowed by her musings or her aching knees, by the time Sis got to the phone, the solicitor was taken aback to hear a living person.

'I was expecting your voicemail,' she said.

Sis didn't care what she was expecting, but it was hardly worth the effort of saying so. Instead, she sat on the faded yellow cushion of the telephone table and let the woman talk. Solicitors were long-winded, programmed to squeeze the maximum time out of the minimum work, but she would get to the point eventually.

After Frank died, Sis had gone and sat in the woman's bright office and let herself believe – briefly, brightly – that the house could still be saved. How many times, she wondered, had Frank sat in the same chair and hoped the same thing? Maybe he hadn't believed it at all or had held it as a bright flower of possibility until the office door banged behind him and his shoes hit the footpath outside and the relentlessness of the world reasserted itself.

She half-listened, drawing her finger along the worn

nap of the yellow velvet. When they got it first, she could nearly write her name in it with her fingernail, but time had rubbed it thin.

'That was the final appeal, I'm afraid,' the woman was saying. 'Do you have—'

'What day did you say?'

'With the appeal denied, the court has given you forty-eight hours to finalise your arrangements…'

The woman kept talking while Sis gently replaced the receiver. Thursday. What more was there to say? She was good with a deadline, she reminded herself. When Frank was sick, she had no patience with the level of care needed until the doctor told her they were talking weeks, at best. With something to aim for, a person could brace accordingly.

Thursday, so.

On her way back to the kitchen to start the letters, her foot caught the edge of the plastic runner and she would have tumbled if the wall hadn't been there to catch her. She must remember to take it up before the bailiffs came on Thursday – they wouldn't have the time to be listening to explanations of Laddy's bladder problems. Through the open living-room door, she caught sight of Frank's desk, covered with untidy piles of this and that. It was where everything ended up, a kind of halfway house between everything coming in and going out. He used to be meticulous about sorting it all out. The first Saturday of the month, he would rise from the breakfast table, remove his jacket and hang it on the chair back, then roll up his sleeves and announce he was tackling the paperwork.

'I'm off to tackle the paperwork, Sis,' he would tell her. 'If I'm not out in two hours, it's bested me and you'll have to call in reinforcements.'

Reinforcements were never necessary. Within the allotted time, he would have it all sorted into tidy little heaps: Do, Bin, Keep. She was happy to let him do it, pleased to be absolved of the forced order of it. Charmed, too, that he had kept the first promise he ever made her. The day they met, she was in the laneway behind the civil service building, crying hot tears of frustration at the meaningless moving of documents from here to there with barely a stamp of a difference. He stopped to talk to her and all she could focus on were his hands. Outdoor hands. Rough and capable-looking. Like waves with the tide on the way in. He used to tease her that she only said yes to him because the civil service marriage ban meant she had to give up her job. She married him for his hands, she told him, and regretted neither the decision nor the telling.

The top of the desk was a sea of paper. Easy to know it had fallen into Sis's keeping the last two years. The simplest thing was to sweep her arm across it and let it all fall into a black sack. One or two envelopes landed on the floor, the courts' harp winking up at her. No point opening them now; the solicitor had told her all she needed to know.

The drawers were jammed full. Orderly clutter, she defended herself. There were gas and electricity bills since God was a boy, and for the weekly bin collection back when they still had one. There was a whole section for those calendars sent by the Co-op at Christmas, with Frank's important dates and appointments in neat black biro. She flicked through the one for the year he was diagnosed, but there was no mention of any meeting with the bank or the solicitor, despite the fact they must have seen one another. With that whole calendar year a lie, it nearly jumped out of her hand and into the black bag of its own accord.

The small drawer, she knew, was filled with Doreen's postcards. A better mother would find a shoebox and stack them snug against one another inside, an index of their relationship. A legacy, Doreen herself might call it.

Sis fanned them out on the top of the desk. 'Pick a card, any card,' she instructed Laddy, who watched her with lazy interest. She closed her eyes and reached out, letting her fingers separate one card from its fellows. As luck would have it, it was one of the more recognisable ones. A mushroom, Sis thought, with tendrils floating above it. Or perhaps a jellyfish. Doreen's words on the reverse shed no light either way. *Humans have between 2,000 and 10,000 taste buds. Which is sadder – to taste less or to want to taste less?* That was Doreen. All drifting questions and no answers. Sis held the card for a moment before gathering it together with the others into a neat stack. She rapped them smartly on the edge of the desk to smooth out the lumps, startling poor Laddy, then wrapped them with a thick orange elastic band. *Did you know that Mercury has shrunk by 20km? That is what comes of having a soft core*, the top one told her. Sis smiled. Poor Doreen. What use was sentimentality where she was going? The past had no oxygen, only what it was let steal from the present.

Right in at the back of the bottommost drawer, she found the folder of house correspondence that Frank had hidden from her. If he did, it was because she turned a blind eye, she reminded herself.

'We agreed there would be no bitterness,' she told Laddy, who wagged his tail and had the grace to look ashamed. What anger there was once was gone into the ground with Frank.

It didn't feel right – she shied away from the word 'fitting' – to put these documents in with the gas and electricity bills. The evidence of the life of the house all mixed in with its death. No, she couldn't countenance it. She could find a box for them, she supposed, but that left the problem of what to do with the box then: to leave them here seemed disrespectful, to take them with her unthinkable. They had ample power already without making a millstone of them.

It would be a kindness to burn the lot, she decided, but it would take her a week to feed it all through the range and that was a week she didn't have. 'Forty-eight hours,' she reminded Laddy.

By the gate at the far end of the yard was a rusty barrel

that for years had collected rainwater. Frank used to talk about using it for something purposeful, but the rain was always plentiful and that 'something' never took form beyond Frank filling buckets from it to slosh over the car when he washed it every second Sunday.

That gave Sis an idea. She got the bucket from under the sink and went over and back from the rain-filled barrel to the gully outside the front gate, filling and emptying, filling and emptying. Carrying half-buckets meant it took twice as long, but eventually there was so little left in the base of the barrel that a bath towel was enough to finish the job. It was a curse to lift out, sodden and heavy. In the finish, she had to enlist the rake from the shed, impaling the towel and moving backwards, step by step, until she could drape it over the lip of the barrel, where its own weight took it to the ground. Should she put it in the bin? Sis wondered. Lord knew she wasn't about to salvage the thing. Wringing it would be the finish of her altogether. She would leave it where it was, she decided. The wind would dry it out and lift it up and away to find its fortune. The birds could tear strips off it and use it to line their nests. 'It'll keep the baby birds grand and warm,' she told Laddy, who was watching from the kitchen, his snout poking over the doorstep. She patted her thigh, calling him to her, but he sighed and refused. He didn't trust the rain barrel and she didn't blame him.

There was no storm forecast, but when Sis looked up, the sky had a faint yellowish tinge to it. 'The sky is going to vomit,' Doreen used to tell Mike solemnly before a storm, and Mike would run, wide-eyed, to the window, ever-ready to believe any old thing he was told.

She had better get something to cover the barrel or else she would have to face into the same dreary task later on. The same buckets, the same towel. The same water for all she knew. After some thought, she went and got Frank's raincoat from beside the front door. Wasn't it as well she kept it aside when Cathy was sorting out his clothes to take to the St Vincent de Paul shop in the city?

'Is that everything?' her daughter had demanded and Sis had nodded that it was, yes. All the while thinking guiltily of Frank's coat tucked inside her own on the hanger. Not hidden, exactly. Salvaged. That was the word. Spared from her daughter's ruthless efficiency.

She draped the coat over the barrel, trapping the sleeves and hood underneath by dint of tipping the metal up an inch using a combination of shoulder and hip that would doubtless haunt her later. At her age, it was a rare evening that hadn't an ache or a pain somewhere and sure wouldn't it make a change to be able to identify the source. By the time she was finished, the air had a snap and crackle to it and poor Laddy was cowering under the kitchen table.

She reached in to fondle his ears. 'You're better than any Met Éireann forecast.'

Sis stoked the fire, put the kettle on and watched the sky darken. The house creaked around her, complaining about everything still to be done. It could wait. This was likely her last storm out here on the edge of the Atlantic. If she wanted to drink tea and enjoy it, that was what she would do.

She was always partial to a thunderstorm. Not a wind storm – that was a different order of fear altogether. But the drama of a dark grey sky lit suddenly by a flash of lime green! It put everyone in their place. If she went in for bucket lists, there would be just the one thing on it: to see the Northern Lights. From time to time, the news said they would be visible over the west coast of Ireland, but she hadn't ever struck it lucky with a cloudless night. *Yet*, Doreen would add, if she were here. Was there ever a word that so cruelly separated the young and the old? So full of promise for one and so fat with longing and regret for the other.

Frank used to say thunderstorms were God throwing

a tantrum. Wasn't it just like a man to assume that there was space aplenty for the luxury of temper? If there was a God, he should have better things to be doing, Sis argued. What hope man, if God was no better than to indulge a sulk? Frank thought her view disrespectful. But then he hadn't lost Bunty. He didn't understand that God's decisions could be unacceptable. It was one of the things they argued about. The things she considered their 'loud arguments'. Her cheeks could still redden at the thought of it now. The two of them trying to outdo each other for hurt. Look at me. See me. Give me this one thing. The wasted energy of trying to convince one another who they were and weren't. She wished the children hadn't had to witness it. Through walls, at keyholes, between fingers. Herself and Frank pushing the limits of their love for one another, secure – smug – that it was boundless. They never once thought that their words might linger. That it might be beyond their power to suck it all back into themselves. The genie out of the bottle and smashed glass everywhere she looked.

Count from the flash until you hear the clap of thunder and that's how far away the storm is. It was three miles away yet when she rose and went to the stuff drawer in the dresser, where odds and ends were rehomed to preserve the thin illusion of their usefulness. Behind the string and Sellotape and maybe-dead batteries and clothes pegs, she found a half-finished pad of Basildon Bond with the lined sheet still carefully tucked into the back. Now there was an idea that should never have been cast aside. For all the resources that were on offer to children in schools nowadays, there was no safety net the equivalent of a lined sheet. A bit more rooting in the drawer yielded three biros, one of which still worked. She sat down and began to write straight away. No matter how bad the empty page was, it would be worse with the words on it. The best way to do it was to do it quickly. Cathy first, because she hated storms the most.

Dear Cathy,

I imagine it is getting cold in Newfoundland these past weeks. Here, it remains mild and we are having a thunderstorm at the minute. Poor Laddy is trembling so hard the whole table is wobbling.

I hope that the children are enjoying their 'Fall' school term and not wishing the weeks away until Christmas. Laddy and I are keeping well.

It was both true and untrue. They were keeping well at the time of writing and that was as much as anyone could say maybe. That they were well in the moment.

Lord but she hated her handwriting. A natural left-hander, a much-derided *citeóg*, she was subjected to the humiliation of retraining in school, her wayward interfering hand tied behind her, where she could feel it twitch wretchedly against her back as her right hand laboured. Her writing had deteriorated with lack of practice and straggled across the page like she hadn't the courage of her own thoughts. If it wasn't for the lined sheet, her words might have staggered drunkenly off the side of the page altogether and Cathy would have to come and read the letter off the wood of the table.

Please excuse my writing. My fingers are not what they once were. No doubt you remember me telling you I was a dinger at the shorthand, top of the class, not that it's much good to me now when no one can read it.

Cathy hated her mother's shorthand, Sis remembered. She used to roll her eyes whenever Sis used her Pitman for the shopping list or for some little reminder to herself.

'She's showing off again,' Cathy would declare. Sis had long ceased being 'Mammy' by then. Or even 'Mam' or 'Mother'. It was always 'she'. Whenever Sis heard people on the radio asking for the right to choose their pronouns, she understood it completely. There was no more sneering 'she' than the one her eldest daughter put on her. Why, she wondered now, hadn't she explained that she was ashamed of her handwriting? That in shorthand her squiggles were no worse than anyone else's? Doreen used to beg her to teach it to her, eager even then for secrets. But Sis refused, unable to shake the idea that Cathy was somehow behind it. That she would agree to teach her youngest girl and Cathy would emerge, crowing, from the shadows, questioning her right to any wisdom at all. Would they have been closer if she had taught it to them? Who could say, after all these years? All she knew for sure was that if they could read Pitman, the letter would already be done and her wrist wouldn't ache from the effort of it. She had to write to them all today, otherwise Cathy might have hers first and share it with the others. Sis could imagine her phoning them to read it down the line. Lording her small power over them. Or perhaps taking a photograph so that they, too, could marvel at her poor penmanship. *Poor Mammy. Poor Sis.* The thought was unbearable. One letter in the post and two in her breast would be no solace. The letters must all be written and postmarked the same day. She could do no fairer than that.

The reason I am writing is because I have some difficult news to share. By the time you read this…

By the time you read this…

By the time you read this…

Outside, the storm had passed. If you could call it a storm. It hadn't been much in the finish. A couple of good clatters of thunder and the rest was all rain. Not a real storm, where the wind off the sea carried salt crystals that could tear the skin from your face. Like gloves made of chipped glass.

She closed the writing pad and put it to one side. Laddy needed his evening ramble. What better time for it than in the dusk after a storm, when the air was worn out and acquiescent, the world newborn and clean around it. She called the dog to her and clipped the lead to his collar before gathering her big coat and woolly hat.

'We'll have the run of the place,' she told Laddy, pulling the back door closed behind her. Who knew but the right words would roll in with the waves and lie down at her feet.

In the yard, Sis was pleased to see that the barrel had survived the worst of the storm. Frank's coat was stretched taut over it still, a testament to its quality. That was one thing she and Cathy agreed on, the wisdom of investing in a good winter coat. Frank had worried about it at the time, whether they had the money to spend, and she wished he knew they had chosen well.

They walked slowly in the dark. Sis didn't believe in flashlights. *To know the dark, go dark*, as the poet said. The Blue House was lit up like a Christmas tree, intruding into her peace. The cleaner's car was gone from the drive. The poor woman had driven home in the lashings of rain, imagine.

At the concrete steps, Sis bent and scrabbled her hand around and was glad when it closed around her stone. Into her pocket it went and down the steps, slowly, slowly, Laddy waiting patiently at the bottom. This time, they turned away from Bunty's Cove and towards the hotel. There was the possibility that the storm had shifted the familiar sand landmarks and a person would be a fool to refuse the extra safety of the light. Independent Sis might be; fool she was not.

The front of the hotel was entirely glass, lit from within as if packed to the rafters with holidaymakers. In reality, it was empty and waiting, its lights designed to deter vandals. When she used to clean the holiday apartments, she had to leave the light on in the stairwells for the same reason.

This time of night, the hotel's quiet was eerie. It brought to mind the *Mary Celeste*, that celebrated mystery of her childhood. She remembered hearing it in school and running home to tell her mother and Bunty, as breathless as if the abandoned ship had just been discovered, the food still warm on the plates of the vanished passengers. Sis had lain awake at night, turning it over in her mind, coming up with theories about how and why those onboard disappeared. Was it like the ships that ran aground in the big storms last winter? she wondered. Or angels? Or God himself, maybe? After all, there was the assumption of the Virgin Mary into heaven, where she was taken up body and soul to join Jesus without ever having to die. Did the same thing happen to the people on the *Mary Celeste*? During a big storm, she tested the idea, sneaking out into the yard when her mother was in bed. She had gone around the gable of the house with her arms aloft and, despite the strength of the storm – *almost a hurricane*, the weather forecast called it – her feet barely budged off the gravel.

She should never have told Bunty about her experiment. Since it was decided her sister was too fragile to return to school, she had turned into a right tattletale. Sis got the back of her mother's hand and then the one punishment her mother could rely on. 'No beach for you, Miss Madam,' she said, knowing it was the worst kind of torment.

The best thing about being an adult was that nobody could tell her she couldn't come here. The day after each child was born, Sis brought them here and showed them the sea, the way it might sing in their blood like it did hers. Poor fool, Sis. She would have been as well off in bed resting, like the midwife told her.

Once Laddy did his business, they turned back the way they came. As Sis replaced the stone on the newel post, holding on for another minute while she got her breath back, a fox came trotting along the verge. He stopped when he saw her, as if freezing might prevent whatever came next. 'I'm no danger to you,' she said, and he twitched his brush and held his ground. Laddy was further down the road, already anxious to be home, and didn't turn at the sound of her voice. Why would he, didn't he hear it all day every day? There was nothing new anymore in Laddy's world.

'Have you no home to go to?' Sis asked the fox, but he didn't reply. If he had, she supposed, she would be in far greater trouble.

Her father had come home one evening and told them he had passed a fox half-dead on the side of the road. He had pulled in, he said, then after a bit of thought, reversed the car back over him, getting out to make sure he was dead. Sis had vomited her dinner and been roundly spanked for the waste of food. Later that night, her mother brought her a plate of toast to eat in bed. 'It'll make you feel better,' she told her, but it didn't.

Maybe that was where Cathy and Doreen got their tendency to eat their upset. They were both bigger than they should be. It was another thing they blamed her for, as if she hadn't raised them knowing that if you wanted to eat plenty of butter, you had to walk and earn it.

After Frank's funeral, the pair of them were picking their way through salads and Sis wanted to tell them to have a proper dinner, for the love of God. But if she said anything, she was the worst in the world.

Whatever they were, it was Sis's fault, it seemed. Hers and Frank's. The girls were brought up with too little and were bound to spend their lives making up for it. She sighed. No matter what a person did, they were wrong.

'I have nothing for you,' she said to the fox. 'You have your place and I have mine. For thirty-six more hours yet,' she added, but he had vanished into the darkness.

'Slim pickings,' she announced to Laddy, closing the fridge door. He was unconcerned. Once she was prepared to share, he would happily eat anything.

'It'll have to be a yoghurt,' she told him. 'Vanilla. Not even one of the good ones.' It annoyed her that they still included it in the four-pack, when it was always paddy-last out of the fridge. She couldn't be the only one, surely. Still, there was plenty eating in a yoghurt. Although the dairy didn't agree with her that well these days, it was a small price to pay beside the years-long fear of osteoporosis.

Leaving Laddy to lick the carton, she turned on the yard light and dragged the black sack of paper out to the barrel. Santa with a bag full of pasts.

The air was calm after the storm and there would be little danger in a fire now. She went back inside to fetch the matches and the firelighters. There was a time she would have been ashamed to need artificial help to set a fire, when needing anything more than twists of newspaper and a few dry *cipíns* was wasteful, and waste, according to her mother, was the worst of all the cardinal sins.

But Sis no longer got to town regularly for the newspaper, so it was firelighters or else do without the comfort of the range.

She brought out the kitchen chair and placed it just outside the door. If she had a sentimental notion of sitting beside the flames, there was no one there to laugh at her.

The height of the barrel meant she had to light the firelighters on the ground before picking them up with the tongs and dropping them in, but it was all managed with little difficulty.

'Not a lot of grace, Laddy, but we got there,' she said, pleased, as the flames began to inquire at the sides of the barrel.

In they all went. The oil bills and the electricity bills. The bank statements and school reports. The Christmas cards and medical appointment letters. The insurance certificates and recipes. The holiday ads cut from the newspaper. The calendars and receipts. Wasn't it a powerful thing, the way the fire treated them all the same? Whether they had brought good news or bad, feast or famine, the fire ate them with equal hunger.

Should she be sorrowful? she wondered. No doubt there was a litany of emotions that should accompany a purge. Yet, as the papers caught and curled and turned to ash, she found little had changed within her. She had chosen her memories long ago and those she would carry with her as long as she had her wits. Everything else was clutter.

Doreen would be the one to appreciate the drama of it. She would have changed into a special outfit for the occasion, something appropriate for howling at the moon. The thought made Sis smile and for a second she wondered if she should have called them to come. If they would have wanted to bear witness. She shook her head at her own foolishness. Witness what? Anything they wanted from this house they had taken with them when they left.

The flames rose into the dark of the sky, their cackling and crackling overtaking the low staticky chat from the radio. Let the woman in the Blue House call the guards if she wanted to. As soon as she told them the address, they would sigh and get off the phone as politely as possible. Barrel bonfires were two a penny in these parts.

Frank's papers she left until last. It was a strange thing to hold them over the blaze. They didn't contain him, she reminded herself. There was no further betrayal here. On the top of the pile were those thick envelopes from the courts and solicitor's office. The ones he had hidden from her for so long. He didn't want her to read them and so she wouldn't. 'Until death do us part,' she had said and meant it. She wasn't dead yet and so her words held. Frank's absence didn't alter the intention.

'He was frightened,' she told Laddy when she had thrown them onto the fire and sat back in her chair, her crochet on her lap. 'A person does strange things when they're frightened.'

It was true. Frank was quiet on the drive to the hospital appointment, claiming he needed to concentrate on the road, making noise about the traffic whenever another car came into view. Sis let him be. You didn't stay with someone for nearly fifty years without knowing when they were afraid. It was only in the doctor's office, when the words had been said, the hand dealt, that she realised he had already known. 'One-in-two,' the doctor told them gently. 'It's the world we live in.'

Frank had taken her hand and said nothing. Even then, she assumed it was death he was afraid of. Still so certain that she knew him. Upside down, inside and out.

Last into the barrel was the letter from the courts, granting the bank the eviction order. The solicitor had read it out to her over the phone, the word ringing in her ears. Evicted. Like something out of the famine. They would appeal, the solicitor said. But just in case, she had negotiated a place for Sis in the county home. She called it something else, of course, and hurried to tell Sis she wouldn't need it anyway. Not with the appeal. God love the girl if she believed it herself, Sis thought. Thank God her mother wasn't here to see it. Or poor Bunty.

She watched the flames lower in the barrel, their fierce heat calming now to a pleasant warmth. In the quiet, the radio came through from time to time, little snatches of the world outside the fading circle of light. Sis went inside to make herself a coffee to enjoy for the final few minutes of the fire. She didn't need much sleep and this time of night was exactly when she felt like a cup. It was thirty years since she had given up smoking, but tonight's coffee tasted like cigarettes.

The coffee made the yoghurt's presence felt in her gut and she shifted in her chair and let a crack go. Laddy startled and barked into the yard.

'Settle down,' she told him. 'It was a poor arse that never rejoiced.' He looked at her and settled back at her feet. He had rejoiced plenty in his time.

Sis sat in her kitchen chair in the doorway, Laddy at her feet, and watched the burden of all the daily resentments and disappointments go up in smoke until embers were all that was left.

Lock the back door. Wash face and teeth, careful not to disturb the clean bathroom. Nightdress. Double-check the door. Sit on the edge of the bed, Frank's side.

Her body wasn't fooled by the routine. Sis got up and crossed to the window, looking out into the dark. It was comforting, the dark, with none of the unreasonable expectation of energy and effort that daylight brought. People talked about dying being like walking into the light, but Sis hoped that when death eventually came for her, it would come trailing a quiet dark.

She walked down the hallway into the girls' room, faintly lit with the light blazing from the Blue House. Every light in the place still on, it looked like. If any stray moth was left this late in the year, they would be driven demented.

The room smelled musty and she opened the window, letting the wind flow through. Nobody had slept in here since the night of Frank's burial. The children had arrived within half an hour of one another, carefully choreographed so that none of them were trapped alone with her for long. Doreen was first, all talk about some play or audition or deadline she was missing. What better addition to her arsenal of *poor-me*s than to lay yet another charge at the feet of the place that had, in her own words, *stifled her creativity*? Such nonsense. Not being taken to museums or given piano lessons were hardly such crippling hardships. And as for her accusations that Sis and Frank between them burned all the oxygen out of a room? Well. It was no surprise that Doreen ended up making play-acting her life.

Cathy would have come from the ends of the earth for the funeral. Not because she wanted to be there, but because she wouldn't give it to anyone else to say she didn't make the effort. She hated to be found wanting, Cathy. She had Mike with her, whether to protect or propel him was anyone's guess.

Mike shifted from foot to foot, finding no comfort anywhere in the house. He had her restlessness, but he was cursed with more options than she ever had. It cost him to come, that much was clear, but it cost Sis too, and, God forgive her, she wasn't able to see past it. He seemed smaller somehow, and forlorn, trailing Cathy from room to room like a deflating balloon.

The night of the funeral, the girls shared their room the way they used to. Cathy took a fresh set of sheets from her wheelie case, shaking them out to flower around her.

Sis watched her daughter strip the bed and remake it. Cathy had stood on the landing of her house in Newfoundland, had gone to her hot press – her linen cupboard, she called it these days – taken out a set of sheets and placed them in her case. All to make the point that her mother's domesticity was unreliable. She had earned that criticism, Sis supposed, and held her peace.

'How was he at the end?' Doreen asked, tonguing her top lip, eager for the details.

All she was short was a camera and a notebook. It was distasteful, Sis thought. But the girl's father had just died and she should be charitable. 'He had no pain,' she said. 'The nurses saw to that.'

'They didn't... do anything they shouldn't?' Doreen asked, peering at her mother.

'They did exactly what they were supposed to,' Sis said wearily.

'Did he say anything?' Mike asked suddenly.

'Wasn't it all said already?' Sis answered and the cruelty was a strange balm.

Mike flushed and rocked on his heels.

'I'll make something to eat,' Sis said and went down the hall to the kitchen. Once there, however, she kept on walking. Out the door, along the road, down the steps, onto the beach. Laddy at her heels, confused and looking for Frank. Her shoes sank into the sand, threatening to hold her in place and, for a split second, panic rose in her throat. Then she simply slipped out of them and walked away across the sand in her tights. At the water's edge, she turned and looked over her shoulder at her ridiculous shoes trapped in the sand. In a thousand years, they would be fossils.

For forty-seven years, Frank had stilled her restlessness. Without him, she might never stop moving.

'What'll we do without him, Laddy?' she asked, but the dog had no more answers than she did.

When she got back to the house, Cathy was cracking eggs into one frying pan, while rashers and sausages spat in another at her elbow. She glanced at Sis and said nothing. She didn't need to. It was all there in the triumphant set of her shoulders, the apron she had packed and brought with her and tied around her waist.

One-in-two for cancer these days, the doctor had said, and of the two of them, it was better that she was the one left. Frank alone wasn't a thought that could be easily accommodated. The deterioration that would rapidly follow. His transformation into one of the poor old fellas he used to pity. No. Of the pair of them, she was the better able to withstand. That much she knew to be true.

Now, Sis shivered in the draught from the open window. She had come into the room for something, but what was it? She climbed into the bed to help herself think better, the sheets damp against her bare legs. The next person to get the place would put in central heating, not realising they were smothering the taste of the sea in the air.

Was there something in here the girls would want? Something she should box up and keep to one side for them? But Doreen already had her books and Cathy had made a point of taking nothing. Even the pretty tablecloth and napkin set Sis had sent for her wedding had been returned. *I'm making my own*, Cathy had written. *Perhaps these could be given to someone who needs them more.*

How was she to take that? Sis wondered. What could a person do when their child – their brilliant, practical child, with qualifications coming out her ears – decided that the life of a 1950s housewife was what she saw for herself? What else had driven her to limit her own precious life in this way, if not fear? There was no way to ask, neither in person nor at a distance of two thousand miles.

In the end, Sis went to the gift shop in town and chose a postcard, a nice image of the beach on a summer's morning. It was no word of a lie to say it took everything she had not to just attach the return receipt for the linens. *I wish you both much happiness in your life together*, she wrote on the back instead and sent it off.

You had no need of me then and you don't now, she could write to Cathy. *Didn't I do a damn fine job rearing you to be your own woman? Who knows but you were right to want it all, just not at the same time. You'll come back and visit, I know, but wait until you're ready. I'll be here and we can walk and talk and find peace in one another, maybe.*

LYDIA

Did you ever wake and mistake the sound of the sea for the rush of blood in your ears, Mary? For the monstrous quiet that races in after a thud? The whoosh-thump that for eternal seconds nothing can penetrate? Like wearing headphones full of your own fright. You had no such quiet, I imagine. There was that one phone call followed by many many more, an exponential curve of shock spreading outward from the kerb of the street not one mile from your house. Then the hospital, with its lights and its squeaks and its beeps.

The loudest night in the world.

[Delete. Delete. Delete.]

It was foolish, Lydia knew, the way her heart started to race the moment she pulled the curtains and placed her hand on the cord to raise the blinds in the living room. There was nobody out there, she told herself. Nobody at all.

The world was safely outside her window, the sea securely contained within the aluminium frame. Nothing had changed while her eyes were closed and she was away wherever it was the human mind went when the body gave itself over to sleep. Outside, grey sky met grey sea, the horizon imperceptible. The Earth an incontrovertible sphere. Anyone who believed in a flat Earth should be brought here to see the evidence of their own eyes.

Through the open door to the kitchen, she heard the drone of the coffee machine give way to the series of high-pitched bleeps that meant it was finished. The designers knew that anyone waiting for their morning coffee would need to be summoned the minute it was ready.

Mary had good coffee in the mornings. Lydia knew this for a fact because she had sent her an expensive machine. The twin of her own, as it happened. A little note tucked inside the wrapping, *Thinking of your family.* Written on a compliment slip from the supplier, implying that it was a community gift. Even so, Lydia watched her online banking app carefully to see if the money was refunded. It never was, and so she could think fondly of Mary in the mornings when she made her coffee. Was it such a stretch to imagine they were sharing a cup?

Lydia took the tablet box from the window sill where it lived in plain sight, whether because she lived alone, or as part of a performance of having nothing to hide, or as a reminder. She didn't care to parse her motivations.

She opened the little Tuesday window and shook a blue tablet into her palm. Lydia loved her dispenser. The mint-green box was a tiny gift each morning, an Advent calendar that started afresh each week. She liked it so much, she bought a second box. That one lived in the drawer beside her bed. A fully loaded comfort blanket. At night, if she needed to, all she had to do was reach for the drawer handle and dry swallow her emergency tablets until her heart retreated back to her chest.

Andrew would advise her to keep a glass of water by the bed.

Andrew could fuck off out of her head.

She was alone and her thoughts were her own.

Lydia took her coffee through to the living room and pressed play. Sea sounds filled the room. Waves lapping on the shore, small and sunshiny and safe. The biddable, sunblock-slick summer sea she remembered from her childhood. Yet when she looked out at that same sea from this same house, it was unrecognisable.

Perhaps the sea, too, had been renovated by Andrew, transformed into something grander and altogether more frightening.

Lydia lowered the volume to listen out for the cleaner's car. Sofia, she reminded herself. Therefore: Sofia's car. The little details were important.

Sofia came on Tuesdays and Thursdays for two hours of cleaning and ironing. Lydia was careful to put the radio on just as she arrived. One of those interminably opinionated morning shows. 'Got to keep up with current affairs,' she said that first day, plastering on a rueful smile and gesturing to her laptop as if alluding to work of some sort.

Sofia had come highly recommended by the agency, but Lydia hadn't even read through her references. All she wanted was someone who didn't live locally. Who didn't remember her from summers years ago. Whose conversation didn't imply they were owed a precis of everything that had happened in the intervening years. Sofia was ideal. Having herself picked her life up and moved it somewhere else entirely, she saw nothing strange in someone else doing the same. Just in case, Lydia was careful to tip her handsomely in addition to her pay. Unzipping a wallet was, as ever, an effective means of zipping a mouth. So runs the world, even here at the teetering edge of it.

Outside, the sky darkened and pulled the sea with it.

Perhaps it was the other way around, the sea the ringleader, the more threatening party.

Last night's forecast had said nothing about a storm, at least as far as Lydia was aware. But awareness was somewhat elastic, she found, once the evening poured into the house.

It would be her first storm here. The past two weeks had been cold and drizzly, the light of the day never convincing. She was certain that her childhood summers here were warm and cloudless, the rainy days that must surely have come having been hung up and dried out by her memory.

Surely the storm was nothing to worry about. Andrew had assured her that his men had done a good job on the house and she believed him. What else was marriage good for, if not to take someone's word that they would keep you safe?

She tapped her fingernail on the side of her cup. The thought that a storm might sneak up unbeknownst to the weather service was somehow disquieting. Perhaps they had different standards for what constituted a storm out here where the land met the sea. Her adult knowledge of the place was embarrassingly slight.

She should call the chemist and have them send her new prescription today. She would phone the off-licence as well, she decided. She could do with another bottle of good whiskey.

You would think me spoiled, Mary. You would look at my life here and wonder where the sacrifice was. Who exactly I thought I was fooling.

[Delete. Delete. Delete.]

Sis Cotter walked into view, her old dog padding alongside her, and Lydia slipped in behind the curtain where she couldn't be seen. The woman passed her house four times a day, twice each morning and twice in the evening. Lydia had recognised her immediately. Despite the twenty-five years that had elapsed since her last summer here, she saw that lean figure in the distance and the name *Sis Cotter* appeared with the ease of a daily prayer. Sis Cotter. As a very young child, Lydia had assumed it was a single name, like Anne-Marie or Mary-Rose. It was only when she was a little older that she realised it was her mother's way of referencing her disapproval, although disapproval of what, exactly, was never made clear, even when Lydia eavesdropped on her parents' post-dinner brandy chat while pretending to read.

Sis Cotter wore the same patterned skirts and tights as she had back then, but it wouldn't be true to say she was unchanged. She wore the years on her shoulders, her head tilting forward like a runner at the finish line. Her skin was fresher than any woman her age had a right to – Lydia's mother, if she were to see her, would be driven to an envious gin. It was the fresh air, Lydia supposed. The saltiness of it like a daily facial.

Once Sis Cotter was safely past, Lydia would move into the window proper and watch her progress along the road until her hatted head disappeared around the curve of the bend.

The steps would appear ahead of her on the right. Steps that Lydia used to dawdle down, staring at her feet and wondering how she would fill the time until her mother let her come back inside for her lunch and afternoon rest.

Was Sis a pet name? A throwback to a time when the old lady on the road was the pet of her family? Perhaps the beloved and much younger baby sister to a gaggle of rough-and-tumble boys. She must have a real name, too. Eileen, maybe. Or Margaret. Something that breathed generations. Lydia wondered if she had grandchildren. A little Katie or Rosaleen somewhere, named for beloved Granny Sis.

Below her, Sis Cotter reappeared on the beach. Some days she turned left, others right. If Lydia took note, she could probably discern a pattern. People were never as mysterious as they liked to believe.

Perhaps she and her dog were trying to get their steps in, but unable to do it all in one go. Did steps apply to the elderly? Ask her again in thirty years. Forty, maybe. People lived longer now, age – time – increasingly malleable. Far more likely Sis simply didn't sleep a lot anymore. Lydia remembered as much from her grandmother, who had lived with them briefly when she was a girl.

Briefly being the operative word. Nobody had thought to forewarn Lydia that Granny had moved in so as not to die alone, and part of Lydia still felt it as a faint injustice.

'Darling, you must have known,' her mother said when an adult Lydia asked her. 'Why else would she have come?'

Did old people wake early because they knew they would shortly be sleeping for all eternity?

All eternity, what a menacing expression. Lydia shivered slightly, her arm hair rising to meet the fine wool of her sleeves.

Do days feel like an eternity to you, Mary? Getting Nick up and washed and dressed and fed in the mornings and then the same in reverse in the evenings. Your strong, beautiful boy as dependent on you now as the day he was born. A painful comparison, I imagine. One you might wish gone from you. Like that film where the couple broke up and each tried to permanently erase one another from their memories. What kind of a life can be squeezed from the middle of all that wiping?

[Delete. Delete. Delete.]

Lydia couldn't call to mind the name of that particular film. She wondered if this was what it would be like to have dementia. It didn't run in her family, to the best of her knowledge, but surely all diseases had to start somewhere. Some flick of a genetic switch upon meeting some environmental pressure.

Life couldn't be as simple as the eternally lucky and the endlessly damned. Could it?

The rain began to tap on the window outside. Cold fingers

looking to find a way in. Her little blue dove had taken flight in the rivers and channels of her blood and her thoughts were streaming in all directions like seaweed in the shallows. She would sit if she was at all certain her legs would obey her. Still, there was something so pleasant about standing there, looking out to sea, swaying as if she were on a ship. She took a step forward and pressed her forehead to the glass.

They went on a cruise after her father's funeral. Andrew thought she needed the break. Something to give her a lift, he said. Let other people mind her for a couple of weeks. She gave in gratefully, knowing he needed to make amends for the funeral fiasco.

Her mother had been hysterical the night before the Mass and Lydia stayed with her to calm her down. Andrew brought Lydia's clothes to her the following day, the regulation black skirt and shirt she had asked him to pick from her wardrobe.

It wasn't his fault he didn't realise there were different shades of black.

'You can't possibly wear that,' her mother said. 'You look colour-blind. No. No no no no no,' she repeated, as if stuck.

Lydia rushed home to change and cried all the way back to the church. When she opened the heavy entrance doors, the Mass had already started without her.

'Everyone's staring,' she hissed to her mother when she slipped into the seat alongside her.

'At least they won't be commenting on your outfit,' was all her mother said.

Outside, the wind joined the rain. A little impromptu jam session. Sweeping imperiously to the front door and rattling the letter box as if it had every right to enter.

She wished Sofia would appear, filling the house with chatter and that clean lemony smell. Scattering the air of loneliness.

'You should get a companion,' her mother kept telling her.

'I'm not a Victorian lady,' Lydia said. 'I can manage perfectly well.'

Living alone was the point when a person wasn't safe to be around others. But she had said it so many times that it had become meaningless to her mother and to Andrew. It shouldn't matter to her that they didn't understand. A true penitent wouldn't care. Those old folks that climbed Croagh Patrick in their bare feet and rose above the raised eyebrows and sniggers.

How did a person even go about finding a companion? It was hardly app material. Print seemed a more likely place to find something – someone – so quaintly inclined. An ad in *Ireland's Own* magazine, perhaps. *Seeking unobtrusive presence for occasional silent company. Thick skin and lack of curiosity an advantage.*

Who would answer that, other than someone with designs on divesting her of her organs, or, worse, keen to be divested of theirs?

As if summoned by the power of Lydia's thought, Sofia's little car flashed the lights at her as she pulled into the drive one-handed, the other hand holding the phone that appeared to be somehow essential to her continued existence. Lydia had yet to see her arrive or leave without a phone call to keep her company. She could order her a hands-free kit for Christmas.

No.

The shutters came down on the traitorous skip of her heart at the prospect of holiday shopping. That would be far too personal. A card with a cheque inside was an appropriate gift. An arm's-length gift.

She crossed to the stereo and shut off her sea sounds, switching instead to the pre-programmed political digest of the day's headlines.

'She's something to do with international affairs, I think,' she imagined Sofia telling whoever it was to whom she told things at the end of the day. Or perhaps in the next house that she went to clean. A cheerful house in an estate in a dormitory town. With an SUV outside the door and a woman with laugh lines and an untidy topknot who urged Sofia to join her for a quick coffee before the school run. 'I haven't spoken to a grown-up all day,' the imaginary woman laughed, gesturing to the infant asleep in a buggy in the living room.

Or maybe this was the only house Sofia cleaned. Perhaps she left here and did something entirely different. Youth services. Evening lectures. Entertaining in the old folks' home. Online sex work. Who ever knew the truth of another person?

Sofia didn't get out of the car. So much for summoning her by the power of thought alone. Lydia could have been on the floor, choking on a grape or a peanut or a memory, time fast running out. Sofia remained rooted in the driver's seat, one hand clutching the phone, the other tapping the steering wheel for emphasis.

Thought couldn't summon anything.

It wasn't as if Lydia hadn't tried before.

'Sorry, sorry!'

Sofia arrived in the hall, a whirl of colour and noise and glistening raindrops. She smelled of outdoors, Lydia thought. As if she had just been walking a dog or a child or sweeping a yard. The full sensory smorgasbord that no scented candle could ever quite capture.

'My mother was on the phone.' Sofia hung her coat on the

peg with one hand while making talk-talk-talk gestures with the other. 'Always a drama. Mothers, you know?'

Lydia did know. 'Tell me about it,' she could have said, rolling her eyes cosily. 'Every year on my birthday, my mother would claim she wanted to die. She said she couldn't possibly live knowing she had a ten-year-old. A thirteen-year-old. A sixteen-year-old.'

But there was a risk that Sofia would think Lydia minded. That the light-heartedness would be lost. That no amount of reassurance – that by the time she was sixteen, Lydia was confident her mother didn't mean it – would shake the impression of fragility and damage.

There was a danger, too, that once uncorked, fizzing emotions might not go quietly back into the bottle.

'I hope everything is okay,' Lydia said instead. Her voice was stiff and formal. An ugly, uptight voice.

'Everything is fine.' Sofia shrugged. 'Just drama-drama.' She moved into the kitchen, chattering away all the while, drawing Lydia after her.

She could casually ask if Sofia wanted a coffee before she started, Lydia thought. She could do that. All she had to do was open her mouth.

'That old lady.' Sofia was shaking her head. 'Mrs Cotter. She thinks she owns the road. Standing in the rain like that – what does she think will happen?'

Nothing, Lydia thought. Sis Cotter thinks nothing will happen. That nothing can happen. She thinks herself invincible. As the star of her own story, it was impossible for her to think that a hybrid car could come silently around the bend and sweep her off her feet and up into the air, a futuristic love story of metal and flesh.

The offer of coffee died in her throat and Lydia watched as Sofia gathered the cleaning things from the utility room, inspecting the wicker caddy to make sure she had everything she needed before setting off upstairs.

What would they have talked about, had she asked and

been accepted? Absent the need to place one another, to comb through friends and acquaintances for overlaps, what else was there? Lydia's work was fictional. Sofia's what Lydia chose not to do herself. Chat didn't come from nothing. A vacuum was, by definition, devoid of matter. Empty of anything that mattered.

A thud from upstairs. Dull and heavy. Despite her blue dove, Lydia flinched and waited for the noise to rise out of her ribcage and overtake her. The metallic screech of car frame meeting bike frame.

In the silence, her own breathing restarted, a sudden greedy intake.

'Sorry!' Sofia called down. 'Just the bleach bottle!' After a moment, she shouted again. 'It was closed! Don't worry about the carpet!'

'Just the bleach bottle,' Lydia repeated, but her heart thundered in her ears and her body paid no attention to words or logic. When the fear passed, anger flooded in. 'Sorry,' Sofia had said, as if an apology was called for. Such careless use of language. It was no wonder sorry had lost its power.

The experts said that hearing was the most lasting of the senses. That even coma patients could hear those around them. With her last gasp, would that awful reverberating bang be the sound that accompanied her out of this world?

The urge to know what Mary was doing swept over her. One little look wouldn't hurt. Just one. Lydia's hands on the back of the chair were white-knuckled, gripping an imaginary steering wheel. She pushed her feet into the floor, toe by toe, and counted until the feeling passed.

The bedsheets could do with freshening, Lydia decided. She could exchange one plain cream set for another, let their snap release the electricity in her fingers. She would look forward to climbing into bed tonight. The weight of freshly laundered cotton. The crackle of the goose-down duvet as it settled around her.

She was holding the duvet cover when Sofia came in and took the opposite side, unpeeling inside and outside with clinical precision.

'You don't have to.'

Sofia shrugged. 'Why do it alone when I'm here?'

Lydia would have preferred to do it alone. Ceremonially. But there was no way to say so without appearing rude.

They worked together for a few moments, pulling and flicking and smoothing. Sofia hummed while she moved. Humming was, to Lydia's mind, the surest evidence of lightness of heart. The casual exposure of it. The certainty that the world would welcome the sound of you moving through it.

'Did you hear the cinema in town is reopening?' Sofia said.

'No. I didn't realise it ever closed,' Lydia said, as if town were an option she occasionally took up.

She had gone to that cinema weekly during her childhood holidays. Her box of sugar-coated fruit pastilles. The plastic seat sticking to her bare legs. Staring straight ahead for fear any of the locals, those hot-cheeked boys and wild-haired girls, would sit beside her or try and talk to her.

'It was closed, but now it will open again,' Sofia added.

'I didn't think you lived in town,' Lydia said. As light as the faint prickle of fear in the small of her back.

Sofia shook her head. 'I saw it on social media. So useful. You join?'

Lydia shook her head. 'I'm not on social media.' She dropped the pillow she was holding and held up her two hands, palms out, as if vouchsafing her own honesty. 'It's too distracting when I work from home.' She hoped she wasn't painting a picture of herself as snobbish. Together with the laptop and fancy coffee machine, it would surely be another mark against her. 'The old lady – Mrs Cotter, is it? – she certainly seems to like the beach. I see her down there all the time.' So casual the suggestion that she saw her while she herself was there. One neighbour bumping into another, what could be more natural?

'Mrs Cotter is part of the furniture on the beach. Her family always lived here. Before the hotel. Before everything. Except the sea itself.' Sofia made a curious whistling noise with her teeth. 'It is a shame she is leaving.'

'She's leaving? Why?'

'Something with her son. I am not sure.' Sofia busied herself tucking a pillow into its new case.

'I assumed she lives alone.' She didn't add that something about the way she carried herself spoke of self-reliance. Of invisibility and freedom.

Sofia sighed. 'I did try not to listen, but the dry cleaners is just so small, it is impossible. Her son moved away years ago and I think maybe she is going to live with one of her daughters now. So you will have a new neighbour.' She gave a final snap and pat and went off to do something else.

One of her daughters. There were two, Lydia remembered. The older one, bossy and harried, trailing a younger brother. The source of the something that was causing Sis Cotter to move away.

And a girl closer to her own age. A strange girl, who never spoke to Lydia but who, day after day, performed dance routines from *Top of the Pops* while checking to see if Lydia was watching. How odd to think of that girl grown and gone. Living a life somewhere else, a life sufficiently open to admit her elderly mother.

If Sis Cotter was leaving, that meant a new neighbour. A lone stranger would be best. A family, at worst. One child or two or three. Daring each other to sneak up her drive and peep in the window. The crazy lady that eventually became part of the stories they used to scare themselves. A Halloween legend. A living witch.

Doreen, that was the girl's name. Doreen and Cathy and

Mike. Shouted across the sand, Sis Cotter in her doorway, waving her arms to attract their attention.

Lydia waited until the car had pulled away – Sofia on the phone once more, talking talking talking. What on earth could one person find to talk about for so long? Lydia wondered where she had left her own phone and eventually found it on the window sill in the living room. She must have had it in her hand earlier this morning and put it aside without realising. It was a side effect of the tablets, the way time seemed to move through her instead of her moving through time.

The chemist was kind on the phone, assuring her that her prescription would be ready for collection within the hour. The off-licence, too, was easy-going. 'Will I throw in anything else for you?' the girl enquired.

Lydia thought of the poor customer service she had endured down the years. Whoever would have guessed that the day would come when a stranger's cheery 'anything else?' was such a comfort? She pinched the skin between her thumb and first finger and watched it turn white and bloodless.

Her final phone call was to CAB505 to arrange for a taxi to collect from both places and deliver them to the house.

'Will it be before the storm, do you think?' she asked, forcing a little laugh into her voice. 'We open right on to the sea here.' Automatic, that 'we'. As if it wasn't just Lydia and the ghosts of lives past.

'Ah sure that won't be much of a storm at all,' the voice on the other end told her and despite the kind tone, she felt caught out.

A foolish outsider, that was all she was.

Maybe that was why she answered when her mother phoned, instead of pressing mute or dropping the mobile into the sink.

'Tell me you've come to your senses,' was her mother's opening salvo. 'Poor Andrew is half out of his mind. He says you're still phoning him and refusing to say anything. Heavy breathing like a stalker, Lydia. His words.'

They weren't his words and they both knew it. And she wasn't refusing to speak. She had simply recognised that talking to each other made things worse. All the words over all the months lay between them, the pile growing until they had to peer around the edges to see each other, then, finally, gratefully, obscuring their view of one another entirely.

'After everything he's done for you,' her mother continued.

Lydia wasn't surprised her mother thought Andrew too good for her. From the moment Lydia brought him home, her mother liked him better.

'Your flirting is shameless, Mother,' Lydia had told her as she kissed her goodbye in the hall after that first meet-the-parents weekend.

'What can I say, darling? I always wanted a son.'

Lydia was briefly glad that she was a daughter and a disappointment. Imagine the psychological damage her mother would have wrought on a small boy, with her eyelash flickering and endless innuendo.

'I can't understand what you think you'll achieve with all this. An eye for an eye leaves the whole world blind, you know,' her mother pronounced.

'That's revenge, not penance,' Lydia said while wondering why she bothered getting drawn in.

'Whatever word you put on it doesn't change the fact that it's nonsense. You'll die of loneliness. Or boredom. I suppose that's the idea.'

'You loved it here, as I recall,' Lydia said.

'The summer is different,' her mother said. 'There are more of our kind of people in the summer. It dilutes the locals. Makes things a bit more palatable.'

'Speaking of locals, I saw Mrs Cotter earlier today.'

'Sis Cotter? I suppose she is an old biddy like myself by

now.' Her mother laughed the tinkly laugh that called forth a compliment.

'She looks very well, actually,' Lydia said.

'Where did you see Sis Cotter?' her mother said sourly. 'I thought you were afraid to step outside your door in case you accidentally kill someone.'

When Lydia heard experts advise someone to talk openly and directly, not to dance around the hard topics, she had the urge to scream. For openness and vulnerability to be useful, they had to be handled delicately. Her mother might claim that voicing her daughter's fear aloud robbed it of its power, but her mother had always conflated rudeness and honesty.

'A friend of mine told me the cinema in town is reopening,' Lydia said, judging it sufficiently neutral to steer them through the remainder of the conversation.

'Oh, darling,' her mother said, and Lydia could hear the rattle of ice cubes as she sipped her drink. 'The cleaner is never really your friend.'

Having got her mother off the phone by telling her she had to secure the house before the storm, Lydia wandered from room to room, wine glass in hand. It was early for a drink, yes, but to impose an arbitrary rule – no alcohol before 5 p.m., say – made her uneasy. A rule suggested a need for it. Motivation was the thing. A person should know why they were drinking, and a person – any reasonable person – understood that a phone call with their mother would drive anyone to drink. Means, motive, opportunity. Wasn't that an Alcoholics Anonymous thing?

No, she realised. That was murder.

Around she went, tapping window seams the way Andrew would. She didn't know what she should look for, so all she achieved was a build-up of static in her good Moroccan leather indoor shoes. Not slippers. Never slippers. Slippers would be giving up.

Lydia put her glass on the window sill and placed one hand over the other, stroking it the way Andrew did. She missed him. Missed the idea of him. The bottle-opening, window-checking, solid reality of him. Of who he used to be.

The day of Lydia and Andrew's wedding was all about her mother. 'I'm the mother of the bride,' she kept saying, even to Lydia herself. It was hilarious, Lydia told her three bridesmaids, while hating them for not rescuing her from it. For not slapping her mother across the face and telling her to get a grip. To her relief, Andrew came and whisked her mother away, telling her that there were guests that needed her special attention. Lydia watched them cross the room and knew her way through life would now be smoothed. She no longer needed to be the one running ahead beating back the bushes.

What was your wedding day like, Mary? A small affair, perhaps. The two of you surrounded by a handful of true friends intent on showering you with love? Are your memories tainted now that your husband has gone and left you to manage everything by yourself?

I'm alone too and this house doesn't feel like home. Perhaps it never will. If I am honest – can I be honest, Mary? – the idea that I will rattle around here until the end of my days, continually feeling a little dispossessed, is not unpleasant.

[Delete. Delete. Delete.]

The house darkened around her. *Hardly a storm at all.* She repeated the words like a prayer, but the sky and the air felt like they might know something the girl on the phone didn't. She stood a careful distance from the window and looked out to where the wind was plucking handfuls of branches and shaking them as if to avenge some almighty wrong. The tree trunks held tight and refused to yield their progeny without a fight.

Lydia drew back into the dark of the hall when the lights of the taxi appeared. If the driver saw her waiting, he might expect her to come out to the car. Even so, he beeped the horn once or twice and she had to wait him out. Eventually, she heard the car door open and shut, then the sound of heavy footsteps. She grabbed the cane from the corner before opening the door.

'Thank you so much,' she said, giving her rueful smile and glancing down at her cane. 'I'm so sorry to drag you out in all this.'

As usual, the glance downward was sufficient to soften any annoyance, removing the need for her to lie outright.

'It won't be much more than puff and bluster,' he said confidently.

Perhaps it was some mark of belonging to disbelieve the evidence of his own eyes. Anyone else on her porch right now – a sensible German, say, or a weather-hardened Canadian – would be pulling on hoods and wellington boots, not the thin anorak this man wore.

'We used to come here in the summers when I was a girl,' Lydia said, suddenly wanting him to… to what? It would take more than being here in winter to make her a local. A person was a blow-in until they had someone in the ground in the local graveyard, wasn't that the rule? That would have to be Lydia herself. She shivered.

'I thought you looked familiar. This is a treat for you so – it's at its best when it's wild and quiet,' the man said. 'Once the hotel opens…' He opened his arms wide, as if the scale of carnage to be expected was indescribable.

'Good for the area, though,' Lydia said. As she spoke, she held out her hand and he put the bag obediently into it. A useful little trick Susan, her psychologist friend, had told her years earlier. 'If someone is talking and you hand them something, they'll take it,' she had said. 'The same is true in reverse – if someone is talking and you put your hand out, they'll give you what they're holding.' 'Goodness,' Lydia had said. 'Why?' But Susan's attention had been caught by her husband's hand on someone else's backside (maybe she held it out to him, Lydia thought) and Lydia never found out the mechanics of it. Her ignorance of how and why it worked did not dent its usefulness, however.

A gust of wind caught the front door and threw it against the wall. Lydia stumbled sideways and felt the colour drain from her face.

'It's just the wind,' the man said, looking at her closely. 'Are you all right?'

Lydia nodded and began to fumble in her wallet for money, her hand shaking too much to pull the zip.

'I'm Danny, by the way,' he said easily.

'Lydia.' She finally managed to close her fingers around her money, adding a ten-euro tip to cover her embarrassment. It was a relief to close the door behind him, until it occurred to her that he might think the money was her being patronising.

'And you accuse your mother of overthinking and melodrama?' she chided herself aloud before unpeeling herself from the front door and taking the bags through to the kitchen.

The fridge was well stocked. Her food delivery arrived on Mondays and Fridays, ensuring a constant supply of fresh fruit and vegetables. Even so, nothing in there appealed. The rain was now hammering down outside, so she supposed that something hot might be in order. A poached egg on toast, she decided. Eggs were a penitential food, filling without being joyful. A perpetual air of dregs about them.

Afterwards, she made coffee and lit the single cigarette she allowed herself after Sofia left on a Tuesday, trusting that the smell would dissipate in the forty-eight hours until her next visit. There was something needy about smokers, rooted as they were in their own physicality, that Lydia couldn't bear to be associated with. Unwilling – unable – to open the windows, time was her sole ally in keeping her secret. So far it had worked, helped along by the lack of curtains or carpet in the kitchen.

She drained her coffee and went through to the living room, where she dragged the armchair closer to the window and sat with her hands clasped loosely in her lap. Whatever storm was coming, let it come.

The first flash of lightning took her breath away. To get her heart back under control, she concentrated on counting the beats until the clap of thunder came. Despite waiting for it, bracing for it, Lydia was unsure for a second if the heavy rumble was from outside the window or inside her own clattering chest. Whatever romantic idea she had of watching the storm paled beside the enormity of the sky and the sea. Ancient peoples worshipped and feared their gods of nature in equal measure. Fear, respect, worship. An appropriate spectrum of response to what humanity least understood.

She got up and moved backwards towards the kitchen, careful to keep looking towards the window, as if the weather were a man with a gun and she his hostage.

Whatever was going on out there was not a spectacle.

Whatever it was was none of her business.

The front of the house was shielded from the worst of the elements, making it easier to ignore the shriek and howl as the outside tried to reach in and drag her out.

She could take a tablet. One extra would make little difference. The doctor himself had said there was a little wiggle room for bad days. But she could still feel the morning's dose, a light shudder in her fingertips. Instead, she took the bottle of white wine from the fridge and poured a glass. The slide of it down her throat was a miracle. In the exchange of cold for heat, she could feel her body working. As if it was designed to do this one thing, to let the wine cool and then warm her. To let it move through her as if she were transparent. That was what alcohol did – she almost laughed aloud at the simple truth of it – it made us transparent to others. To ourselves. Our tears, our fears, our aggressions, coaxed out. Slow at first and then all in a rush, like an office karaoke party.

The storm was endless. Or it might have been short.

Slow, slow, quick, quick, slow.

Time accordioning like in a fairy tale.

I heard an astronaut interviewed once, Mary, and he said that when he returned to Earth, he could feel gravity itself. A weight on him, he said, as he lay in bed at night. Time, too, has weight. A lifetime of it. All that we have done or not done.

[Delete. Delete. Delete.]

Lydia's laptop was on the island beside her and she fired it up, letting its slowness smooth her ruffled edges.

She had no social media apps on her phone. Andrew had deleted all her accounts in the days after the accident, saying that they brought out the worse in people.

Lydia simply logged into his account whenever she wanted to watch Mary. His password was unchanged, GalwayRaces07.

Mary's account was public. Her sunflower avatar there for all to see. Reading her posts was not lurking, and even if it was, it was Andrew that would appear as Mary's friend suggestion.

There was a lot to see. Mary posted frequently. Affirmations. Animal videos. Charity fundraisers. Trapped at home, Mary's posts had a feeling of a lifeline about them.

Pinned to the top of the page was a statement about what had happened to Nick. Her pride in him. Their struggle. A thank you and a reminder that the link to the GoFundMe page was now closed.

Below it, Mary's posts had settled into a predictable rhythm. The candles and praying-hands emojis that meant it had been a bad day. An overabundance of blue hearts on a good day. Occasional sarcasm, which Lydia inferred as Mary feeling bolshie instead of saintly. Was that new fire in her belly or old? There was no way to know. Mary, too, had scrubbed her account of everything before the accident. Her old profile, her previous self. It was a strange expression, 'scrubbed'. It implied a cleansing, when all Lydia felt was dirty, as though she herself were a shameful secret.

Days out warranted photographs. Nick in his wheelchair, Mary crouched down by his weaker side, the side that tilted against the headrest. Lydia would zoom in close, as if she might find the marks of her car on his body all these months later. As if the traces weren't evident in every altered atom of his being.

Mary never posted old photos or memories. It was for all the world as if her life had begun the day of the accident. She had given up work in the tax office to become Nick's full-time carer when he left hospital. When the powers that be judged that he was rehabilitated to the extent he ever would be. So she, too, was at home all day. In another world, Lydia thought, they could swap recipes, meet for coffee or a Pilates class.

In another world, of course, they would both still be at work, their lives never overlapping.

Sometimes, Mary posted her thoughts on whatever book she was reading. Lydia was proud of her then. For her energy. Her commitment to escape. Sometimes she ordered the book, if Mary had particularly liked it, but she had yet to read any of them. She would get as far as opening the covers and the words would lift themselves from the page and scramble over one another until her head hurt.

In January and July of each year, Nick went into a local

nursing home for respite care. Mary never went far for her weeks off. To her sister up the country, usually, or to a small hotel with a leisure centre. Lydia imagined her stroking thirty minutes of slow lengths up and down a twenty-metre pool, then climbing out, unselfconscious in her old swimming togs, to go and sit in the jacuzzi for ten minutes. The pinnacle of relaxation for her now, thanks to Lydia.

But it was also true that, sometimes, Lydia envied her those weeks. Woke at night and cried with ugly self-pity. It was Nick who had no respite, she reminded herself. Nick's life she ruined. Thus, it was Nick's life to which she must compare her own and be grateful.

I miss cathedrals, Mary. Cathedrals in foreign cities, where I could become part of the quiet, my head raised or lowered by their beauty. No different to anyone else.

What do you miss most in those weeks when you are away from him, away from home? What is it you long for?

[Delete. Delete. Delete.]

Lydia took a pill and poured another glass of wine and was back at the window when Sis Cotter was due to pass by on her evening walk. Seeing the woman gave her a fleeting sense of connection or something close to it.

But Sis Cotter was leaving and taking all of her certainty and comfort with her.

Lydia would not panic. She would not. She would not. She would not.

She could feel her edges softening around the repetition. Outside, the damp grey-blue of the paving stones stopped her from wondering if the storm had happened at all. If perhaps she had imagined it all. The gaslighting that was Irish weather.

From the picture window she could see right down onto the beach. That was the first thing she insisted on when they began to plan the remodel. Evenings spent planning, wine replacing coffee as they scanned interior-design websites. Weekends spent browsing furniture and fittings showrooms, followed by dinners full of laughing agreement about this or that.

Like the low stone wall they agreed would maximise the view. The yard paved in the expectation that there would be weekends when they brought down both cars 'in case they each wanted to do their own thing'. How smug they were! How had they borne themselves? How she wished they had kept the dense greenery her parents had planted that had screened the house for years. Trees whose height and breadth would shelter her from the world.

When the accident happened, the interior of the house was barely started, awaiting marble from Italy for the hall, a claw-foot bath from Finland, a log-shaped postbox at the gate with their name on it that they had ordered on holiday in Canada, a single-pour concrete worktop from wherever the hell such things were brought forth.

When she told Andrew she wanted – needed – to move in straight away, he reminded her it was unfinished.

'It doesn't need to be fancy,' she told him. 'Just fast. Flat-pack furniture. Second-hand. Whatever you can find, I don't care.'

'When do you want to be in by?' he asked and, just like that, it seemed her marriage was over.

The sea was nearer than usual. She was certain.

Not in a tide-is-in kind of way – she was no city girl that would fall for that illusion – but as if the ground had eroded during the storm. For the first time, Lydia wondered what would happen if the tide were to come in and simply continue, to crest the small dune with swift ease and close its jaws around her door. She closed her eyes and pictured it. She in the living room, glass in hand – much as she was now – while the water rose to her ankles, her knees, her thighs, her elbows. Would she hold still? Would she welcome it, invite it in, stroke its white tips like the fox that crossed her yard at night?

As a child, she believed – with a fervent and deeply held certainty – that time was running out. That the world and everything in it – Lydia herself, her house, her street, her school – would be eaten alive by acid rain. She could picture it, her skin bubbling and fizzing as she melted under its power, like the Wicked Witch in *The Wizard of Oz*.

She listened to teachers and newscasters and her parents talk worriedly about sulphur dioxide in coal-fired power stations and pictured the noxious clouds rising and joining forces with the rain in the sky, like some big celestial gathering, before corroding the Earth with its own stupidity. Beneath it, buildings would crumble, forests would turn to ash and seas boil. She had too much imagination and too little common sense, her mother scolded, after yet another night was ruined by Lydia's nightmares and clawing need for comfort.

She was a teenager before she realised that acid rain had faded from view. She worried briefly that it had become such a problem that it was no longer discussed in front of children, but that seemed absurd based on the evidence of her mother's regular lunch parties. Once adults had a glass or two of wine, they had little control over what they did or didn't say. She had lost count of the conversations full of what adults intended to be meaningful silences and attempts at eyebrow-raised discretion, but that in reality meant someone had an affair and was caught, or had cancer and there was little to be done. Even so, she was nervous approaching her science teacher to ask him.

'Sir? Whatever happened to acid rain?'

'Now there's a thing!' He beamed at her and launched into an explanation of the changes in regulation, in power stations and car manufacturing, the miracle that was the catalytic converter, the innovations through which a handful of the determined, it appeared, had conspired to save humanity from itself. A temporary stay of execution, as it would turn out.

After acid rain, she worried about World War III, fuelled by casual anti-Russian sentiment seeping in from American movies and books. Then the Twin Towers fell and Lydia had the sharp sensation of the world shifting uncontrollably, driven by a politics she did not understand and never would while she sat in rooms, learning French verbs, Descartes, and the life of Julian of Norwich.

There were no nightmares. Instead, for the first time, she was frightened into sleeplessness, sitting up in bed clutching the packs of iodine tablets the government had issued to protect against… what? Even they weren't sure. Against panic, maybe.

Lydia's peace of mind was bought for short intervals by virtue of her age and feeling of invincibility. It was true, too, that the novelty of disposable income bought forgetfulness. Or perhaps it was more accurate to say it bought cheap flights and expensive clothes and a related merciful distraction.

In the months and years before the accident, climate change became a creeping fear, prompting her to change to a hybrid car. With its environmental credentials, its undeniable status, its tax breaks.

Its lethally quiet engine.

Lydia opened her eyes and looked at the sea again. It was definitely closer. She was glad, suddenly, for the low wall. If sea level rise was to be the end of the world, at least she would see it coming.

The thing to do was to order iodine tablets. She snorted a laugh and clapped her hand over her mouth.

Focus, Lydia.

The thing to do was to take a sight line. Something fixed that she could monitor daily. On the left, that rocky outcrop where the seagulls perched as if waiting for some sort of signal. From that to... she swivelled her head. To the ridge of Sis Cotter's roof to the right. She shut her right eye, turned and looked. Shut her left eye. Turned and looked again. She had it now. She had its measure. Had it by the short and curlies. She laughed again and realised the wine had gone to her head.

'A plan, Lydia. You need a plan,' she told herself sternly. 'No good sipping wine and watching the end of the world lick your front door. Fiddling while Rome burns.'

If giving up her car was too late to save her, then she would have to save herself. High ground would buy her some time. And where higher – and readily available to her – than the attic? It would be a brave sea that would rise above eight metres.

She tapped her fingernail against her wine glass. What did a person pack for the slow end of the world?

In the bedroom, she opened her wardrobe, surveyed the contents, and began.

Fleeces, torches, books, notebooks, whiskey, biscuits, tissues, pillows, blankets. Two identical piles grew on the bed and she placed each in its own box, naming the items in a long list, like that children's game, I-went-to-the-shop-and-I-bought, with each additional item requiring her to start over and list everything from scratch. She took the biro from her nightstand and wrote their names. *Lydia* on one box. *Mary* on the other.

My psychologist will have a field day with me, Mary, if I ever see her again. It is, on balance, unlikely. I do not believe there is room for her on our apocalyptic adventure.

[Delete. Delete. Delete.]

Adventure. Lydia sat down. Suddenly exhausted, as if she had already scaled the wall of water.

After the accident, when it still seemed Nick would most

likely die from his injuries, Andrew engaged a solicitor for them. For her.

'The best outcome, Lydia – may I call you Lydia? – would be a coroner's verdict of death by misadventure.'

Oh, words. Was there anything sharper and more deadly?

Lydia closed her eyes. 'The best outcome, *Dominic*, would be a full recovery for Nick. Or, failing that, the ability to go back and decide to get a taxi home that night. Or, better still, not go out at all.' She didn't say that, of course. She didn't even properly think it until weeks later, methodically slamming her fist into the tiled wall of the shower while the rainfall showerhead pounded water on her spine.

That day in the solicitor's office, she sat meekly while Andrew asked questions and jotted down answers, as if her lapse in judgement were a test he had to pass.

Nick did not die. Did that mean he was alive by misadventure?

And what of Lydia? Was she herself alive by misadventure, too?

She lost interest in her project and piled the boxes in the corner of the room behind the door, out of sight.

Downstairs, Lydia took another tablet from the box. Her whole evening, from music to dinner to toothbrushing, held in the palm of her hand. She swallowed and consulted the clock on the oven. She should eat now or risk having to sit upright in bed until the early hours. Yesterday was... she cast her mind backwards, trying to find something that would differentiate the days. Yesterday was almost sunny and she had a salad. She remembered because she had taken off her cardigan while she ate, and thought that in another life, she might have gone for a walk. If yesterday was salad, then today was stir-fry. Roughage and more roughage, for all the difference it made to her poor innards, slowed to a crawl under the weight of the medication.

If a person had innards, did that mean they had outards?

Lydia gathered together the bits and pieces she needed to cook. Wok. Chopping board. Large-blade knife. Then carrots, bell pepper, courgette, onion, broccoli, mangetout, side by side in sacrificial silence. Salad and stir-fry had mindless preparation in common. Chopping and tossing. A dash of lemon juice on cold. A dash of soy sauce on hot.

It was a small, pale version of long, luxurious days of cooking for their friends, the kitchen warm with music and happiness.

That was what their group of friends did; they took it in turns to cook for one another. A standing monthly arrangement, each couple in turn. No takeaway, no children, no excuses. A mild degree of one-upmanship that saw Andrew and Lydia book a long weekend in a little village devoted to the existence of a celebrity chef.

They took a cookery class with the chef himself, a three-hour affair in which they learned to make food to impress. Aspirational cookery. At least one vegetable neither of them had ever heard of and would struggle to find in their local supermarket. The man himself came and checked their progress. Andrew needed to relax into it, he said, while Lydia needed to work on her timing. When they sat down to eat, they toasted themselves for complementing one another so beautifully. Together, they agreed, they made the perfect team.

The final morning, on her way back from breakfast – full fresh honeycomb, omelette station, champagne – Lydia took a wrong turn through an unmarked door and found herself in a pantry. Amid the staff scurrying to fulfil every spoiled request was a woman stacking canisters with tears rolling down her face. For a moment, Lydia wondered if the canisters were full of her tears. Nobody saw Lydia except the crying woman, who was too miserable to care. Lydia mouthed an apology and returned to her table. All day, she couldn't shake the sensation that life – real life – was whatever was happening in that back room, and she herself was the illusion.

About a month after the accident, when Nick was out of immediate danger and rehab had begun to seem a distinct possibility, Andrew encouraged her to have her friends over for dinner. He would cook, he said. He would invite them, he said. He would leave them in peace to catch up and then come back in when it was time to clean up, he said.

He would expect it to fix her, but he did not need to say that.

All afternoon, she lay on the couch with a book unread in her hands, while the rich smell of a red-wine reduction wafted through, followed by the delicious comfort of garlic and onion sizzling in the pan. Her favourite smell in the world. She used to joke that she started all her recipes with it, even dessert.

For a while, she thought she might manage the evening. She rose and went upstairs, showered and perfumed herself, dried her hair. Standing in her bra and pants in front of the open wardrobe, the smell of the lamb shanks wound upwards and under the door. Roasting flesh, in all its fatty horror.

She vomited in the en suite and refused to come out or to let them come in.

Over time, she taught her friends not to reach out to her, but to wait for her to get in touch. From there it was a simple matter of reducing her contact to a phone call when she knew they wouldn't answer, to a quick text, to nothing at all. A slow war of attrition on years of tears and laughter. Of weekends away, shared gripes, shopping trips, husband-bashing, exchanging holiday tips, manicure tips, hairdressers' contact details.

In this war, Lydia had something they did not: she still knew who they really were.

Andrew couldn't understand her withdrawal from her friends, her life, from him.

He with his knife-like logic. He who was so discerning.

He with the careful way he parsed her words, looking for cracks that he could fill and fix. Over and over, their failure to hear one another, so that her only choice was to say nothing, to give him nothing that he could twist and turn, trying to see the light in it.

Above all, his failure to understand that he himself was made unbearable, his judgement questionable, by the fact that he didn't recoil from her, from her continuing presence in their house, her feet in their slippers, her backside in their chairs. That his persistence of faith in her was the opposite of acceptance.

Fuck. She had sliced her fingernail alongside the courgette and lifted a long inch of skin with it. Repulsed, Lydia stumbled backwards and knocked the chopping board from the worktop. It landed on the floor with a dull crack and she instinctively waited for the screech of metal as bike frame met bumper. Instead, there was a silence so loud that her ears rang with it. Tears threatened, but she would not give in to them. 'Tears of self-pity are not earned, Lydia' – her mother's dictum something to hold on to here in this wintry kitchen at the edge of the world.

She went to the sink and rinsed her finger, wrapping it in kitchen towel before picking up the board and resuming her meal preparation.

Do you make an effort to cook at home, Mary, when it is just the two of you and Nick cannot eat what you make? Do you plan meals or batch cook or take the time in the kitchen as a daily escape? When you take Nick out to eat, how can it be a treat when it looks like so much work?

[Delete. Delete. Delete.]

Lydia held the ball of wool in her left hand, her right hand winding from the loose skein draped on the chair. A decade ago, she would have wondered irritably why they didn't just sell the damn wool in balls, but these days the monotony of it was comforting. Soothing in the way the knitting itself would have been if she ever actually started. For now, the wool itself was the thing. A two-handed focus that let her mind drift until the evening vanished. She thought again of fairy-tale time. How there were years of nothing and then whole lives flickered in and out in the blink of an eye. One bite of an apple. One kiss.

One glass.

And nothing was ever the same again.

Outside the window, night had fallen. Before moving here, Lydia had said those words and heard others use them and believed herself to understand what they meant. But it was here in winter that the truth of the expression lived. Where night came from above and the sky threw down its curtain of dark and stars with the suddenness of spilled liquid.

She wound her wool and she thought about Mary. About the pictures she had posted earlier. Nick by the fire in a café. A cup with a straw on the table in front of him. Mary beaming, love in her eyes. Nick looking straight ahead. *Sunday afternoon in the snug*, Mary had captioned it, adding *#timeout #grateful* for good measure.

Despite her smile.

Despite her knee-aching crouch beside him.

Despite her arm wrapped around his shoulders.

Lydia didn't know which were worse – the days when

Mary posted nothing and she was left to imagine their lives, or the days when Mary posted a picture and she was left in no doubt about the eternal child that she had gifted Mary.

One bloody book club for a bloody book she hadn't even bloody read.

But she hadn't made it to the last one or the one before and she felt guilty and she missed seeing her friends.

One stupid glass of wine because she was working hard and deserved a break.

No.

Tell the truth, Lydia: one stupid glass of wine because she had caught Andrew cooing at babies in restaurants instead of rolling his eyes and tutting in frustration. Cooing when they had agreed, right from the start, that children were not for them. A decision that was absolute, or so she had believed.

So. One stupid glass of wine because they had already had this conversation, had already agreed it wasn't what they wanted, and yet now whenever he came and sat beside her, she was afraid of what he would say. What he would ask for.

One stupid glass of wine because it was her body, dammit.

Witness for the defence: she sipped slowly. She ate cheese and olives and crisps.

For the prosecution: she held out her glass. She drank the wine.

Without it, she would have left earlier. Nick would have made it home in one piece.

Instead, there was her mood and the wine and then the thump, the screech, the body, the wait, the sirens, the questions. The gaping hole in reality. The bizarre impossibility of undoing something. Time's insistence on moving relentlessly in one direction.

The endless whooshing in her ears as if she were underwater.

But when she breathed in, all she got was air.

Nick was alive and Mary was alive and so Lydia's life would mirror theirs. Having decided that living was to be her penance – having, in fact, gone to church for the first time in years and whispered it, like a vow, in the quiet of the confessional – it was a little much to complain about her lot. If Mary could endure, so too could Lydia. Until she was old and grey and forgotten.

Like Sis Cotter.

But Sis Cotter was not forgotten. She was going to go and live with her daughter.

Lydia could walk down the driveway and stop her on the road. 'What is the worst thing you have done in your life?' she could ask Sis Cotter and search for absolution in the answer.

'Tell me honestly,' she could beg. 'Tell me how to survive it.'

PETER

'Fintan was moved to the hospice a few hours ago.' Peter repeated the words back to Caroline as if they might make more sense coming from his own mouth. As if the work of shaping them and emitting them, smoke-like and coiling, would let the truth of it through.

What else was there to say? Questions seemed crass, hinging as they did on inevitable projected timelines, on declines and plateaus and the daily balance between pain management and hope. He got out of bed and reflexively pulled open the curtains, but 1 a.m. on a November night offered no comfort other than orange street lights and the reflection of his own pale face and untidy hair.

He cleared his throat so Caroline would know he hadn't hung up.

'A few days, they think,' she said.

A few days. What did that even mean? This weekend? Next Tuesday? Again, the questions that came to him were all unhelpful.

'He'd love to see you,' Caroline said.

'Absolutely. Absolutely. Yes. In the meantime, if there's anything you need, just let me know.'

Peter turned on the downlights over the kitchen island and slid a pod into the coffee machine. The thought of going back to sleep seemed unconscionable. He watched his hand pick up the pod, slide back the drawer, insert the pod, close the drawer, flip the switch, and it was like he was no different to the machine. A series of mechanical movements to obtain a desired outcome.

The coffee machine was a gift from Noel and Sheila when he bought the house. They would never have dreamt of such a gift themselves – they gave him money and told him to treat himself to something he wouldn't get otherwise. It was worth the money. Eight years and still going strong. Never a bad cup yet.

He wouldn't dream of seeing Fintan like this. With nothing in his head except vacuous shite about coffee machines.

What Fintan needed was what he already had. Caroline's calm. Her practicality. Nothing fazed her. Peter saw her lose the head once. It was the week before she married Fintan, when her father told her he had invited a few more from the town at the last minute and the hotel would just have to find room for them. Wasn't the hotel opening up specially for them? he said. They would have to make room.

Peter took a sip and winced. The coffee was bitter and unhelpful. He tipped it down the sink and leaned against the worktop.

Tea, Peter thought. Tea was what was called for. Sweet and milky, the way Noel and Sheila taught him to like it. He filled the kettle and put it on to boil. Took down the teapot, a fresh mug, Sheila's navy-and-white-striped tea cosy.

He had to go and see Fintan. Sit with him. Hold his hand, even. Jesus. Fuck. How had it come to this so quickly? It was a bare handful of weeks since Fintan rang – itself as rare an event as Halley's Comet in the days of the casual text message – and told him.

'How bad is it?' Peter had asked. Thinking, in his naivete, that they might have to take one ball. Both, at worst. No babies would be a hard blow for his friends, but sure they could adopt. Or pay someone to have a child for them, if they had the money. If they didn't, he could pitch in a few bob. He had a fair bit put by and they would be welcome to it. Ten per cent into the bank every fortnight. Sheila's unshakeable influence.

'That's a matter of perspective,' Fintan said. 'From my side, about as bad as it gets. For Ted next door, who's had his eye on Caroline since we moved in, it's the chance of a lifetime.'

'Good man, Ted,' Peter said, but his heart wasn't in it.

If he had been able to find something to say then.

Or, failing that, if he had done something.

Got in his car and driven to Fintan's house and knocked on the door and sat with him. Taken a punch if that was what Fintan needed or taken him for a long spin or to the driving range or taken him out to get so fluthered he couldn't tell his testicles from a teapot.

If he had screwed his courage to the wall. Balls to the wall, you might say. If he had said that to Fintan, at least he would have made his friend laugh and lightened the load for him.

But he said nothing. Just nodded and nodded and nodded as if Fintan could see him.

'How's work?' Fintan said eventually.

And what did Peter say? What had our big thick lug to say for himself? What words of comfort could he muster for his best friend of thirty-odd years? 'Yerra. Same shit, different day. You know yourself.'

Same. Shit. Different. Day.

As if he had heard nothing Fintan said.

The shame scalded him off the phone and the days passed and he kept telling himself he would phone again when he had his head wrapped around it. When he knew what to say. When he could be a help rather than a hindrance. In the meantime, he sent Fintan the odd text message now and then, as if nothing had changed.

He didn't contact Caroline at all. He could think of no words that didn't involve the standard 'let me know if there's anything I can do', to which she would rightly respond that he could pick up the bloody phone and talk to his friend.

In time, he told himself for days. For weeks.

All in good time.

And now there was no more good time. Very little time at all, in point of fact, with Fintan in the hospice and Peter in his own house. Too late to be the right kind of friend. The kind that knew it was better to be there and say the wrong thing than to stay away in perfect silence.

He should at least have offered to phone some of the lads, save Caroline a job. He looked at his watch. He couldn't phone her now; she might be trying to get a bit of kip in what was left of the night. The relief disgusted him. Even had he phoned, he would have been hoping for their voicemails, hoping not to have to actually say it out loud.

They were the same, mind you. After Fintan told them all his diagnosis, they had met in the pub on a non-table-quiz night, already lopsided without him. The All-Rounders in a suddenly-too-small circle. The name was a joke in normal times, given the gap in their collective knowledge of soap stars, reality TV shows and the like. Al's default answer to everything was Cindy Crawford, that was how out of touch they were. 'Who was…' the question would start and Al would nod once and whisper *Cindy Crawford* and they would crease themselves laughing and have to wait to hear the full question in the recap.

They got the drinks in to cover the fact that nobody knew what to say and for the first few minutes, it seemed that they would spend the night exchanging *Jesus*es and *fuck me*s and go home again no more relieved or reassured than they had started. Their slumped shoulders and mute headshakes were equal parts devastation and guilt at their own luck. Eventually, Peter asked the barman for the darts and they gathered around the board, glad of the focus. It riled them up, though. The darts flying with a little more power behind them, the quibbling about a toe over the oche a little more heated than usual. The whole thing felt like betrayal rather than solidarity and there was a distinct air of relief when Al drained his glass and said he had an early start in the morning, giving them all the chance to do the same.

They had missed four or five table-quiz nights since. Peter wondered if that was the end of it or if they would gradually go back to it. After a decent interval.

After.

Tea didn't go with anger. He poured it down the sink and, ten minutes later, found himself leaving the twenty-four-hour petrol station with a naggin of whiskey in a brown paper bag.

The first shot of whiskey made no dent in things, but the second knew its business well. By the third, he was able to press play on an old episode of Fintan's TV show.

It wasn't his show at all, Fintan insisted, which only made it all the more enjoyable to wind him up by calling it that. It was an eight-parter on the use of biomedical engineering to help people who struggled with their everyday lives for different reasons. In the first of Fintan's episodes, an older woman who had had a stroke was struggling to regain a range of motion in her hands and arms.

'The real problem,' her daughter confided, 'is she's a bit depressed.'

The thing about Fintan, Peter noticed again now, as he had the first time he watched the episode, was that he spoke to the woman rather than the camera.

'I'm Fintan,' he said to her. 'I'd say you're bored out of your skull without all your favourite things to do. Tell me, what are you missing most?'

It was the first time she had smiled in weeks, her daughter told the camera.

That was Fintan. Nothing about himself, all the engineering qualifications, the lectureship in rehabilitative technologies, the innovation team he led at the university. Just straight in there, seeing who she was and what she needed.

Peter topped up his glass and watched screen-Fintan in his lab, working on a simulated knitting game. A ball of energy moving from one table to the next, pushing his thick hair impatiently out of his eyes.

'We've uploaded over a hundred patterns for jumpers and cardigans and cushion covers,' Fintan told the delighted woman.

'I'll knit one for you,' she promised him.

'You knit it and I'll wear it,' he said, and they shook hands and laughed.

Where would it all go, all that personality, all that life? Fintan would go from a breakout star of last year's series to a caption at the end of the next series' credits. *In loving memory of* and a photo of him filling the screen. His tangible clutch-it-in-two-hands identity gone, replaced by memory, with all its frailty and fallibility and liability to damage by other people.

The second episode was the one with the child and the video gait analysis. 'Will you run for me?' Fintan asked, and Peter wasn't able for it.

Maudlin. That was the word. That was *exactly* the word. If he was waiting for anger, he would be there yet.

Peter's eyes felt like they had been peeled. While he had apparently managed to make it to his bed at some stage, he hadn't had the foresight to close the curtains again and the sun – even in its weakened winter state – was lasering through his skull. He was as raw and exposed as bare feet in the snow.

Oh, alcohol was all promises of a protective layer of righteous anger, but mute on what happened afterwards.

He sighed and tried to sit up in the bed. There was no way he'd manage the office like this. Never mind a site visit.

Let people hold on to their homes for one more day.

'Food poisoning is so rotten,' Anita said when he phoned the office.

He accepted her sympathy and her promise to rearrange his day and let everyone know who needed to know. In exchange, he endured her story of a bad takeaway, nodding and mmhming in the appropriate places, reminding himself to be grateful he was known for not being much of a drinker.

When he hung up, he was surprised to find it was still early. What was he to do with his day? He could go to the gym, he supposed. Sweat it out. Cycle the stationary bike until his blood hammered loud enough to drown out the Artane Boys' Band clashing their cymbals in his head. It would be an appropriate punishment for his lack of judgement in drinking whiskey.

Whiskey on a weeknight. On what people with children called a school night.

He didn't like the gym on the best of days. Who did? Wasn't the whole thing designed for people who didn't like themselves? Who else could look into the wall-to-wall mirrors at their own red, sweaty, unappealing faces. 'You're not the worst-looking I've dated,' a woman told him once, a backhander that came back to him every time he emerged from the changing room and into the gym proper.

He could go out on the real bike, he supposed. Get some fresh air. But that felt increasingly like taking his life in his hands. All those unnecessary SUVs, with their drivers chatting away on their phones as if hands-free meant they could throw their concentration wherever they liked, like ventriloquists.

He unlocked his phone and scrolled through his social media feed. Misery, anger, despair. Charity fundraisers. Empty exhortations to be kind.

How did Fintan pass the time these days? Knowing Caroline, she had something programmed for him. A podcast, something humorous, maybe, or soothing. Whatever it was, it would be exactly the right thing. That was the beauty of knowing someone inside out.

A wasted hour later, he managed to get himself up and into the shower. Since he had time to spare, he felt around his balls, tried to get a little something going. There was an actress he'd seen in a movie a few weeks back who had stayed in his head. The fearless, focused type. With added leather trousers in case the fearlessness and focus were too subtle. Instead, he found himself probing for lumps.

Jesus. Fuck. There was the will to wank vanished and gone. Was nothing sacred?

The couch ate the morning, then lunchtime, then the afternoon.

Daytime television was all the same. Middle-aged people moving house or doing up their house or clearing out their house in the hope of finding a fortune they hadn't had to work for. He didn't know whether it was intended to be motivating or dispiriting.

Whatever the intention, the effect was an oozing dread that this was where they were all headed. That everyone had the same compulsion towards magnolia walls and gravel driveways once they hit a certain age. Peter muted the ads and looked around at his own walls, two crisp white walls and two a rich dark red. Looking at it now, he wondered if it was a bit masculine. A bit dark and off-putting. Especially with the black leather sofa. At the time he had thought it pleasingly minimalist, but now he wasn't so sure. Perhaps a warmer white for the walls, and maybe ochre for the chimney breast. Something that would be a splash of bright whether morning or evening.

It would take a bit of work to cover the red. He could get someone in to do it, of course. Save himself the bother of dust sheets and masking tape. But at the first hint of a tradesman about the place, Noel would be at the door with his stepladder and his van full of bits and a neighbour prevailed upon to sit with Sheila. No amount of reasoning would convince him it was a bad idea to be working at a height at his age. He could do it without telling him, Peter supposed, but that would be to deprive himself of a lively topic of conversation for their weekly phone calls. A life in small details. That was how he and Noel kept in touch.

He should phone him, Peter knew. He was very fond of Fintan and no doubt news of his move to the hospice would be all around the parish by now. Noel would be worrying. But there was no way to talk to Noel without asking for Sheila. Without having to hear the pride in Noel's voice as he told him she still knew him, still perked up when his name was mentioned, although she was liable to ask when he was due in from school or whether himself and Fintan were out gallivanting. There was no way to talk about her when she was all but gone and he wasn't yet finished needing her.

He would phone Noel. He would. He just needed to get out and do something with the day first.

The pelting rain meant the driving range was empty save for one older woman meticulously whacking balls into the far distance. She didn't so much as glance up as Peter set down his bucket and swung his arms in an approximation of a warm-up.

The first few shots were disastrous by any objective standard, even for a sometime pitch-and-putt player like Peter. As the bucket emptied, Peter's rage surged and he abandoned all pretence at technique in favour of simply belting them as hard and as far as physically possible.

Fintan wasn't angry.

Unfathomable, given the pure misfortune of it. The lack of anyone or anything to blame.

He doesn't want to waste his time and energy on anger,

Al reported. He was the first of The All-Rounders to brave a visit to Fintan's house after that night of darts in the pub. Peter wondered if he had sent the same text to everyone individually, now that their quiz WhatsApp group had been quietly retired. *Doesn't want it around him, he says. Or around Caroline. Corrosive, he says.*

So Peter couldn't be angry. He had no claim to a fury his friend believed damaging.

He looked out to where the balls lay scattered on the ground. Pity the poor fucker who had to go and pick them up in the downpour. The place was quiet, though; they would likely leave them where they lay until the rain eased.

'You're not hurling, you know,' the older woman called across to him. 'Nobody is going to come and take the ball off you. You can take your time.'

'Thanks,' he muttered without turning. If he had, he might have been tempted to tell her that all his hurling was done from the ditch.

Going to hurling matches was his and Noel's thing almost from the start.

Sheila took care of the practicalities of settling him into his room, getting him his school uniform and books, asking about likes and dislikes, schoolwork, hobbies, whether or not he had made friends – the kind of practical care that Peter came to recognise as love.

Her questions about whether or not he had made friends made him squirm. The little crease of worry that appeared on Sheila's face when he had no answer in response. 'You can invite a friend to tea, any time you like,' she repeated. 'This is your home now too.' Peter nodded and tried not to worry about her worry.

Noel was more of a background presence for the first few weeks. After a year-long stint with his mam and Ken, his mam and Lee, his mam and Tony, Peter was a bit wary of men in general, if not Noel in particular.

Noel knocked on Peter's bedroom door one Sunday morning. He respected a closed door, Noel had told him the day he arrived. Peter's room was his own and nobody would go in without his say-so.

'Up and at 'em,' was all he said.

When they pulled into the car park of the GAA grounds in a town about an hour away, Noel climbed out. 'Grab your coat and come on.'

He paid for the pair of them at the gate and had a good look around before leading Peter to the grassy bank behind the goal.

'Who's playing?' Peter asked but missed the answer in the wave of disappointment that crashed over him at the sight of the two teams coming onto the field brandishing hurleys. Hurling! He knew nothing about hurling! At least with football he knew some of the rules.

'The important thing is to be here.' Noel winked at him. 'You'll see.'

When the referee blew the whistle to start the match, Peter did his best to follow the action, but the ball was so small that he had to look to the swivelling heads in front of him to know where to look.

After a while, he noticed that when someone in the crowd shouted something, Noel sometimes repeated it, to a chorus of agreement. Not all the time. Every few minutes, maybe.

'Well. And what did you make of that?' the man beside them asked when the whistle blew for half-time.

Noel threw his eyes to heaven. 'Might as well give the ref a jersey,' he said.

'You said it!' the man laughed, thumping Noel on the arm. 'Did you ever see anything like the number of steps before he thought to pass it?'

'Might as well glue the sliotar onto it,' Noel agreed. 'Listen, the young lad here is dying for a slash.'

'Say no more.' The man raised his hand and ushered them on.

They were back in the car before Noel spoke again. 'Half a match is a good start. You're living in the country now, Peter. The matches are part and parcel of it. They're not the worst, you know. Gives you something to say and someone to say it to.'

For the next two months, they went each Sunday, graduating from half-matches to waiting for the final whistle. Different teams, different towns. Noel always used the same handful of phrases and Peter could soon tell when he was getting ready to throw one out. 'Ah, come on!' 'Sake!' 'Keep pulling.' 'Our arse is out in the wind.' It got to the stage that Peter joined in with the occasional comment. More of a mutter than a shout, it was true, but still.

'That'll do you,' Noel said. 'Not everyone is a shouter. If they were, the players wouldn't hear the whistle.' He lit a cigarette from the car lighter, opening the windows on both sides as if Sheila wouldn't be able to smell it the next time she sat in the car.

That was Noel. He saw more than he let on.

Peter sighed. Noel. He should phone him.

Instead, he went to pay for another bucket of balls, earning himself a raised eyebrow from the woman with a sedate third-of-a-bucket still to play.

The vegetables were chopped and ready and the oil was heating in the wok. Peter filled a pint glass of water from the tap, slugged its coldness down into his belly and refilled it again. Something in the action of refilling the same glass, the stack of bright peppers and carrots and red onions, was suddenly unbearable. Monk-like nearly. Peter decanted the lot into a Tupperware box and took himself off to the pub.

Flanagans was quiet in the early evening. What he needed, Peter decided, was something deep-fried. Something battered and sorry in yesterday's oil. He ordered a fizzy water while he waited, and a beer he didn't want and wouldn't drink. It was easier to order one than to have people thinking he was judging them. A beer on the table let everyone stand easy.

There was a clatter on the table and Peter found himself looking at a fine piece of haddock, fresh from the fryer, the batter crisped up to look like a tail, and all perched on a mound of chips. His usual. His stomach groaned at the sight of it.

He and Lynn used to come here a lot. She often stayed over on a Sunday night and they got in the habit of dropping in for their dinner. Sunday nights needed a bit of a lift, Lynn declared, and Flanagans was handy.

Everything about their relationship was convenient, but it took Peter a while to see it. Lynn worked in the tax office, over on the other side of the council building, which meant she knew what a sheriff was and what he did. It saved him having to explain. To pitch himself, as he had come to think of it. Lynn already knew the score and was, like many council employees, more interested in what people weren't doing than what they were.

They had met at the council's sports-and-social Christmas drinks and shared a taxi home when they discovered they lived in the same area. In the back of the taxi, she kicked off her shoes and took out her phone and Peter thought, with a sudden rush of interest, that he had never seen anyone quite so sure of themselves. Emboldened, he leaned forward. 'Since you have the phone handy, I'll give you my number,' he said, and was delighted with her huge laugh.

Things were easy with Lynn. That was one reason they lasted two years. She liked being part of a couple. It suited her.

It suited him, too, no point pretending otherwise. It

was nice to have someone to take with him to Fintan and Caroline's for dinner on a Friday night. Fintan liked everyone, of course, but he properly liked Lynn, who read a lot and wasn't shy about sharing her opinion. The pair of them would invariably get into an argument about something – whether direct provision or artificial intelligence or the right order to watch the *Star Wars* movies – and Caroline and Peter would retreat to the kitchen to do the dishes in companionable half-chat, half-quiet.

That was how Peter knew Caroline liked Lynn, because she was happy to let Fintan loose on an argument unsupervised and with all pretence at politeness vanished.

It was very easy. Too easy.

The steps were all there in front of him, all he had to do was walk them. A few dates. Staying over a night at a time, then two. Dinners with his friends, dinners with her friends. Graduating on to weekends away in Ireland in a nice quality hotel. Lynn liked to dress up for dinner – high heels, her hair up and her earrings brushing her neck. She was one for making the effort and, to give her her due, it was always worth it. Peter's weren't the only eyes that followed her across a room.

Peter met her parents in a series of well-reviewed restaurants, where her father ordered good wine and pressed Peter to leave the car and get a taxi home.

Lynn met Noel and Sheila, who were half-scattered with delight, falling over themselves in their anxious efforts to make an impression. Lynn had her phone out and was showing them this and that, in that way she had, and it was suddenly all Peter could do to stay in the chair. A dog waiting patiently for a statue to throw the ball for him. '*He doesn't know it's a statue!*' Lynn crowed, as if she thought they were too dim to figure it out for themselves. The loud sound of a motorbike that turned out to be two men on a moped, one driving while the other sat behind him blowing a slide trombone, like the world's smallest parade: '*It's a trumpet, look!*'

Peter watched Sheila, sitting in her armchair at the head

of the table, reaching for words and missing them. 'Having a back-in-five,' Noel called it, still ready to believe it was nothing. He would lay the full flat of his hand on the tabletop as he said it, give it two quick little taps and smile. Lynn, fully apprised of Peter's concern and Sheila's refusal to discuss it, chatted away easily as if nothing had changed, repeating it all again word for word when Sheila asked the same question a few minutes later.

It was all easy until it wasn't.

Peter began to notice he was unsettled. He told himself he was tired, he was agitated, he was worried about Sheila. Anything but admit he wasn't happy. Anything but ask himself why, if he didn't want to share those worries with Lynn, he was with her at all.

In Flanagans, they ordered their usual – Caesar salad for her, fish and chips for him – and while they waited for the food to come, Lynn started to show him videos of her niece, toddling towards the camera saying some shite or sitting in the bath and saying some shite. She might as well have taken a biological clock out of her handbag and stuck it on the table between them.

'I think we should break up,' he said.

'You don't know what you want,' she said, hours later when they were still going over the same ground. The same *why*s and *I don't know*s.

'We've come to a natural end,' he kept saying, a phrase he felt managed to be both firm yet respectful of the time they had spent together and the expectations that might have arisen.

Lynn did not agree with his assessment. Nor was she exactly complimentary about his suggestion that it was fairer to her if they called it quits now, when a baby was the next step in her plan for her life.

'I thought you would be mad for a family of your own,' she said, and he would have admired her directness if it hadn't been smothered in a cruelty that did nothing for her cause.

It took some convincing for her to see that just because he

94

didn't know what he wanted didn't mean that she could fill the gaps with what she wanted.

'Congratulations,' she said in the finish. 'If what you wanted was to obliterate our relationship and make me feel as if I never knew you at all, then you can consider that a goal achieved.'

It would be little comfort to her to hear that he wasn't sure he knew himself at all either.

'Are you certain you aren't just panicking?' Caroline asked him, and he wondered for a minute if Lynn had asked her to ask. Not that it mattered where the question came from. He was sure.

Peter took the few remaining chips in a doggy bag. He liked to put them in the garden for the seagulls that ventured in from the harbour, a blatant bribe so they would leave the bird feeder to the sparrows and wrens.

Despite not even lifting the bottle of beer to his lips, he drove as carefully as if the L-plate was still on the back window, stopping completely at every roundabout and yield sign he met.

The hospice car park was nearly full. He drove between the lines of cars belonging to people who had done their day's work and then come to help their loved ones die easier. Caroline's red Mini was in the second-to-last row and he hoped that she would leave while there were still people around. He didn't like the idea of her crossing the tarmac in the dim light thrown by the overhead lights.

He turned off the engine and took a minute to compose himself.

He could go in.

Could he go in?

If he went in, what would he say to Fintan? No amount of history could paper over the gulf that now existed between them. Talk of the past would put it in neon lights that the past was all Fintan had now.

They met one lunchtime in the schoolyard. It was a couple of weeks after Peter's first day. That nightmare day when everyone crowded around and shouted questions – *where are you from? Why are you starting in the middle of the year? Who do you support?* After a couple of weeks, the interest in him had died down and he was left alone. He stood in his usual spot by the wall, in the shade of the big tree. Far away from the football game to avoid the danger he would be drafted in. Someone would have had to be looking for him and he knew nobody was.

'Give it time,' Sheila told him in the mornings when she dropped him off, already alert to his habit of assuming the worst. If he was giving it time, it was for Sheila's sake. He hadn't been with them long, but they seemed decent and the food was good and plentiful.

Anyway, there he was at his wall, when a skinny boy walked over, frowning at nothing, in a way that would become more familiar to Peter than his own face.

'Hold this for me,' he said, holding out a piece of string.

Peter suspected some kind of a trap, he just didn't know what. Some kind of practical joke. 'Hold it yourself,' he said.

'I can't,' the boy said patiently. 'I need to hold the other end and my arms aren't long enough to do both.' The boy stretched his two arms out as far as they could go, wiggled the tips of his fingers and dropped them back to his sides.

He looked at Peter then and Peter waited for him to say, 'Hey, you're the new kid,' but he didn't. Instead, he said, 'Look, if you don't want to hold it, can you at least stand on it to stop it moving?'

Peter thought for a moment and decided it was probably safe. When the boy placed the end of the string on the ground, Peter trapped it under the sole of his new black runners. He was glad that Sheila hadn't insisted on the regulation school shoes. 'They all look the same to me,' she had said in the shop when she caught him looking at the wall of shiny new runners. 'Pick whichever one you like best.'

'What are you doing anyway?' Peter asked as the boy began to move away.

'Measuring,' he said and Peter wondered if that was the trick: to make him ask.

But then the boy stopped and turned and his eyes had a kind of shine to them. 'The length of the base of the smallest pyramid in Egypt was three hundred and thirty-five feet. I wanted to see if it would fit here.'

'Why?' Peter asked.

The boy shrugged. 'It'd be cool to know.'

That evening, Peter went into the dining room, where Noel and Sheila kept their books. The bottom shelf of the bookcase was taken up with a row of encyclopaedias, *The Joy of Knowledge*, they were called. He took 'P' from the row and began to flick through.

'Great to see them being used,' Sheila said, passing through on her way to do something else. She never seemed to stop or to sit, except briefly when eating. 'I'd say we never cracked the covers.'

'Why do you have them?' Peter asked, then cringed at how cheeky it sounded. He meant it genuinely – the idea of having something you didn't need was alien to him.

But Sheila smiled. 'They were one of those offers. You know – collect one a fortnight and then after two years you have the full set. We started and I suppose it became a habit.'

Peter nodded and went back to his reading. Sheila patted his shoulder. 'The next time anyone asks why we have them, I can say "they're our Peter's".'

I never told you that the next day at school, I waited in the yard for you to find me. I had it rehearsed in my head. 'Well,' I said casually. As if my heart wasn't thundering in my ears. 'Will the Menkaure pyramid fit or not?'

That was you all over, Fintan. Forever gathering titbits and friends and bits of this-and-that, drawing us all into your life.

Even as he said the words aloud, Peter knew they would go no further than the quiet of the car. The time for easy reminiscing was gone, leaving only the prospect of awkward pseudo-eulogy. With no future to speak of, there were simply no good words.

He saluted Caroline's car before driving home to tea and the telly.

SEA

SIS

The light was all wrong when Sis woke, and it was only the familiar weight of Laddy on the bed beside her that kept her from calling out in panic for Frank. Silly of her to fall asleep in the girls' room. And with the window open, too. No wonder her neck was stiff and sore.

She rolled onto her side, shifted slowly to the vertical, swung out her legs and stood.

She could do with Cathy right now, she thought as she dragged pillows from pillowcases. But no. This was her job to do and do it she must. And step lively. She tucked the linens into one of the pillowcases and left them in the kitchen. She could wash them after breakfast. There was good drying out; they would be ready to come in off the line by the time she got back from town. If they weren't too wrinkled, they could go straight into the bag for the St Vincent de Paul shop. She had seen several of those bags in the stuff drawer yesterday. Press them into service and that would be two things cleared.

The sky was in two minds about itself this morning. Heavy with cloud and the sun a bright fist trying to punch through. The sea remained a stubborn brown. Its hackles-raised look, Sis thought of it. The sea with a growl in its throat. The real sea. Enjoying its power and temper. Not like the summer sea in its party dress, all blue-and-white frills and performance.

She and Laddy were one as sluggish as the other as they headed out the gate for their walk. It wasn't until they reached the peace of Bunty's Cove that she could take a full breath. Drawing the air down deep, feeling her lungs crackle with life. If she was honest, she regretted missing the night in her own bed. Their bed. 'One to go,' she told the waves and they sucked in their breath and held it for a respectful moment before lying down at her feet.

The sea always had the power to make her feel better. Even as a child, when the problems of her little world seemed huge and insurmountable: the door slammed behind her father, her mother white-faced after the doctor saw Bunty, her sister's eyes growing ever bigger in her thinning face. The sea with its murmurings and rhythms soothed the worst of her unquiet.

It might have been yesterday that she was pulling at her mother's skirt, asking – whinging, she realised once she had children of her own – to go to the beach. 'Can't you go yourself?' her mother had snapped and there it was. A lifetime of freedom thrust at her in a busy moment.

Young Sis wasted no time. She took none of the usual trappings that accompanied her mother on their walks to the beach. The handled basket stuffed with towels and sun lotion, a blanket and book for Bunty so that she might sit safely in the shade and not have to be brought home almost immediately after arrival, a flask of tea and a stack of enamel mugs that scalded the mouth off you.

Instead, Sis ran, on winged feet it felt like, across the yard and out the gate and scrambled down the bank as quickly as she could before her mother could change her mind and call her back. Or – worse – ask her to take her sister with her. Sis loved Bunty fiercely, but Bunty wasn't much fun at the beach anymore. She was slow now, preferring to walk the long way around by the path rather than tumbling down the sandy bank and landing on the beach in a giggling, breathless heap the way they used to. Bunty was easier to like before she was sick, Sis thought, and the guilt made her itch inside her clothes. She would find the nicest shell for Bunty, Sis decided. The very nicest one. Even if she loved it herself – even if it was the very nicest shell *she ever saw* – she would give it to her sister. The thought of it, her sister's joy, her own sacrifice and goodness, sent Sis skipping along the beach, eyes cast down, searching.

It wasn't a shell she found in the end, but the perfect stone, worn smooth by the water before landing in a warm rock pool where it could no longer be dragged in and out by the waves. Sis had been following the rainbow that lingered after an earlier shower – the shell for Bunty long forgotten – when it vanished into that selfsame rock pool. She had lain down on her stomach in the sand and trailed her fingers in the warmth of the water, hardly daring to breathe in case her fingers closed around the pot of gold. Instead, the stone slipped into her hand. It was the perfect size for a small palm, with a ring of white circling one side, marking it out as chosen.

Bunty's eyes – so dark now, like two burnt holes in a blanket, their mother said, in the special voice she used when she was pretending not to worry – shone when she saw it. 'I'll feel I'm there with you on the beach,' she said, taking Sis's scratched hand with her own cool one.

After the funeral, Sis snuck in and took the stone before her mother cleared out Bunty's room.

'I'll feel you're here with me,' she whispered, but there was no trace of Bunty in the still air of the empty bedroom.

It was when Sis got to the beach that she understood that this was where Bunty was, in the shelter of the rocks, among the sigh of the waves and the whoosh of the salty breeze.

The stone had sat on Sis's bedside locker all the years since. It was in the instructions she had left for the solicitor: she was to be buried in her wedding dress, with Bunty's stone clasped in her palm. People would think it strange. Might wonder if they knew her at all. But Cathy, Doreen and Mike would remember the Sis-and-Bunty lore they had grown up with. They would understand and that was what mattered.

Out in the sea, she could see Danny Creed's head, seal-like, among the waves. Rain, hail or shine, he swam the width of the beach, Sailor the dog trailing him, barking all the way. In excitement on the first lap, Sis thought, and in encouragement on the return leg. Dogs knew what a person needed. The day Tom Creed was buried, Danny landed in front of his father's coffin with his hair dripping seawater onto the shoulders of his suit. When Sis shook his hand in sympathy, she could smell the salt on him still.

She leaned in and gave him the only thing she had.

'We learn to live with it,' she said, and he raised his eyes to hers and nodded.

That was the sea for you. It made enough of itself to go around.

She had thought of asking Danny Creed to take Laddy for her, but he was too old to swim and too stubborn to stay on the beach and wait. Stubborn and set in his ways.

Sis ran her fingers over the wooden sign proclaiming *Bunty's Cove*. Her mother had been near-hysterical in the months after Bunty's death, going each day to the graveyard to see if her headstone had been erected. 'Using most un-Christian language,' the parish priest said when he called to tell her father something needed to be done. Her father's response was to show him the door and disappear out to the henhouse. When he came out the following day, it was with a small wooden sign carved with the words *Bunty's Cove*. He took her mother's hand and led her down onto the beach, to the sheltered spot Bunty liked best. The council left the sign where he put it, a grace extended because of her mother's long history in the place. The weather was less kind, touching and stroking the wood until the letters were worn smooth. Sis traced them with her index finger; they were as thin and delicate as Bunty herself. Accidental artistry on her father's part.

'That is the one comfort in getting old,' she told Laddy, who was snuffling half-heartedly through seaweed. 'Things that would destroy you when you're younger are no more than a drop in the bucket.'

The woman was standing inside the big front window of the Blue House, looking back into the room behind her. Sis wondered if she ever sat in the sheltered cove of the beach and asked who Bunty was, why she was gifted the one sheltered spot in a sea of wildness. As if in answer, the woman turned and Sis knew her, suddenly, as the same child who used to come in the summers long ago. The parents came for years, bringing their own food and drink and friends, so they never had to mix with the locals. When the work started on the house, there was talk it had been sold, but then it all ground to a halt and was forgotten until recently. Yet here was the same girl, a woman now, and the house evidently not sold at all.

The girl was a poor watchful little thingeen, Sis had thought at the time, forever peering sidelong at Cathy and Doreen and Mike as if they might take a bite out of her. She had the same big dark eyes and narrow shoulders now as she had then, dressed in a neat little jumper that would never keep the wind out. An indoor jumper.

What was she doing back at all? If Sis was staying, she might have made it her business to find out, but she had no time for questions today. There were jobs to be done yet.

When Sis opened the back door, the stillness rushed out to meet her. That was the way of it sometimes: when the sea was loud, the house felt shy by comparison. What she wouldn't have given for such quiet when the children were small and the house rang with their wanting. The most rewarding job in the world, people said, as if to expect time off was pure greed.

She made herself a cup of tea and settled down to write her

letters. She needed to get a grasp on things if she was going to finish on time. Tomorrow, she thought, suddenly. *Before tomorrow.* Which meant even less time for nonsense. She would write Doreen's letter, Sis decided. Doreen's would be the easiest.

Dear Doreen,

How is the new play going? Although I see from the calendar that it is not due to 'open' for another three weeks, so I imagine you are only in rehearsals yet.

It stood out on the page, that 'only'. She could write the third secret of Fatima underneath it, but that 'only' would be all Doreen saw. She was a great one for imagined slights.

Sis and Frank had gone to see her in one of her plays once, when she still lived in Dublin. In a damp little apartment she shared with a woman she called her 'friend' as if Sis had come down in the last shower. Doreen said it with a smirk, delighted at the idea she was getting one over on her mother. It was easier to let her believe it. As if Sis – as if anyone! – cared who stuck what where anymore. Whatever the friend was to Doreen, they weren't able to stay with her, which meant booking into a hotel. The waste of it had Frank in a bit of a spin. She didn't know why at the time, of course. Either way, they argued about it. Sis wanted to stay somewhere nice and central – she was no shopper, but the atmosphere of the capital wasn't something a person had the chance to soak up every day. Frank insisted on being out near the train station, even though their return tickets were booked and all they had to do was show up on time. They fought a full day and a night over it, Sis wondering if they were each secretly enjoying taking sides after the years of relative calm between them.

They went backstage after the show and if they were looking for glamour, they were disappointed. It was all dirty cotton-wool balls and piles of sweaty tights, and people falling over one another to get to their belongings.

'I hope you don't leave your purse in here,' Frank had said, looking around at the chaos, and Doreen flushed scarlet. If it wasn't for that, Sis thought, they might have had a nicer evening. Gone for drinks with the cast, maybe. Frank could have had a coffee. They might even have talked about the play itself, let Doreen have her triumph at wrong-footing them with her onstage nudity. As if they hadn't washed every inch of that beloved body for years. Instead, Doreen marched them silently back to the distinctly dingy restaurant in the basement of their hotel and ate a bare mouthful of her salad before 'remembering' that she had an early appointment and needed to get home.

'I'm glad she's gone,' Frank said and reached across the table to take Sis's hand. It would be mean-spirited to agree out loud, but she squeezed back and when the waiter came over, she asked for another glass of wine.

The nights are drawing in and with the hotel closed, the road is quiet. That suits myself and Laddy, as you know. A woman has come to stay in the Blue House – she used to come in the summers as a child. You might remember her to see. You were about the one age, as I recall. It's funny to look at her and easily believe that she is a grown woman, when, to my mind, you're still the small girl you used to be. She hasn't set foot out the front door yet, but there's little life about the place in winter, as you would no doubt remind me.

Seeing the woman in the Blue House, Sis wondered again what it might have been like to have Doreen living next door to her. An idle thought, with neither power nor future to it. This place would suck the life from Doreen. Hadn't Sis let her go in the full knowledge that it would take failure or disaster to bring her back again? That this, to Doreen, was a place of last resort. A place for people whose life had gone wrong on them.

They broadcast your play on the radio a few weeks ago.
Myself and Laddy listened with great enjoyment and fondness,
although the sound of your voice made him lonesome. He kept
getting up to see were you outside in the hallway. You were the
best thing in it, but I'm sure you know that. I hope you know
that. I hope you're proud of yourself, the life you've built, the
choices you've made. You should be.

In the background, the radio announcer told her it was coming
up on the hour. She pushed the notepad to one side and got to
her feet. 'The morning is gone on us, Laddy,' she said. There
was no time to finish the letter, nor to get the sheets washed
and on the line. Not if she wanted to get into town and be sure
of getting home in daylight.

'There's no good looking at me like that,' she told Laddy.
'We'll have no dinner if I don't get to town.'

She would have the evening long to finish her letters.

Sis wheeled the bike out of the shed and leaned it against the
wall to check the chain and the tyres. It was a week since she
cycled it to town and a person could pick up a nail unawares
and be in trouble before they were half a mile down the road.
She used to take Laddy with her, his lead looped around the
handlebars, but he was past that now and preferred to stay at
home with the radio. They had an unspoken deal: he pretended
not to notice her leaving and she pretended she hadn't gone.
It was, in its own way, a version of marriage.

She angled her leg carefully through the frame of the bike.
Gone were the days of standing on the pedal and pushing until
she was coasting along and could swing her leg over with no
loss of momentum. There wasn't a day she didn't want to

go back and catch her younger self by the hand and tell her to savour the power of her body, no matter the job. Whether sweeping the yard or painting the gable or pushing out babies. But if the young only played at memory, then nostalgia and regret were old people's diseases. There was little middle ground, it seemed, or what there was passed unnoticed.

She shook her head. Lord, but she was away with the fairies today. If she wasn't careful, tomorrow would find her still here, half-on and half-off the bike and the sheriff knocking at the door.

Once she was out on the road and freewheeling down the hills, the wind blew through the wool of her cap, tickling her scalp and taking the years with it. She was twenty-five, thirty-five, forty-five years old, pedalling and laughing, Frank beside her on his own bike. They had the car by then, of course, and cycling was just for fun.

And, oh, what fun it was!

Off they would go, the two of them, with a picnic tea in the basket of the bike and Cathy warned to keep the younger ones out of trouble at home. The three of them bribed with the promise of ice cream if all was well when they returned. 'An hour,' Sis would tell them. 'We'll be no more than an hour.' Hadn't they earned it? After hardly seeing each other all week, a Friday evening wasn't much to ask.

On Cathy's last visit, Sis had suffered through her endless circular talk about 'parental guilt'. It was, as far as Sis was concerned, just another plea for attention. The desire to be told she was doing great, when she was simply doing what needed to be done. You fed your children and clothed them. You taught them to read and sent them to school. You hit them or you didn't. Guilt didn't enter into it.

On the far side of the last bend, the town reared in front of her as if she had come around the corner shouting *boo!* People were forever talking about the life and colour of the place.

The truth was when the council first started the campaign to brighten the place and attract tourists, giving grants to paint businesses pink and blue and green and yellow, it all looked a bit unnatural. Sis would come flying around the corner on the bike and see the town pushing itself in front of the countryside, like a badly reared child that didn't know its place.

Over time it grew on her. There was a determined kind of cheer to it. A bravado. It reminded her of Doreen with her bright scarves and earrings. Showcasing the best of itself. Besides, something about the primary colours made the sky more stately in its shades of grey.

She got off the bike and walked it to the rack in front of the supermarket. She had never bothered with a lock and she didn't intend to start now.

'Morning, Sis. How's things?' Tilly Daly called from where she was watering the hanging baskets that gave her an excuse to be out in front of the flower shop rather than in behind her counter. It was a shop Sis never understood. People needed a place to go for their funeral flowers, granted. But when did flowers become the be-all-and-end-all gift for Mother's Day, childbirth, birthdays, leaving parties? Flowers, flowers, flowers. It puzzled her, this insistence on marking new starts with something whose life had been cut from it. Like turning up with roadkill. But Tilly wasn't the worst, foolish shop notwithstanding. She stood tall after her husband hightailed it off to England with a girl barely out of school, and was one of the few to look Sis in the eye after all that business with Mike.

'Morning, Tilly. Grand out today.'

'It is. No Laddy today?'

Tilly would notice, of course. Her own Trixie was gone these past six months. She had to take her to the vet in the finish, Tilly said. She wasn't allowed to stay, imagine. Sixteen years and she had to pat her and walk away, leaving the dog crying and confused. What was worse, she had to spend the evening at home wondering was it done yet. Never again, she had told Sis, the tears standing in her eyes. It was plants and flowers from here on out.

'It's too far for him these days,' Sis said.

'True. Fine day for a bit of exercise all the same.' Tilly gestured to Sis's bike.

Sis nodded. That was more of it. That determination to exercise. It was a sad day when being out in the fresh air, rejoicing in the health and strength of your body, was something that had to be scheduled. In her day, life kept you busy enough that you had no need for going running indoors.

The air inside the shop was warm after the wind on the bike. Sis took a basket from the stack by the door and put her woolly hat into it. Later, she caught sight of herself in one of those big overhead mirrors that make everyone look like a bank robber and realised she had been walking around with her hair standing in a little puff at the back of her head. Never mind. Sure, who would be looking at her anyway?

'Mrs Cotter, how are you?'

'Can't complain, Katie. How's yourself?'

Sis nodded and smiled while Katie talked at dull length about her children and their various activities. It was the same story whenever she came into town. Katie worked in the supermarket and pounced on any chance to stop work and chatter. She used to be in school with the girls and was forever mad for news of them. Sis was careful to have a little titbit each time. She wouldn't give it to Katie Nolan to say that she didn't know what her own children were up to. And sure, if some of the news was a little out of date, what of it? Katie would never know. Neither Cathy nor Doreen were much good at keeping up their girlhood friendships. Sis was grateful for that now. It meant her news – the court and the county home and the whole sorry mess of it – was her own to share with her children as she saw fit.

Katie tailed off from whatever slight or wrong to one or other of her offspring she was recounting. 'How are the girls?

How's Cathy? When I have to get my five up and come into work, I think of her with only two to mind and that big house to do it in. Didn't she land on her feet!'

Sis knew a backhander when she heard one. Katie saw no further than Cathy with the luxury of being at home, where she herself longed to be. Sis thought of her own mother, who had brought work into the house when she couldn't go out to it, washing other people's smalls and ironing their shirts so that her own children might have shoes to wear to school. Cathy was smarter than that.

'Her old firm are mad keen for her to go back,' Sis said. 'Even part-time, but she's having none of it. Babies aren't babies for long and she'll have all the time in the world to pick up her career again then.'

'She'll be lucky to go back at the same level, things move so fast,' Katie said.

'Her heart might be set on something else by then, who knows?' Sis's smile cost her dearly. 'She's determined as ever, our Cathy.'

'And how's Doreen? Will we see her in anything soon?'

'It's all theatre with our Doreen.' Sis mustered a merry laugh. 'She's a purist through and through. Nothing so humdrum as TV.' She leaned closer and said conspiratorially, 'Nothing so well paid, either. Poor as a church mouse she is, but it's all about the quality of the role.' Satisfied that she had made a virtue out of Doreen's poverty, Sis made to move on, but Katie wasn't done with her yet.

'I hear you have a new neighbour. Or should I say an old neighbour? That funny O'Gorman girl who used to skulk around town on her own. She's as strange as ever, I hear. Tell me, is it true she arrived in the dead of night in a blacked-out van?'

Sis blinked. 'I couldn't tell you. She could have ridden in naked on a Shetland pony for all I know. Whatever way she came, it was quiet. Other than that, you're as wise as I am.'

Katie didn't like that. 'She won't be your neighbour for long, I suppose. You're on the move yourself shortly, I hear.'

She would be damned, Sis thought, if she let this little madam have the last word. 'Onward and upward, that's me. I'll be spoiled for company, I believe. They tell me I'll be hoarse from chat and deafened from news. You'll have to call up. They do a smashing afternoon tea on a Thursday, I'm told. Sparkling wine and everything. Sure, why not start the weekend early when we can?' Her jaw creaked with the effort of holding her smile as Katie walked away.

Just like that, the day soured on her. The saving grace was that Katie didn't ask about Mike. Even she wouldn't be so brazen. He was the family's private business, which meant people only talked about it behind their backs.

Unable to face the remaining aisles, the endless breathing of other people's air, Sis took her basket straight to the till and paid for her potato and carrot.

'Fine day today,' the young lad behind the till said, smiling up to his two ears. 'Won't be long now till Christmas is on us.'

No doubt it was part of his training. *Be nice to the old biddies. They might not talk to anyone else all day.* As if she couldn't tell the difference between sociable and patronising. As if a person's years were in inverse proportion to their cop-on. For heaven's sake. It wasn't like the one starved the other.

She yanked her hat down hard on her head and looked around for Laddy before remembering she hadn't brought him. For a second she was lonesome for his warm welcome and considered going straight home while house and dog were still there to greet her. But she had things to do and no one to do them for her.

She placed her shopping in the basket on the bike, moving her library book to make space. The hen might grace her with an egg later to go with it. No, she decided suddenly. If this was going to be her last dinner at home, she might as well go out with a bang. With a steak from the butcher, no less. What of it? Weren't her teeth all her own?

Crowleys butchers was at the other end of town. Coogans was closer, but they were very pass-remarkable and she didn't like giving them the business. Everyone that darkened their door brought in gossip the way Laddy tracked in mud and it was as well to stay off their radar. No doubt Coogans had word of the eviction up and down the town before she heard it herself.

She would go to the library first, Sis decided. It wouldn't do to have time run out on her and miss the window before they closed for lunch. She was never late returning with a book and she wasn't going to start now.

Inside, she was pleased to see Noreen behind the desk. She was a nice woman, great for news but not in such a way that it left a person feeling grubby.

'Sis! How are you, pet? I was wondering if we'd see you this week.'

'I wasn't sure I'd make it in before you closed.'

Noreen rolled her eyes. 'That's all pushed back. We can't close until two o'clock now. Customer-focused and all that.' She leaned confidentially over the counter. 'It's a long morning, I don't mind telling you. My belly thinks my throat's been cut.'

'Can you keep a packet of biscuits or anything back there discreetly?' Sis asked, herself no stranger to the growl of hunger.

'Firing offence.' Noreen rolled her eyes. 'If I was a smoker, nobody would bat an eye if I stood outside the door for five minutes here and there, but food? Don't make me laugh.'

'Could you claim a food addiction?' Sis asked.

Noreen took a theatrical step back from the counter and waved her hand up and down the rasher-length of her body. 'The evidence is against me,' she said, beginning to laugh.

Sis joined her in a giggle. 'Stacked against you, you might say.'

'Well, it certainly isn't stacked on me,' Noreen said and that started the pair of them off again.

Behind Sis, someone cleared their throat. Noreen reached under the counter and took out a pair of dice. 'I'll be here when you're ready,' she told Sis.

Noreen had turned to the next person before Sis had a chance to tell her she wasn't taking out a book today. Instead, she went and sat at her usual corner table with her back to the wall. These days it was less quiet than when she used to come with the girls when they were tiny. One on the front carrier of the bike and one on the back. The library was a place to bring them when she had nowhere to go and no money to take them, but she would have liked it anyway. It had a cheerful purpose to it, with its book clubs and knitting groups and people researching everything from diseases they might have to places their running-away money might take them. A line of middle-aged men sat at the bank of internet access points, pecking at keyboards with thick index fingers, the cracks of their backsides a defiant display of optimism. There's only so much a person can change, those arses proclaimed.

Sis rattled the dice in her fist. Behind the counter, Noreen gave her a thumbs-up and Sis felt a flush of something. Warmth or sorrow or something akin to one or the other. Noreen was the best of them. Her mother must be right proud of her. What would it be like to have one of the girls working here? Sis let herself imagine for a moment that it was Cathy behind the counter and she was waiting for her to close the doors to the public so that the two of them could go for lunch. Over to the new café, maybe. The one with the old-fashioned cake stands in the window. Sis hadn't liked the look of the place for a while after it opened – she had thought the cream cakes in the window unhygienic and then felt foolish when she realised they were plastic cakes, but it was the kind of thing Cathy would like. A fancy coffee machine that took up half the wall and a row of different fancy milks in the fridge. Sis sighed. Her imagination got her as far as carrying her coffee and cake to their shared table but, faced with conjuring a casual conversation between herself and her eldest, it gave up.

Back to the task at hand. Sis rolled the dice gently on the table. A four and a three. She got up and made her way along the stacks to the fourth aisle, where she touched two books at random, then withdrew a third. It was a book on the Spanish Civil War, with the most beautiful sunrise on the front cover. When Frank was sick – towards the end, when he had hardly the will to open his eyes – she would describe the front cover of a book to him before ever reading a word aloud. A little throwback to their game of years earlier, where she would bring home a book and he would try to guess the content from the cover. Small pleasures, it was true, but no less pleasures for all that. 'Why can't you just pick a book like a normal person?' he would say, shaking his head and laughing. She didn't mind the teasing, knowing that the truth was he delighted in her little idiosyncrasies.

If she were to take this book home, it would tell her what it was like to be a young man fighting a war he didn't agree with. If Sis was honest, it wasn't too much of a wrench to put it back on the shelf. She had read plenty like it in her time. Still, she gave the spine a quick stroke with her fingers, a poor replacement for bringing it home with her – a little like being asked to dance in the last song of the medley. Better than nothing, but you weren't sure what exactly you were supposed to be grateful for.

'That's the last of the books you had checked out. You're all clear with us now. No point tempting you to a recommendation?' Noreen said. 'I've a lovely little detective series just in. The lead character has a dog that's Laddy down to a T.' She paused and lowered her voice. 'The library above in the…' She paused, searching for a word. 'The library above is small, but I can order in anything you like. I'd be delighted to drop it up and bring anything else you fancy. It'll cost you tea and a biscuit, though.'

The news must be well out, Sis thought. Her business known and discussed the length of the town.

'Coogans,' Noreen said apologetically. 'I left my meat on the counter and walked out. Not that that does you any good.'

It didn't and yet it did. Poor Noreen, forever reaching out to everyone. Sis wanted to take her by the hand and lead her down to the beach, stand her in the shallows and tell her that good or bad the ocean saw her.

It was a kindness to offer. An equal kindness to refuse. Nothing killed a friendship faster than one person burdening another. Friendship depended on both parties being free to choose to be there. Never be beholden, her father used to warn her.

'Let me get settled first and I'll be on to you then,' Sis said. She put the dice back on the counter and smiled at Noreen.

'Hang on to them,' Noreen said. 'You can give them back to me when I call up for that cuppa.' She paused and smiled back. 'Once you're settled.'

But when she turned away to deal with another customer, Sis left them where they were.

It would serve her right if Noreen was straight up to Coogans with the story. Sis Cotter: every bit as rude and sulky as they all said she was.

She might even get a free housekeeper's cut for her trouble.

Emerging into the daylight, Sis understood suddenly what it was that made Laddy stand in the yard and howl some nights. It wasn't the moon itself; it was the realisation that the world was at once too big and too small and altogether out of your hands.

Laddy. She should get home, enjoy the time they had left together.

She had asked in the nursing home if she could bring him with her. Of course she had. If you didn't ask, you didn't get. But sometimes you didn't get even when you asked.

'We have a guide dog that comes in the first Monday of the month,' she was told. 'He's the king of the place and gives everyone a great lift.'

'If Laddy was a guide dog, could I bring him?' Sis asked, but the woman had already moved on to talk of something else.

The church door was open, the warmth pouring out. More waste than metaphor, but Sis wasn't so foolish as to refuse the free heat.

She made for the tiny side chapel – not a chapel as much as an alcove with a single bench and a stand of votive candles – and sat down with a sigh. Welcome though the brisk skies were, the cold got into her bones that bit more this year than last. She who was always a winter person, sitting here mooning after snowdrops and early light. Funny how a person could have the season of their soul changed on them.

In the quiet and the warmth, she felt herself opening out the tiniest bit. Enough that she could admit there would be snowdrops and daffodils and crocuses to admire in the garden of the county home. And a dog to pet once a month.

She dug in her change purse for a coin for the candle box. There wasn't much in there. Two crisp fivers and a handful of change. Shrapnel, Frank called it. By the time she had food and heat and light for herself and Laddy and a bit put away for the graveyard groundskeeper to keep her parents and Frank looking spruce, there wasn't a lot left over. Frank's life insurance had gone to the solicitor. They couldn't work for free, they told her several times, as if she was looking for charity.

The shrapnel didn't add up to two euro for a candle for

Bunty, but if she put in fifty cent just this once, there was nobody around to know which or whether. Let God or the other fella keep her in purgatory a day longer. Knock a day off her eternal reward.

The candles were real night lights, boxes of extra-long safety matches left on the ledge at the front. The risk of burnt fingers evidently greater than that of arson. There was still more good than bad around the place. Or the belief in it at least.

Sis lifted the lit candle in the back left corner and moved it further along the row, clearing a space for Bunty. It had to be the back left or it wouldn't work. No point analysing it; it was just one of those strong feelings. Bunty loved the look of candles, but they scared her, and Sis was called on to do all candle work, whether lighting a birthday candle or the range. After Bunty blew out that last birthday candle, Sis lit it again when their mother's back was turned so Bunty could have a second wish. She wouldn't tell Sis what she was wishing for, no matter how Sis pleaded or tried to tempt her with promises of handing over any and all future treats.

'It won't come true then,' she said, her eyes huge and dark in her pale little face.

'It won't come true anyway,' Sis said meanly.

She got her arse reddened for that. She tried to explain that she didn't mean Bunty would never get better, that mightn't even have been what she wished for, but her mother wouldn't listen. She refused to speak, even, other than to hiss that Sis should pull her skirt back down and get out of her sight.

After Bunty died, Sis would talk to her. A word here and there at first, then, gradually, longer, more detailed conversations. Her mother must have told her father, because he called her into the kitchen and told her that if he ever heard her talking to Bunty again, he would have her committed to the asylum in the city. The look on his face was one she hadn't seen before and it frightened her. She was just a child, he told her, so people would take his word for it.

Cathy had something of the same look, a kind of fear mixed with disgust, when they were out with friends and the other mothers were chatting among themselves while Sis sat on a wall and looked into the distance. 'Why can't you be like a real mother?' she would shout when they got home, then run upstairs and slam her bedroom door, Mike toddling after her.

A swishing sound up the aisle caused Sis to look around. The black and white of the Carmelites was unmistakeable. It irritated her, the ostentatious pseudo-humility of it: yards of black to denote their sin and a tiny bit of white for their goodness. As if inviting everyone else to disagree with them. Such thoughts felt disloyal, suspecting as she did that Bunty, had she lived, might have been a nun. No other future was imaginable for her gentle sister. This would have been her place.

Sis sighed. If she were to pray, what should she ask for? What did she deserve?

God was all-merciful, they were taught. Sis thought she might have more to say to a cranky old God. A God tired of living, tired of human shit and talk and havoc and nonsense. Will I pour the tea, she could ask him, knowing he was sugar-sick of levitating it with his mind. They could talk about their children. She was sure Old-Testament God might have thoughts about his hippie long-haired son, with his notions of peace and love and forgiveness. Anyone who thought peace and love were worth a damn never lived off the edge of the Atlantic.

The church never felt like the place for the kind of thinking prayer required. It was designed to make a person feel small in all the wrong kinds of ways. Meek and guilty and creeping. No. If she had a request, it was into the sea she would cast it. God helped those who helped themselves.

The parish office was in the far corner of the churchyard, but there was no answer when she knocked. If she wanted to see the caretaker, she would have to go up to the graveyard and find him. She could cycle there grand, but it would mean walking the high hill back into town afterwards and her legs mightn't have a third walk in them today. It felt like she was cheating on Laddy, but she had no choice. There wouldn't be time to come back into town tomorrow. 'You're on the clock, Sis,' she reminded herself.

She would have to find a different way to pay the caretaker next year. She had them taken care of for the year coming; she could do no more for the moment. She would sort something out. Someone *there* was bound to know. Sis was hardly the only one with more family behind her than ahead of her.

Waiting at the pedestrian crossing, she watched the door of the bookies open and close, open and close, open and close. It was a revolving door the place needed. It had been repainted lately in the more sombre green of modern Ireland, the leprechaun tones and brighter pre-recession shades long gone. Now it was a more grown-up green. A sober green. A we've-matured-into-ourselves-and-learned-our-lessons green. She had to hand it to them. Clever, whoever they were. The marketers. Or was it marketeers? Oh, they were clever all right. The kind of clever that never saw the inside of a jail cell.

Open and close went the door. Open and close. They said it was only the dabblers who ever went into the place nowadays – the hardliners were all at home behind their computer screens. No doubt a terrible shock to their families when it all came out. At least she knew where Frank was on Saturday and Sunday afternoons. After his bath, he would put on his good suit and freshly polished boots. He paid Doreen to shine them on a Friday night for him.

She used to look forward to him going. Relished being alone for a few hours. A chance to catch up with herself. Down to the beach she'd go, rain or shine, and walk the length of it once or twice, with her shoes in her hand and her skirt rolled thick around her waist. What did she think about in those days? Little that she could remember. The sand between her toes. The breath in and out of her lungs in keeping with the waves. The silence before and behind her, save for the high lonesome call of a seagull or a dog barking in the distance.

'Are you all right there, missus? The light is green again.'

The lights must have changed several times and she was blocking the footpath. She shook off the well-meaning arm and stepped into the road just as the light turned red again. She ignored the horns beeping. What great hurry did they think they were in?

On the opposite side, she didn't stop but walked directly to the door of the bookies and pushed it open.

Open and close.

Sis outside.

Sis inside.

A line of men stood against one wall, watching the big screens – horse racing, football, Grand Prix, greyhounds – while the women sat inside the little windows waiting for punters. When Sis entered, the heads all glanced at her before turning back to their business. Whatever they were doing, she thought, it didn't look casual. It didn't look like fun.

Her purse still held the same two fivers, the same ten-euro note. Sis eyed up the women behind the counter before approaching the oldest of them.

'Can I get a list of horses for the next race?' she asked.

The woman – no name tag and sure what need among a houseful of regulars – smiled at her. 'That'll be Clonmel. Here you go, love.' She passed over a newspaper, folded to show the names. 'Take your time with your pick. You've six to choose from.'

Sis scanned through the names, her scalp prickling the way it did when Laddy sat up on the bed at night with a low growl in his throat.

'Family Business to win, please.' She hesitated a moment then pushed her ten euro under the gap in the Plexiglas. It had to be enough that she would feel it. Otherwise why bother, after all this time? Herself and Laddy could share a steak.

The woman passed her slip back under the counter to her. 'They go to post in ten.'

Sis stood quietly by the wall. It was warm and she was tempted to take off her coat and hat, but she didn't want to draw attention to herself. Not that there was any danger of attracting notice from the men lining the place – at her age, she would have been invisible even if she stripped to her knickers in the middle of the floor – but from the universe itself. Who knew but that was the gateway Frank stepped through all those years ago? All those tears ago. One quick bet, he might have thought to himself, then off came the coat and he was lost.

Or it might have been the suit. The fact that after a week of dirty work, Saturday came and he could feel like someone. The clothes maketh the man. Ah, but how quickly they could unmake him, too.

Seven minutes to post. Sis followed the signs to the toilet. It was a single cubicle inside what might have been a broom cupboard back when places had such things. Washing her hands, it was hard not to catch sight of herself in the mirror. Her face had long ago creased into the seasons. Brown in summer. Spring, too, if they were lucky and had a good run of weather. Ruddy in autumn, runny-eyed in winter. Were she to stop going outdoors, she would be hard-pressed to tell what time of year it was at all.

There was one mirror left at home, the cracked cabinet door in the bathroom. A crack ran diagonally from corner to corner so that she was used to seeing herself in two halves and it was odd now to see herself straightened out and whole. She had smashed the mirror herself during a fight. That last, terrible fight, when it all came out, everything Mike had lost and what Frank himself had done to try and get it back. The unthinkable choices he had made.

'Listen to me, Sis, will you listen to me?' Frank had shouted.

'Listen to what? More of your promises? Your lies?'

'It wasn't for me. It was for Mike,' he said. 'They were

going to break his legs, Sis. They told me that to my face. Our boy, Sis. With his two legs broken. What other choice was there?'

'But our house,' she keened. And then, worse, so much worse. 'My beach.'

'It'll be grand, Sis. I'll sort it out, you'll see.'

He was so certain, Frank. Right or wrong, he was always certain. Forever thinking that doing well was a sign of his own talent and good judgement, while his losses were put down to bad luck. He really believed he could beat the system.

'We'll get the better of this thing,' he said, and that was when her hand found the soap dish, a Connemara marble thing that one of the girls had given them some Christmas. Cathy, of course it was Cathy. Doreen habitually claimed either that she 'didn't do' presents or that the post must have been mislaid. Anyway, the marble was there to hand, its weight convincing in her fist. Frank saw the intention on her face.

'Seven years bad luck, Sis,' he said, holding his hand out to her, palm down, like she was a dog to be calmed. She knew already that it would be worth it. That the wild satisfaction would carry her wave-high over whatever misfortune would follow her. She brought her hand to shoulder height and hurled the dish. Soapy water dripping onto her good skirt and she not caring. How enjoyable it was to hate him there in front of her, the pants and jacket already starting to hang off him if she had taken the time to notice it. Frank's mouth dropped open like an *amadán* and his hand lifted to shield his face. The shock written all over him and her own feeling of triumph. The hot, pleasant gush of earned shame searing through her.

She was calm then, once it was done. And when Frank told her he would fix it, he would have Mike's debt cleared in no time, it was a money problem with a money solution, she believed him. A fool for him, even after all the years. He had a gambler's conviction.

His own system beat him in the finish. She sat with him in the doctor's office and watched him pale as the doctor steepled his fingers and listed all the cubbyholes in Frank's body into which the cancer had crawled and nested. Then he died and it became clear, finally, how much he had lost to keep the worst of their son's badness from her. She came straight home from the solicitor and got rid of all of the mirrors. There was no point looking in them and pretending she was whole. The bathroom mirror was true and so it alone stayed put. Crooked Sis and her crooked self.

She would have to get used to mirrors again in the county home. If she didn't, she supposed she could break them. She had form, as they say. She allowed herself a smile at the aptness of the joke, then turned away and wiped her hands on the paper towel.

The atmosphere in the room had changed when she emerged out into the bank of screens. There was an expectant air, a hum of chat as the men muttered about form and colours and weights, while the six horses were caged into the metal shafts that would spit them out into their futures. Did they ever refuse to run? Sis wondered. Simply stand there when the door rolled back and dig in their heels. Stay where they were. Insistent. Waiting to be carried out of it.

She supposed not. They were animals, bred to live by sheer instinct.

It was all over in a matter of minutes, Family Business beaten as if it was ordained. Sis felt strangely bereft. It wasn't that she thought winning would bring her closer to understanding Frank and Mike, it was that losing placed them beyond her reach altogether.

'It's no different to the bingo or the lottery,' Frank had snapped at her once, thrusting his fist into the arm of his coat.

'I don't do the lottery,' she told him smartly.

'You're a saint,' he said, his hands clasped, mocking, in front of him. 'The only saint in the country. Saint Sis.'

She patted her pocket to make sure her purse was still there and turned to leave. Whatever of her husband and son she was looking for, she wouldn't find it here.

There was rain coming, the sky crouched low over the town and the air had a blowsy, barely held feel to it. It was a couple of hours away yet, she judged.

Enough time yet, provided she kept moving.

Crowleys was busy. From the back, it was a wall of navy, black and green polyester. Sensible country colours on sensible country shoulders. A wall of dark lightened by scarves of various hues. Any Tom, Dick or Harry could put on a scarf and call it style.

Sis stood inside the door, waiting her turn and listening to what everyone else was ordering. A person's order gave away their age as surely as their knuckles would. Young people didn't trust themselves – minced beef and chicken fillets were as far as their ambitions stretched.

People her own vintage asked for the classics: a house-keeper's cut, a rump, a loin. Things learned at a mother's knee.

All of it had been too much for Bunty. Her constitution could stomach nothing more than a few shreds from a ham hock, boiled until the meat was fairly falling off the bone. There were plenty of days when Sis or her mother would sit beside Bunty, trying to tempt her with a guggy egg or a plate of pandy. Sis's mouth would water just looking at it, the mashed potato made creamy with milk and butter, with salt to give it a flicker of surprising taste.

Sis herself had to use the butter sparingly or feel the wooden spoon across the back of her hand. 'Do you think we're made of money?' Gluttony was nearly as bad as waste, in her mother's eyes.

When she got to the counter, Bill Crowley himself came to serve her.

'Sis Cotter, the very woman. How's Laddy doing?'

Before Frank died, Bill used to ask, 'How's himself?' It was a mark of service – the kind of careful, knowing service that had all but disappeared – that the very first time she set foot in the shop after Frank's funeral, he had moved smoothly to asking for Laddy, bypassing the ignorant assumption that she was lonely and the new awkwardness that nested between herself and the world.

'He's grand, thanks, Bill. I'll take a couple of slices of cooked ham for him, and a nice bit of steak for myself.' She thought of the meagre pickings in her change purse and added, 'Nothing too big, mind you. Plenty eating in a couple of ounces.'

'Little and often, isn't that what the experts say is good for us?' he said automatically, his hands pulling and cutting and weighing.

She had wondered if Bill would take Laddy for her, but he had his plate full with his son-in-law eaten alive with cancer almost overnight. She couldn't hand him another problem.

Poor Laddy didn't deal well with change anymore. After Frank died, he was bad-tempered with looking for him and not finding him. The postman came off badly, it was true, but his pants were thick and the dog's teeth old and soft. He threatened to report Laddy to the dog warden and have him put down. The bad bastard. Sis ran at him with her own teeth bared and that sent him packing quick smart.

He refused to deliver the post to the door after that, instead leaving it on the gatepost. Making a production of drawing the van up to the gate and leaning out as if his life was in danger. The eejit.

Sis would have been happy to let the wind take the lot of it – what need had she for his leaflets about half-price turnips and free eye tests? – but the solicitors were involved by then and she didn't like to think that Frank's business might blow into a nosey garden. She refused to wait at the window for the post van, she wouldn't give him the soot of it, but it galled her to know she was around the house with one ear cocked for the sound of the engine. The hovering was as bad as the time Doreen ran away to England on the boat and they were three full days and nights waiting to hear if she was drowned or dead or worse.

'There you go.' Bill took the money and put the paper package into a blue plastic bag. 'The tree huggers will have my guts for garters, but there's rain on the way and we don't want you dripping steak and followed by every dog in town.' He held the bag in his hand and looked at her before handing it over. 'I get up the nursing home way a couple of times a week doing deliveries. There's a seat in the van for you any time you fancy a spin out.'

Everyone knew her business. 'Jailbreak already, is it?'

Bill's face shifted, the sorrow flickering for a moment. 'Sure we all need a timeout now and then.'

The opening was there to ask and Sis took it. 'True for you. How's Caroline doing? Is Fintan any better?'

'There'll be no better,' Bill said heavily. 'He's gone into the hospice. Not much left in it, I'd say.'

'I'm sorry to hear it,' Sis said, and she was. They were a fine young couple, and she would forever be grateful to Caroline for that last-minute invite to her wedding. The last time herself and Frank had danced together, as it turned out.

'The hospice will see her right. Give her my best, won't you? Tell her we're thinking of her.' She wanted to add that Caroline was lucky to have the help. That if a young man had to go, it was as well not to go at home, where the memories of the end would grow like ivy over the memories of the beginning and darken the whole thing.

'I will, Sis, thanks. And I'll see you someday soon. We can start with a spin and see where the road takes us. Bunty's Cove or wherever you like. Ladies' choice.'

'Ladies' choice,' she agreed and turned for the door.

Poor Sis, they would say when she left. Poor Sis Cotter. Frank's part in the whole sorry story known no doubt and little pity for him. There was a pair of them in it, she wanted to tell the town. It wasn't one single decision that got her where she was; it was a lifetime of them.

She made it back down to the supermarket with the minimum of nodding and smiling. With rain coming, people were hurrying on their way with their heads down, sparing her the need to come up with excuses to keep moving. She collected the bike and set off out of town. The wind was a cold biting at her ears and she hunched over the handlebars, her spine warning that she was calling on muscle memory she no longer had the muscle for.

Close to, the wheel looked impossibly narrow and she marvelled that it could bear her weight at all. She cycled east, through the first roundabout, then a second and a third before arriving at the top of the hill down into the valley that housed the bones of the local dead.

Once upon a time she would have cycled hard until the hill overtook her.

Once upon a time and now. It felt like the bike moved of its own accord and she was coasting, she was flying, faster than she could control and her body forgot itself and it would be worth every penny of the price she would pay tomorrow. She had the urge to shout to the dead: *Ready or not, here I come.* But when she opened her mouth, the wind snatched her voice and flung it and she had to be satisfied with sending her thoughts ahead of her instead.

Dismounting at the graveyard gate, she smiled despite the ferocious wobble in her legs. She should have known better, but just think what freedom she would have missed! Wasn't that life in a nutshell? Doreen would appreciate that idea. She must add it in a PS to her letter before posting it.

The caretaker's van was parked outside and, as luck would

have it, he was sitting in the passenger seat having forty winks after his lunch.

When Sis knocked on the window, he woke with a start and had several failed efforts to buzz down the window before realising he needed to start the engine. When it was eventually achieved, Sis thrust a little roll of notes in the open window at him. 'You'll look after them for me for another twelve months,' she said. 'Frank and Bunty.'

He pocketed the money. 'You're a step ahead of us all, Sis. We're in November yet.'

Sis nodded. 'You might as well have it rather than me minding it at home.'

'Afraid you'd be tempted to put it all on the—' He stopped and reddened the shade of a winter morning.

'My thanks to you for everything,' she said and walked to the small gate to let herself in.

Frank's grave was in the new section and neat as a pin and Sis forgave the caretaker his awkward mouth on the spot. Well worth wearing out her good winter boots and not replacing them. Keeping Frank and Bunty cared for was a heartier kind of warmth.

She sat on the lip of the gravestone. Another thing that still fit her, and she allowed herself a moment of small pleasure at the thought. Neither of her own girls would be able to perch here; they would spill over the two sides like porridge out of the saucepan. She had asked Doreen once – tactfully, she thought – if she would find it easier to get acting parts if she lost the weight. 'Jesus Christ, Mammy,' was all the response she got, and Doreen's ample backside flashing at her as she stomped from the room. It was true and pretending it wasn't was no favour to anyone.

She had considered bringing Laddy and leaving him here. She would have had to beg a lift from someone, but that wasn't what stopped her. It was the thought of him making his slow way home, then standing hungry at the back door, thinking she was inside and ignoring him. That would be no way to go.

'It's done,' she told the stone now. 'This time tomorrow, I'll be off to pastures new.'

She wondered if Frank, wherever he was, knew already. Another thing he knew before her. She shook her head at her own foolishness. Marriage was an article of faith. If Frank didn't turn out to be who she had imagined, it wasn't his fault. He had no more control over the excesses of her imaginings than she had over the shortcomings of his behaviour. People were who they were.

'I would do it all again,' she said, pressing her palm to his name on the flat of the stone. Just his name and dates. No epitaph. His loss too big to put words on. 'I would do every day of it again with you.'

The grass was wet and her shoes were dark and sodden when she got to Bunty's grave. She kissed her fingers and rubbed the side of the headstone, the way she used to rub the frame of Bunty's bedroom door towards the end, when her big eyes and short breaths meant Sis had to keep her distance for fear of passing on her germs.

'How's my girl?' she asked, then stopped at hearing her father's words, drawn from some distant place inside her. That was the problem with clearing out the house; everything else was dragged with it.

It was to Bunty Sis came when Mike had his day in court. Frank drove her to the graveyard gate and waited for her there. He didn't mistake the kind of support she needed and for that she was grateful.

'It's over, Bunty,' she told the stone. 'Mike was found guilty. And oh, Bunty! To have to sit there and listen to what they said about him and know it was all true and yet not true at the same time. That his decisions were his and yet not his. That he was never his own man, but always trailing someone else. That he never had faith in who he was or who he might be.'

Even a month later, when the judge handed down a suspended sentence and Mike walked out with them, it didn't change what he had done or the fact that the whole world knew it. It didn't erase the memory of the Garda drug squad searching the house and car and leading Mike away. They were spared the handcuffs at least. Everyone agreed that Mike wasn't violent. Just weak enough to be useful to those who were.

When they got home that day, Sis stood by the range and listened to Frank telling Mike that it would blow over. That all he needed was to wait it out and things would go back to normal.

It was with the greatest precision that she walked to the table and placed her two hands on it. 'You'll pack your things and you'll go, Mike. There is no place for you here now.'

In vain did Frank claim on the boy's behalf. He was as much to blame, he said, and why should Mike be shown the door when he himself was equally at fault?

Sis had looked at her son, still in his court suit, and he could have been eight years old and about to make his First Holy Communion. That day, too, had brought its own shame. Mike and another boy had held the host on their tongues until they got back to their seats and it was safe to pocket it. Sis and Frank and the other poor parents sat there fondly watching their boys' hunched shoulders, their praying hands clasped to their mouths, and had seen what they wanted to see. It wasn't until the following Monday in school when the teacher caught them about to flush the host down the toilet that the truth came out. It was a dare, Mike said. Because the host would bleed if it was really the body of Christ. Refusing to say who dared him only endeared him to the wrong kind of young lad. Gave him a name for being a useful sop. But that didn't become clear until later. At the time, the wooden spoon across the arse and an apology to his teacher and the priest had seemed sufficient to handle it.

There wasn't a wooden spoon in the world big enough to sort out today's mess.

'I'm going for a walk,' she told him. 'I don't want you here when I get back.'

'Where is the lad to go?' Frank called after her, but she kept going. She was running by the time she got to the steps, clicky hip and all, kicking off her two shoes and letting the waves take them. If she never stood in shoe leather again, she would be all the better for it.

When she got home, Mike was gone. She never asked where and Frank never said. If he stayed in touch with Mike, he kept it to himself, understanding that to do otherwise would be to risk her resolve. It was too late to undo what was done, but staying away gave Mike a chance. When the period of suspension was up, Cathy told her he was gone to Spain, where he was working in a hardware shop.

'For half-nothing,' she said accusingly. 'Wasting most of his wages on rent.'

Better to be working for nothing than idle for nothing, Sis thought, but let Cathy's anger blow itself out on her.

For her part, she thought the hardware shop a smart move – someone else's idea, most likely – because there was little there that might lead him astray. Spain was a place for summer people, Sis thought. Her boy had shed his winter self and turned his face to the sun. Let it warm whatever little gap was at the centre of him that time and life could put right. She had done her best and the rest was up to him. Even God himself had no dominion over free will – wasn't that what higher minds than hers believed?

The crunch of gravel made her look up. A couple was walking along the little path on the right-hand side, chatting as they went. Sis stood – her knees clicking and cracking – and pretended to be picking weeds from the base of the stone until they had safely passed by. She had things to say to Bunty and precious little time to say them without being interrupted by strangers.

'Doreen is in a new play,' she told her sister. 'Postmodern, she says, which I gather means it doesn't make much sense. She sounds very excited about it – she sent a postcard last week.' It was one of those 1950s Brighton prom ones. A woman and a man sitting together on deckchairs, with a skeleton beside them. The caption read: *So what's the food like at your hotel?* It was hard to know how to read it. If Doreen was in a mood buying it, she might have meant it as a dig for what Sis had said about her weight that time. Or it could have been an olive branch, a way of saying she was over it. Doreen was generous with her happiness ever.

'If you were here,' she told Bunty now, 'we could go over to London to see it. Imagine the pair of us: two old biddies in our sensible shoes but a pair of elbow gloves for you and big earrings for me, just to feel we were making the effort, in some uncomfortable little theatre, like the ones above in Dublin, with your knees nearly tucked into your ears. Desperately uncomfortable it would be.' But it would be many other things besides – fun and funny and memorable. They would laugh until they wheezed, with no need for oxygen tanks or fear.

Doreen would have been Bunty's favourite, although she would never have admitted it. Bunty was made to be an audience.

Even after all the years, it was hard not to wonder how the trajectory of all their lives would have been altered if Bunty had survived to adulthood. What would her children have been like with their Aunty Bunty to love and spoil them, to listen to them and make their little childhood issues feel big or their bigger adult issues feel little? Bunty would have done both effortlessly. She had the knack of listening well, so it wasn't until afterwards you realised that you had actually solved it yourself. Such was the quiet power of her company. Was it because her sister did less that she was a better noticer, Sis used to wonder, or was it that being ill strengthened her power to see the world clearly? But without Bunty herself, there was no one to ask.

'I'd best be getting on,' she said. 'There are things to do and no one else to do them.'

All the same, she lingered another moment. 'They would have been better with you here,' she told Bunty. 'We all would.'

The hill was punishing and the bike heavy and it took all Sis's tricks to best it.

First, she looked at the ground rather than the rise in front of her, watching her feet meet the tarmac and telling herself that the going was flat. But if her mind believed it, her shoulders surely didn't and she had to stop part-way up, lean the bike on the ditch and stretch the ache out of them. She rolled them forward to meet her ears, then back until her shoulder blades nearly met in the middle and that helped. It did.

She took the next section in intervals. Like someone in a gym, she told herself. She counted to sixty aloud, then thirty, then ten, as the words vanished with her breath until she had to stop and rest. Truth be told, she wasn't sure that time that she would get going again.

But get going she did, this time in stages. Just to the corner. To that gate. To the tree up ahead with its branches stretched out to her like you'd see in an airport arrivals hall. Would her children have come home more, she wondered, if that was the welcome she had for them? When the work restarted on the Blue House, she let herself imagine that it was Mike who would be moving in. An older Mike, with an ease to himself and a word for everyone. With a wife or a girlfriend – no prude, Sis! – and a job and a plan and maybe a child or two. If wishes were horses, beggars would ride.

If wishes were horses, the streets would be full of shit.

If wishes were horses, Mike would lose his shirt on them, too.

And she had no interest in minding children at her age.

Dear Mike,

It is my sincere hope that this finds you well. Cathy tells me that you are working again and I am glad for you. Don't take that luck for granted.

A day's work is never anything to be ashamed of. You'll remember, as a boy, not wanting your friends to know that I worked as a cleaner in the hotel from time to time. I said nothing at the time, as you were too young to understand, but I'm sure that you see now that shame has no place in a day's work. Maybe I should have impressed that on you better at the time.

Maybe that was my mistake.

It was as well that she breasted the hill just there. There would be no peace made if things descended into blame. She would write it out when she got home. With Laddy beside her, she would put the right words on the page and leave all the wrong ones out.

The sky had darkened now to a shade of purplish grey that was the exact match of the winter coats she had for the girls when they were little. It took her until spring to pay them off, but they got two years out of them and Cathy's coat did Doreen for another two years after that, and Mike had both, when his turn came.

Afterwards, she would think that it served her right to come off the bike. Hadn't she literally her head in the clouds? Her mother's words brought painfully to life. But if her lack of attention was one factor, so too was the sand at the edge of the road, which shifted beneath the wheels of the old bike, turning the front at an awkward angle that she was too slow to catch, tipping the bike into the gully and her with it. It wasn't far to fall, but it was hard enough that it shook the breath from her chest. For a split second, she thought Laddy's lead must have become entangled in the chain before remembering that she hadn't brought him. She lay with the tears gathering behind her closed eyes and wished he was there with her – the comforting warmth of him would get her to her feet. But he was at home, his nose to the back door, waiting to hear the squeak of the brakes as she rounded the final bend before home.

If Frank were here, he would give out to her and tell her that this was why she should have learned to drive. That at her age, a bike was the next best thing to a death sentence and who better to know than himself, eaten up with cancer as he was?

Illness softened him, opened him up or broke him down or whatever damn thing. Made him a little better at talking about things directly. She occasionally caught him looking at her and when she turned and asked, 'What?', the answer might be to a question that was years in the making.

'It made me feel better,' he might say and she would know he was talking about the gambling. Better about what, she wanted to ask, on days when the care and keeping of him was dirty and tiring and his moods were hard going. What was there in his life so difficult to deal with? Hadn't she loved him better than herself? Kept his house, his children, his interest?

But when he was clean and dressed – he supping soup, exhausted in the bed, and she spooning it into him, exhausted in the chair – she knew that it was the same stress that everyone felt. The gap between the way things were and the way a person wanted them to be. She could blame his friends – indeed she had, for a long time – for leading him astray. Those men in suits with money who told him he was the salt of the earth, who made him feel most like a winner when he was putting it all on the line. But that would just be Sis choosing an interpretation that suited her, at the cost of the truth of him and her together.

When the last slide overtook him, speeding up and up until he was finally gone, she was overcome with a powerful tiredness. 'That's after all the running around after him,' Cathy said, as ever leaving her own baggage for others to trip over.

It wasn't that at all, Sis wanted to tell her. It was that grief had weight, it had heft, and a person had to carry it around with them, day in and day out.

Grief was the same tape, playing over and over. Some days

soft in the background, others loudly. Stones in their pockets were what people used to kill themselves when they were too tired to live anymore. Sis wondered if the stones were symbolic – the weight of grief alone could sink a person surely. Oh, Frank. She loved him all the harder for all the mistakes he made.

If he were here, he would catch her under the two arms and lift her to her feet, never once complaining about the weight of her or the disease-eaten pain of his spine. He would set her on her feet and hold her two hands. 'You're all right now,' he would say. 'I have you.'

Ankles, one and two, moving inside her boots. Knees, one and two, moving inside her tights. Elbows, one and two, moving inside the sleeves of her jumper. Wrists, one and two, she could see them moving. She moved her head gently from side to side. No dizziness, no throbbing. So far, so good. With a bit of effort, she sat up, shuffling until the weight of the bike no longer pinned her in the dirt and muck of the roadside. Back moving. Ribs staying put. Rest here a minute. Let life course through her. The knowledge that this was not the moment when she and her body parted ways. Her old body. Her old friend.

Her tights were ripped, she noticed. They would need to go in the bin when she got home. One less thing to wash, she thought, and felt a bubble of laughter rise. She swallowed it back. If a person let go now, there was a danger of hysteria and where would she be then? With the rain starting to insist and Laddy at home waiting for her and letters to write.

She held on to the saddle of the bike and, sorry for its betrayal, it let her lever herself upright against it. The front wheel was buckled and she had to push it the remainder of the way home. If she were a different generation, she would leave it behind her. Doreen would have thrown it in the ditch for someone else to worry about, but that wasn't Sis's way. It could go in the shed, she decided. Let it be the next person's problem. It was a blessing that nobody passed her on the road – she would have been the talk of the town with her muddy coat and stiff stagger. The fewer people that saw her in that state, the better.

Between the fall and the walking, she was still on the road home when the heavens opened. With the hat plastered to her head and her shoes squeaking with water, she must have been a sorry sight. She stopped to pull the brakes at the corner. 'Nearly home, Laddy,' she said, knowing the words were for herself.

He was happy to see her; wet or dry made little difference to him. She let him follow her around while she took off her wet things and hung them over the range and dithered over whether or not to run a bath. In the final weighing, the difficulty of getting out didn't hold a candle to the need to ease the deepening stiffness in her bones. She would be damned if she couldn't walk out of here tomorrow on her own two legs. They could have her house – they were the ones that wanted it – but her pride didn't come with it.

She pulled the step-stool alongside the bath and put a towel and her phone on it, switched on just in case. She left the bathroom door open as well, to be on the safe side. Laddy lay down on the other side, glad of the company after the long afternoon on his own.

Undressing was slow, like everything else. A striptease that nobody would want to witness. Skin in pouches and pockets. Little gathers of herself. Such care people take of their bodies in their youth and in their life-giving years. Here I am, their bodies say. Know me. And all the precious carefree years concertinaed into short middle-age. Then old age and, again, the treating of the body as something fragile and priceless, except this time it was a crumbling map to a place nobody else remembered. She lowered herself into the water, glad to disappear from her own eyes.

The bath was her refuge when the children were small. The one door she could shut and know that it would stay shut. The water was rarely fully hot and she could still hear the children fighting – it was a door, not a miracle – but at least she could close her eyes and dream. What did she dream about back then? She could hardly remember. The usual things, she supposed. A little holiday, a break from everything. Winning the lottery and finding a way to keep it from Frank so that he wouldn't disappear one morning and reappear a week later with his pockets as worn out as a hoor's hanky.

When she told Mike that honest work had no place in it for shame, it was her own experience she drew on. It was what she had told them up at the new hotel when she went in looking for a job, doing her best to project confidence rather than desperation.

'You'd surely find something more suitable in town, Mrs Cotter,' the manager, Denis, said smoothly, knowing full well that she wouldn't be there if she didn't have to be. God forgive her but she hated men who let the little mean bit of power they had go to their heads. There was no excuse for it. As if every human being wasn't entitled to respect.

But Frank was who-knew-where since she showed him the door in temper when she went to the old flour tin and found her careful Christmas savings taken. '*Stolen!*' she shrieked, not caring if the children heard her, or the neighbours, or Almighty God himself. Enough was enough.

'This will be just fine, Denis,' she said. 'An ideal opportunity for us both, in fact. I'm as near to next door as you'll find, if you are ever short-staffed.'

Talking him into it, imagine!

He couldn't leave it there though. He had to rub it in. 'We get a lot of girls coming in thinking they can start off in the housekeeping team' – housekeeping team! Did he ever listen to himself, Sis wondered – 'and then move into the restaurant or' – a little giggle of amazement here – 'into reception, even. So it would be important to know from the start that we all tend to stick to our own niche. Within our own skill set, as it were. I wouldn't want there to be any misunderstandings.'

Sis held her hands behind her back, pinching the skin between her thumb and forefinger until the pain roared louder than her anger.

She left with an invitation to come back the following day 'for a trial'. She wouldn't cry, she told the sea. They had nothing left. Less than nothing, having had Christmas almost entirely on credit. In the butchers', when the young

Crowley girl, home from college and full of self-importance, told her that the turkeys were cash only, she nearly wept on the spot. Bill Crowley came out from the back, wiping blood and feathers from his hands, and told his sister to go away and not be annoying their regulars.

'Mrs Cotter has that turkey paid for long ago,' he told her before turning to Sis. 'We have your grand vegetable box put away upstairs as well,' he told her and she said thank you, that's lovely, thank you, then stood there, her eyes burning, while that kind soul went up to his own kitchen and filled a cardboard box out of his own fridge. It was all there, down to the gravy powder. Mrs Crowley must have killed him over it.

She told herself it was a new year and a new start and cleaning wasn't the worst.

But with Frank gone, she couldn't draw a full breath. There was an expectancy in her. A waiting. A feeling of something left undone, the front door left unlocked. Still, the work was solitary and quiet and she could throw open the windows as wide as she liked in each room, the way the sea could tell her it would be all right. Working at the hotel meant she didn't need anyone to mind the children. Doreen was a youngish seven, but Cathy had a good head on her for nearly nine. She could lead them home from the school bus stop and keep an eye on them for the hour until Sis was finished. And if anything went wrong, well, she was right next door.

Day one, she was already behind. Cleaning a hotel bedroom, it turned out, was not like cleaning a room at home. There were continental quilt covers to be reckoned with – nothing as simple as a sheet and blanket – and toilet roll corners to be tucked under, telephone receivers to be dusted (who would have ever thought of it?) and pencils to be sharpened. There was a cough and there was Denis behind her in the room, and Doreen behind him, her face blotchy with tears. Sis's blood ran cold at the sight of her.

'What is it? What's wrong?' she said, falling to her knees in front of her daughter. Denis didn't move, she realised afterwards, just stood there, her breath practically warming the zip of his trousers. 'What's happened, Doreen?'

'Cathy was making our tea and she said I couldn't have a sugar sandwich and I said I could and she said she was the boss and I said you were. Just because you're working here doesn't mean you're not the boss, sure it doesn't, Mammy?'

Was it awful to wish there had been an accident – nothing fatal, of course – instead of this embarrassment? Sis's face burned as she got to her feet, her knees cracking.

'Go home and have whatever you like,' she said, keeping her voice even. 'You can tell Cathy I said so.' Anything else would, she knew, simply prolong the agony of her snot-caked child appearing like a wraith in her new workplace. 'Go on now.'

'That won't happen again,' she told Denis as she turned to go back to her work.

'See that it doesn't. I'll be docking you fifteen minutes for time wasted,' he said, turning on his heel.

It never happened again. She slapped Doreen's legs black and blue when she got home. Not even with the flat of her hand, but with the hairbrush. 'If I lose this job, what will we eat?' she hissed, punctuating each word with the heft of the hairbrush. She felt shame then and she felt it now.

She let him come back – of course she did – made sane again by the settling deep within her. They agreed that she would not ask him to leave again, that he would give her no reason to. A wordless agreement, it was true, forged in hot breath, panicky fingers, the sweet easing of an ache. When Mike was born, nine months later, she held on to the job by dint of convincing them to let her work the late shift. The days were long, but she had the beach to herself in the early hours when she finished work and was on the way home.

They stayed together. She kept her word and Frank did, too. There might be few places in her life where pride could perch, but that at least couldn't be taken away.

It's a little late for me to be giving you advice, my dearest Cathy. You and I both know that. So we won't call it advice. Instead, I'll tell you that the experts say it is prudent for a woman to think ahead. To have the house in her name, a little money set aside. Not advice, you understand. Just passing on the words of the experts I hear on the radio. You are smarter than I ever was and that gives me hope that your life, despite appearances, is founded on more modern principles.

There, she would have annoyed Cathy with that, but what else was she to do? She had nothing else to give her.

The water went cold while Sis was away in the past. She should have set the alarm on the phone to make sure she got out while there was some chance it would do a bit of good to her joints. Instead, she was stiffer than ever and she had to roll sideways and grab on to the side of the bath and rise from there onto her knees. Glad as she was for the phone beside the bath, she didn't want to have to use it.

'You could hold me under,' Frank had said one night, catching her hand as she went to help him out. 'Will you?'

It had been a hard day, the cancer yowling against his spine in spite of the painkillers. Sis tried to convince him to let her ring the district nurse, but he wasn't in the humour. They looked at one another for a long moment and she knew there was little would comfort him today except to treat him as the man he had always been.

'I'd never lift you out after,' she said finally. 'And there's no one I could ask to help me,' and he nodded at the bald truth of it.

When Sis was out of the bath herself, safe on the dry

solidity of the towel on the bathroom floor, she was as weak as a kitten. All she was fit for was tea and the radio and Laddy on her feet to warm them up. The bath didn't need to be cleaned, she decided. She had been cold, not dirty, and it would do to give it a wipe around the edges in the morning.

'What have we come to, Laddy, when a warm bath is the height of risk?' she asked him, when she had the tea made and the range roaring and was starting to feel steadier on her feet. 'What have we come to at all?'

The radio was dealing in evening talk. Politics and sport and culture. None of it had much to impact her anymore. With the house gone and only herself left, there was nothing but wind and weather could harm her now. Still, it was better than the afternoon talk of self-improvement gurus making people feel bad about themselves. Or the cranks who, having spent the early part of the day feeding their grievances, emerged with them ready for airing.

Doreen was forever recommending podcasts. Nothing Irish – Doreen didn't listen to them, wanting nothing more than distance from her birthplace – but now and then a postcard would arrive with a scribbled name of some cultural bit or other she thought Sis should listen to. Sis never did. The digital radio Doreen had sent her was still in its box somewhere. It was no wonder young people were so self-regarding, when they chose everything according to their own narrow interests. The point of the radio, she wanted to tell her daughter, was that it was real and it was random. Living, breathing people talking in living, breathing time. Podcasts, by the time a person listened to them, had nobody on the other end. Sure how could they be anything but lonesome? But if she tried to put that on a postcard, it would come out wrong and drive Doreen into one of her sulks.

Sis kept her notebook next to the radio, ready to jot down anything that caught her fancy. It pleased her to remember the shorthand, her own secret code. If someone was to break in, they wouldn't know what she was writing. It could be nuclear codes for all they knew. Or instructions to her hidden millions. Wouldn't chance be a fine thing? It was a rare day there was nothing new to add and even then she made a note of the feeling. Whether it was worry that there might be nothing new in the world or satisfaction that she had got to the end of learning – whatever that was – or maybe even that heaviness of heart and body that came over a person from time to time and left them unable to take in the world around them. Whatever it was, there was a sense of satisfaction in having it there in black and white. At the back, she had written in each of Doreen's podcast suggestions, just in case. Maybe she should dig out the digital radio and take it with her. She might have no need for live radio with living, breathing people around the place to annoy her.

'No walk this evening, Laddy. You can have the evening off.' She scratched behind his ear to hide her upset. 'Even if I somehow got down those steps, I might never get back up, isn't that it?'

Instead, while she cooked the steak, she opened the kitchen door so he could potter in and out if he needed to. Frank used to say that beef without onions wasn't worth a damn, but the smell of frying meat rose in the air and her stomach gurgled, onions or no onions.

The steak spat in the pan and she pressed finger and thumb together to gauge the tenderness. When it was still soft enough that it wouldn't upset any ageing teeth, she took it off the heat and let it rest on the plate.

She crushed all the sleeping tablets, to be on the safe side. There were a fair few – she had just filled a prescription when Frank went downhill that final time. She didn't cod him with talk of how he would rally. Such lies would have been an unkindness – whatever it was he needed to say, it was her place to let him say it.

'They'll have to let you keep the house now,' he whispered

and the triumph on his face told her what he himself had never admitted: that he knew all along he was ill but waited until it was too late for the bank to do anything about it. 'I promised I wouldn't let you down.'

'I know, my love,' she said and nodded just the once so that he would know she believed him.

With the sharp knife, she cut a deep trench down the middle of the steak and patted the powdered tablets into the meat, pouring the fat from the pan over them, watching them fizz and buck. It was the right thing to do and the kindest way to do it. Even assuming Laddy had it in him to love someone new, he would never cope with the loss of the old.

She had given the bath one last consideration – the water was still in it – but his life had begun when he escaped the water butt and she didn't like the idea that it had finally caught up with him. As if his whole life had been an accident.

That old riddle from her childhood: *would you rather be nearly drowned or nearly saved?* Nearly saved, she had said too quickly, without grasping the meaning. How the older children had laughed at catching her out. There was nowhere to put that shame except to pass it on, and no one to pass it on to, only Bunty. But it didn't work. Her sister was already used to considering those questions and, rather than being absolved of her own mortification, Sis had to carry it alongside the smarting red cheeks for having upset her sister.

'Too much water under the bridge, Laddy, isn't that it?' She set the plate down by the door and watched him eat.

Cathy had brought her children here just once, after Frank was diagnosed. She wanted them to meet him before he died, she said. No soft-soaping there. The eldest was two and a half, looking sideways through her fringe at everything, forever pulling Cathy's skirt and whispering to her. 'We don't whisper in this house,' Sis told her and she started crying and Sis was suddenly the worst in the world. The younger one was no better. He was just a baby, at that stage of half-crawling, half-dragging himself along the floor, picking up every bit of lint and dirt in the place. Grim-faced, Cathy pulled the hoover out of the press and spent an unnecessary length of time dragging it from room to room, pulling out furniture as if the child could possibly get in behind a locker or an armchair. She never lost it, Sis thought, forever anxious to prove she was the better mother.

The worst thing was that when Sis's back was turned, Cathy had Laddy turfed out into the cold, claiming he was unhygienic. He wasn't the one wiping his snots under chairs and on the corners of the tablecloth, Sis wanted to say but didn't. Frank was tired and needed a quiet life. Instead, while Cathy was fussing with naps and bottles, she snuck Laddy into the back bedroom, where he jumped up on the bed and sighed himself to sleep on Frank's arm. It was hard to know which of them was more grateful for the comfort.

It was unforgivable, Sis knew, to snap at her grandchildren, no matter what they broke or tore or disregarded. She apologised – oh, she apologised – but they cut their visit short, leaving two days ahead of schedule. *Not wanting to tire Dad out* was one reason given. *Showing the children their heritage* was another. Sis had to hold in the snort when she heard that one. What heritage had they beyond what was under this roof? The truth was that Cathy couldn't – or wouldn't – reconcile her past and present. Or maybe it was simply that her performance of parenting had her worn out.

'Go easy on her,' Frank said as they stood in the door and watched the car pull away. 'She feels she has something to prove.'

She told herself that it was because he was ill that he didn't wonder what it was Cathy had to prove and to whom. 'You might be right,' she said and slipped her shoulder under his to help him back to bed. The truth was that it was a relief that Cathy was gone, and her disappointments with her.

The radio was low and playing classical music. Listening to it was a habit from when the children were small and Sis needed comfort rather than agitation.

Doreen was particularly prone to night-time vomiting. She never felt ill going to bed, but it would come on her in the night and she would wake and pad into her mother's room, covered in a pool of sick. For a time it was so bad that Sis dozed in a chair in the kitchen so that when Doreen came up to her, she could strip and wash her in the kitchen sink without waking the whole house. Under the guise of letting her hair dry, Doreen would snuggle into her lap while Sis hummed and rocked and savoured the closeness and the quiet.

There was something primal about the need for mothering that arrived, savagely, during illness. Sis could still remember the feeling of being poorly and wanting her own mother. Not that she got her – with Bunty's condition rising and falling at the slightest thing, Sis tried hard to keep her sickness to herself so as not to add to her mother's worry. When Mammy was worried, she lost time and forgot things and Daddy didn't like that. She would hear his hand against Mammy's face, the sharp crack of it echoing through the house and upsetting Bunty. Sis would climb into bed beside Bunty to reassure her, but she had to be careful not to fall asleep there, or Mammy would be cross and pass on the slap. Sis could have any kind of germs, Mammy would say. Sis could kill Bunty, she was so dirty and dangerous.

Sis had her own faults as a mother – and plenty of them – but she did her best to make sure that Doreen felt the full weight of her love on those restless nights. As she got older, Sis needed only check she had her purple plastic basin and brown towel beside the bed when she tucked her in. Sis was glad to have the full night in her own bed, Frank's warmth stretched out beside her, his hand heavy across her belly.

It wasn't like losing myself, Doreen, although I know you'll appreciate the dramatic sentiment better than anyone. It was more that the bits of myself that I liked were all wrapped up in the idea of who we were together. Your father knew me as young and old and all the ages in between. Every fibre of my being and my becoming. You children only ever saw me as fixed and finished. Children never see the road. I hope you won't take it the wrong way if I say that that's part of the problem and part of the solution, too. Maybe you will find that out for yourself someday. With Alice, maybe, if she makes you happy.

Mentioning the unmentionable. Doreen would likely stop reading right there.

She looked over it. It was not an apology, not quite. What good would that do anyway? If Doreen needed somewhere to put her anger and regret and resentment, the least Sis could do was hold it.

'We do the best we can with the information we have at the time, isn't that it, Laddy?'

His head was heavy now and it was impossible to imagine getting him to the bed. Impossible to countenance sleeping in the bed without him. Sis could stay out here with him, beside the range, where he was happiest. Wasn't it where she slept that whole year after Bunty came home from hospital and needed the bedroom to herself so she could have the window open, rain, hail or shine?

She took two blankets out of the blanket box beside the range and sat on the floor, putting his head in her lap. She put one blanket around her shoulders and the other over him. That was all he wanted.

'Frank will be waiting for you,' she told the dog, fondling his ears, now growing cold around the tips. 'Tell him everything is fine. Look after him the way you looked after me. Tell him I'm grand. That you would have never left me otherwise.'

LYDIA

Lydia woke with her hands buried in her crotch. A childhood habit that had recently returned. Maybe it had something to do with sleeping alone again, although she couldn't swear she hadn't done it before Andrew, when, as a serial monogamist, she was briefly in between boyfriends. Maybe because she had seen an orange glow in the sky the previous night and, before realising it was a bonfire, thought for several panicked seconds that hell itself was coming for her.

The spare room was cold, her breath making special effects of her first few minutes on the exercise bike. Her warm-up programme had an early gradual incline and she leaned into it, pressing her feelings into the pedals and watching her heart rate climb.

When she was a child, her mother had a particular way of dealing with that distasteful sleeping habit.

'I caught Lydia with her hand in her twinkle,' she would announce at the breakfast table while Lydia cringed into her Rice Krispies. 'What do we say to that?'

Her father was nonplussed the first time it happened. 'Twinkle?' he said. 'Isn't that the magazine she gets on Fridays?' He turned to Lydia. 'Have you been reading under the covers with a torch again? How many times do we have to tell you you'll ruin your eyesight?'

Lydia's mother, having failed to convey the necessary information through a series of significant eye movements, leaned over to whisper in her husband's ear. God forbid the word *vulva* would be spoken aloud in their house. The floor would open and deposit them all among the fiery hobs of hell. Through her eyelashes, Lydia could see her father's face reddening at what he considered inappropriate table talk and knew she would pay for that as much as for her transgression. Her mother displayed her to her father as if she were a project they had taken on together and thus should share the disappointment equally.

Lydia leaned her head on her folded arms and pedalled into the pitch-dark of her sleeves.

Up the programmed hills, steep and punishing, then on to the short and merciful flats.

The saddle firm beneath her buttocks, her legs going round and round until her back blazed and her thighs burned and her lungs were fit to burst and finally, finally, she felt clean.

In the shower, her legs shook pleasantly. Evidence that she had not wasted her morning. Proof for the imaginary audience that was her mother, who, in Lydia's mind, was waiting outside the door, timing her daughter's shower and wondering if she was up to anything she shouldn't.

All of these issues would be made smaller by her mother's death, she reminded herself, as her therapist had taught her. They would be compressed small enough to fit into the box with her.

That knowledge brought Lydia comfort rather than guilt.

She hadn't room for any more guilt.

Outside the living-room window, Sis Cotter made her slow way past, the dog plodding at her heels. It took little effort for Lydia to superimpose her memories of a years-ago Sis, not much older than Lydia herself was now, striding out, crackling with energy and purpose. Lydia had looked at Sis then and wondered what powered her. Inside the window, Lydia's own mother would be draped across the sofa or a chair, as languid and liquid as her diet. Gin and oranges, Lydia did not know then, did not accommodate vibrancy. Yet for all her bright blazing, Sis Cotter now walked no quicker than anyone else. Whatever she had been in such a hurry to get to or from all those years ago, life had slowed her and forced her into step with the rest of the world.

Had Lydia herself ever felt such urgent life? What was there in her working-shopping-coffees-lunches-dinners city life to prompt it?

The woman who enjoyed those things seemed a stranger to Lydia. Impossible to imagine that her life once overflowed with work and leisure and living. Inconceivable to think back to her skewed priorities. All those hours on the road, driving from place to place for work. All those meetings, hotels, conferences, phone calls imbued with a ludicrous self-importance. All those nights she would go on and on about how hard she worked, how she was 'simply exhausted'.

Out in the sea, someone is swimming, Mary. A man, bare-chested in the Atlantic, imagine. The same man every day. His dog swims behind him, chasing him, it seems like, until they both turn and retrace their strokes, this time the man chasing the dog. I wish you could see them.

There are two sides to everything.

Almost everything.

[Delete. Delete. Delete.]

Lydia watched the two distant figures safely on to the beach, the man wrapping the dog in a towel before attending to himself.

Stupid loyalty everywhere she looked.

I wish you could see them, she had thought. What would Mary think if she were here?

Lydia walked her house with Mary's eyes, stopping in each room to imagine what she might say to Mary, what Mary might say in return.

'No dishwasher?' Mary might enquire, looking around the plain white kitchen.

Lydia shook her head as if Mary were really there. Gave a brave little lift of the chin. 'There's no need when it's just me.' The brief solidarity of Mary's hand on hers before she moved out into the hall.

Unable to cope with the new demands of their lives, Mary's husband had left her and Nick. Although Mary didn't address it directly, a series of uplifting posts suggested she had few regrets. *Once you realise you deserve better, letting go will be the best decision ever*, one proclaimed. Lydia's heart had stopped on reading it. Visions sped through her mind, of Nick in a hospital bed, on life support, a tearful Mary with her hand on a plug, transforming Lydia, finally, from a monster to a murderer.

The post wasn't about Nick at all, but about the man who had left, as men do.

The man who couldn't cope. The man who deserved more. The fucker.

Comments from Mary's friends suggested it was no great tragedy, but Mary refused to stoop to mud-slinging. *Peace begins with me*, she posted instead, accompanied by a vase of lilies. Apposite, Lydia thought. If a little funereal.

Lydia stood in her hallway and looked around her. Mary would inhale nothing more than the clean smell of Sofia's caddy of environmentally friendly products. No need for candles in Lydia's home. There was no smell of long-term care to mask, that unmistakeable mix of antiseptic and central heating and baby powder.

Mary's eyes would drift to the sole artwork. A sombre canvas depicting a long-haired woman nearing the top of a flight of steps, about to pass through an archway and into daylight. Although her back was to the camera, something in the slight downward tilt of her head suggested the weight of the world. A sorrow borne. Lydia had loved it on sight and insisted on dragging it home from holiday with them, much to Andrew's puzzlement.

'Is it not a bit grim?' he said, but she shushed him, laughing, and said she would hang it in her office where he never had to see it.

The night she moved here, she had taken two pills together and fallen asleep on the sofa in their old house, trusting Andrew to get her here safely.

She had already tried twice to leave the city.

The first time, she made it almost to the car before the panic hit. The world suddenly black and spinning as if something had hit her head. Andrew's voice, echoing strangely. 'Breathe, Lydia. Just breathe through it.'

Through what, Lydia wanted to ask, but there was no breath for questions. The air outside the house was poisonous, it felt like, her body rejecting it utterly.

The second time, she got one foot over the threshold of their front door before the world swam and she made her staggering retreat. Melodrama, she would have thought, had she not lived it. The terror of not knowing when – if – the next breath was coming.

So there was no other way to do it, she knew, other than to knock herself out and trust to Andrew, yet the image of him carrying her over the threshold made her stiffen with shame.

She woke in the new old house and when she walked into the hall, her painting was the first thing she saw. Andrew had taken it from her study, wrapped it and loaded it in the car, doing the entire thing in reverse on the other side. Some days she thought it was a comfort he was unable to give in person. Other days she thought his relinquishing of the space to her was a goodbye letter.

The living room would be the high point of Mary's tour, of course, with its unparalleled views of the sea. 'It didn't used to be like this,' Lydia could tell her. 'When I came here first, there were boxy little windows. Single-glazed. Puritanical.'

Would Mary think the view a hopeless extravagance? Hardly, Lydia reasoned. Even Sis Cotter's house had big front windows. How could a person not?

Maybe Mary would be drawn by the beauty of the unbroken grey.

With Mary beside her, Lydia might have the strength to open the window and let the sound of the waves wash in. She stretched a hand towards the handle, then snatched it back. It was no good. Not without Mary.

The first time she brought Andrew here, they went down to the beach before going into the house. It was a dull wintry sort of day and she could tell Andrew was disappointed that the view wasn't better.

'On a summer's day, you can nearly see America,' she said, nodding in mock sincerity.

'On a winter's day, you can nearly see your own hand,' he said, and they both laughed at the idea, the remoteness of it.

'Your mother told me how much you loved it here, so I bought it from them,' he said. 'It's all ours.'

Her mother told him how much she loved it. Of course she did. Lydia thought of all the lonely days she had spent here. The years of longing for a friend beside her. She looked at Andrew, bursting with delight at his gift. Here he was, the someone she had waited for. And here he would be. Here *they* would be.

'We'll grow old and grey together here,' she said, putting her arms around him. 'Just us and the sea for company.'

That was before the sea came to feel inevitable, relentless as guilt.

Before the grey stripe of sea and the grey stripe of sky began to look like bars. Just because she had chosen it didn't make it any less true.

She could phone Andrew now and speak honestly.

She could tell him that when she phoned the chemist or the supermarket or the off-licence and gave them directions, she told them she lived in the Blue House, the one just before the hotel.

She could tell him that his name for the house never crossed her lips and maybe then he would understand.

She could tell him. She could tell him.

Could she tell him?

But here was Sis Cotter making her way along the road. And Lydia waiting for her. Waiting for the turn of the head that meant she was still alive in the world. That she was seen by someone, something, other than the sea.

The green and white of the post van sent Lydia to the corner of the hall again. What need for a dog when she herself would make Pavlov proud? She hoped the postman was delivering next door and had simply pulled into her drive to get the van out of the way of any passing traffic.

She pressed her clammy hands to her face and waited to see what would happen.

It was worse in the city, she reminded herself, when the postman was on a bike and approached unheard.

When the doorbell rang, she wiped her hands on her trousers and picked up her cane.

'Lydia O'Gorman,' he said when she opened the door.

Was he asking or telling? It seemed an unnecessary power

that he would have her name while he could be anyone. Nameless. Untraceable.

What would he do if she said 'no'? If she shook her head regretfully and closed the door. How many times would she have to refuse her own name before he would give up and send the undelivered letters to whatever postal graveyard awaited them? Three was good enough for Saint Peter, but this postman was in his shirtsleeves in November, suggesting he wouldn't yield that easily.

'Are you Lydia O'Gorman?' he asked again, more slowly, eyeing the cane as if she might not have understood the first time. As if her ears and legs were connected in some fundamental way. They were, she supposed. What else was it her brain did, other than connect the various parts of her into a functioning whole?

'Are you all right?' he asked. 'You're very pale.'

'I'm fine. I'm so sorry. I was away with the fairies,' she said, surprising herself with the expression. Where on earth had she dragged that from? 'I'm Lydia, yes. Lydia O'Gorman. That's me.'

In his hand, he held a small box. The kind that good chocolates came in. The kind she and Andrew used to buy when they were visiting friends.

For a minute, she wanted nothing more than this low-stakes conversation, where honesty could yield to politeness.

'So much for the storm yesterday,' she said.

He laughed. 'You're not wrong there. A shower of rain with notions was all it was.'

Lydia cast around for something else. What was it the taxi driver had said yesterday? 'It won't be long until the hotel is open and the place is busy again,' she said.

'Oh, the summer people won't be kept away,' he said.

Was that how they were seen? All those years her parents talked about the place with a sense of ownership, their weeks of summer holiday as incontrovertible in their calendar as Christmas. All that time, did the locals simply write them off as a single pitiful entity: *the summer people*? Surely the people here loved their place generously and without wishing other people gone?

Well, she was no summer person and he might as well start coming to terms with that now.

'Mrs Cotter and myself had better enjoy it while we can. And her dog, of course,' Lydia said.

The postman's face closed down and for a second she thought he might spit on the ground. What had she said wrong?

'That dog should be put down,' he said.

'The dog is all she has,' Lydia said, surprising herself.

He handed her the box. 'That's no fault but her own.' He turned to leave. 'Bye, Ms O'Gorman.'

'Call me Lydia,' she said, but he was out of earshot.

She took the little box inside and put it on the kitchen worktop. It was heavy. Or dense, perhaps. She never really understood the difference.

She opened the package slowly. When she peeled off the final layer, she was puzzled to find a box of make-up products. An enclosed sheet of paper welcomed her to their subscription service and assured her that each month she would be treated to the very latest and finest trends that the organic beauty industry had to offer.

It had to be from her mother. Who else?

She opened the tiny tins and, despite herself, thrilled at their richness of colour. Should she give up this tiny unlooked-for joy? Could she? What would Mary do? Mary would be too busy tending to Nick's needs to worry about eye creams or miracle non-medical cosmetic treatments.

She would have to ask her mother to cancel the subscription. Nothing else was tenable.

'Cancel it, darling?' her mother said.

Lydia pictured her: one brown-pencilled eyebrow arching above a perfectly painted eye, even this early in the day.

'Why on earth would I do such a thing? I was rather pleased with myself for the idea. I was going to send fruit, but I was afraid you might choke on a grape or something there by yourself and I couldn't possibly have that on my conscience.'

The line fell silent while they both considered her words. To her credit, her mother didn't pretend not to have said it.

'You know I didn't mean it like that, Lydia. Don't be tiresome and take needless offence.'

Lydia said nothing. It was a verbal mess of her mother's own making, so her mother could be the one to fix it.

'Have you seen anyone today? And don't think you can get away with saying the cleaner and thinking I don't know her name.'

'I see the same two neighbours every day.' Lydia didn't know why she was defending herself. Instinct, she supposed.

'I hardly think Sis Cotter and that embarrassment of a husband of hers are anything to crow about.' Her mother giggled, delighted at her own wit.

'She's a widow. Her husband is dead.' They could be widows together, her mother and Sis Cotter. One no better than the other.

'She's better off without him,' Lydia's mother pronounced. 'He gambled the house out from under her, you know.'

'How would I know?' Lydia echoed. She tried to picture the man and couldn't. In her mind, Sis Cotter walked alone.

'Honestly, Lydia. It takes so little effort to be interested in other people's lives.'

There was no possible reply. If Lydia had been the one to share the news, her mother would have told her that gossip was beneath her. 'A man goes swimming in the sea in the mornings,' she said to change the subject. 'With his dog.'

Her mother shuddered. 'What is it with people and their dogs? I cannot fathom how they bear all that mess.'

'They swim along together. It's quite sweet, actually.'

'Sea swimming is becoming very popular. Very good for the skin, you know.'

'I know.'

'I must see if there's a seaweed treatment that I can add to your beauty box next month.'

'Please cancel it, Mother. Please.' Lydia remembered why she had phoned. That was another of her mother's talents, moving so far from the point that a person forgot their own mind.

'Absolutely, darling. I'll cancel it the minute you swim in the sea instead.'

Lydia closed her eyes. 'That's... not possible.'

Her mother tsked down the phone. 'Then it's equally impossible to cancel the subscription, I'm afraid. It's paid up for six months in advance. Or a year. I forget the details.'

'But it's not who I am anymore.'

'Oh, Lydia, darling.' Her mother's voice lost its bright tone. 'We are always ourselves. We just have to find ways to make it bearable.'

After she hung up, Lydia looked at the array of tiny pots and tubes on the worktop in front of her. 'And if we can't?' she asked softly into her silent kitchen.

The house did not reply.

Sis Cotter walked a bicycle out through her gate and appeared to lie it down in the road. Lydia stood on her tiptoes to see what she was doing, but Sis was hidden by the pillar at the end of Lydia's driveway. When she reappeared, she was on the bike and cycling away towards the town, with an uprightness and speed that surprised Lydia. It wasn't until she disappeared around the corner that Lydia realised she, too, had straightened and leaned forward, as if she were behind Sis on the bike.

As a teenager, Lydia and her friends had spent their lives on their bikes. Whole weekends passed in going from one place to another, only to kick the same tyres in a different place, declare it boring and move on. All of them aware on some level that it was being on the bike that counted. That the cycling itself was both the journey and the destination.

Once the boy group and the girl group began to mix, everything changed. Katie McCarthy was the first to start arriving on foot, with some breathless story of a puncture or a loose chain.

'Are you not staying around?' she would ask, crossing one pristine white canvas shoe over the other and looking up at them from under her fringe. 'Never mind. I can walk home.'

The boys would trip over themselves to offer crossbars, saddles, carriers, whatever Katie wanted. Lydia would watch them and wish they would hurry, impatient to be on the saddle and on the road.

When the performance was over, Katie would climb onto the crossbar of the victor and off they would all go. Lydia cycled behind them, watching Katie steer while the boy held her waist, her giggle trailing like a scarf on the breeze. When they came to the big hill – no matter where they were going or coming from, the big hill was a given in their Sunday afternoons – she would swoop past them, low over the handlebars, and feel a smug pleasure that Katie was missing out on the freedom of it. No boy's hands on her waist could make up for the rush of speed and adrenalin.

As the weeks passed, more and more of the girls fell victim to bike trouble. As if some evil fairy were moving through their sheds and garages on Saturday nights, sabotaging inner tubes and gears and brake cables. Crossers and backers overtook the group until eventually Lydia alone of the girls brought her own bike. 'You're a flyer on the hills,' Liam Lynch said, arriving alongside her at the brow of the big hill, but the approval in his tone was undercut by

Katie McCarthy, venomous on the bar of his bike. 'Lydia is just like one of the boys,' she smirked.

The comment spoiled her day and then followed her home and spoiled her evening, too. Katie's words a tick bite in her mind.

The next weekend was the last before the school holidays and her departure to their stupid holiday home. Lydia woke with a heavy feeling in her stomach. She picked at her food, hoping her mother would notice and tell her she wasn't allowed out, but her mother was busy thinking about something else and hardly touched her own apple slices. Lydia wheeled her bike to the front gate, then turned slowly and leaned it against the inside of the wall. She walked to the factory that served as their meeting point, telling herself if she wanted to, she could turn around and go home.

'Bike trouble,' she muttered and waited for someone to challenge her. To ask what had happened, or why she was suddenly as red as Liam Lynch's rugby shirt. But nobody else even bothered with an excuse anymore, merely waited brazenly to be chosen. The boys never faltered, beckoning first one girl, then the next, as if it was all somehow preordained. It was a long time – an embarrassing length of time – before Lydia realised that it was in fact orchestrated. That at Saturday evening Mass, while the girls were inside the church, mentally rating each other and finding themselves wanting, the boys sat on the wall of the churchyard horse-trading names and reputations.

Liam Lynch didn't say anything, just jerked his head towards his bike and waited for her to follow him. He wasn't someone she had ever thought much about. He said little, which made him mysterious, until he opened his mouth and spoiled the impression.

His hands were firm on her waist and Lydia was surprised at the flutter of expectation as she grasped the handlebars and steered them along. Anyone would think she had never cycled before. Impossible to ignore the clench and unclench in her – dread word, her mother never not in her head – in her twinkle. She shut her mother out and wondered if the sensation was his hands or the judder of the bike. At the first crossroads, the boys struck off in four different directions.

'Are you sure you know where we're going?' she asked him, but the wind must have caught and cast her words, because he didn't reply.

His imagination was not that limited, as it turned out. Nor were his hands slow, moving up and under her T-shirt with the speed of someone accustomed to plucking a high ball out of the air in a line-out. He applied the same finesse as he might have to that job – a firm grip with both hands before loosing one to make a bold run for the line. After several blocked attempts, he peeled away from her with such speed it was as if he had heard the final whistle in the distance. He got on the bike and waited for her to readjust her clothes and climb back on the crossbar, then pedalled her back to the corner nearest her house.

'Bye then,' he said, on parting. 'Thanks.'

So that was what all the fuss was about, Lydia thought. At least now she knew. Given the choice again, she rather thought she would opt instead for the freedom of her own bike, the wind in her hair and all the decisions hers to make.

But that was a childish thought. Better by far to be on someone else's bike. To be lovable.

Those childhood friends had proven themselves for what they were, the product of circumstance rather than closeness. For a while after she moved away to university, Lydia would contact them when she came home at weekends, gradually growing tired of being the one to suggest meeting up. Left to them, she felt their friendship would be put to one side. The thought made her burn.

They weren't real friends, she told herself. If they didn't value her, others would. She was surprised and pleased to find that, with that thought alone, her upset lost its form, changed shape, became something else, something hard. The past set in resin.

A valuable lesson, it turned out. Imagine how lonely she would be now had she not had a lifetime of learning to let people go.

Lydia began to set the table while the soup was heating on the hob. She had refused Andrew's offer of a microwave for the kitchen. Convenience was the preserve of the busy.

One coaster, one cloth napkin, one knife, one plate, one spoon. She had packed the good cutlery, knowing it meant nothing to Andrew and reluctant to imagine it unused and dull at the back of a drawer.

A lone island of one at the end of the big oak table. A table intended for entertaining that now gathered dust. Lydia had to remember to wipe it down on Tuesdays and Thursdays before Sofia came.

One of everything except glasses: one for water and one for wine.

She never used to drink alone. But if she didn't do things alone now, she would do nothing.

She used to watch the solo drinkers at the Galway Races. Down at the tote, a line of white-faced men spilling their pints as they silently urged their elusive futures towards the post. Had Sis Cotter's husband been among them? All shine and shambles?

The Galway Races were a staple in Lydia and Andrew's year. It was where they met. Introduced by a friend of a friend, the click between them almost audible.

'I've missed one in the last decade,' Andrew told her. 'My

ex booked a last-minute holiday and it felt churlish to refuse. I should have known it would never last.'

Lydia had looked at his hands with their neat nails and thought it a mistake she would never make. 'I missed one as well,' she said.

She hadn't, but she liked the feeling of equilibrium it gave them. 'A wedding,' she improvised, which steered them smoothly on to their thoughts on weddings, carefully couched in approval or opprobrium for the choices of others. All hypothetical, of course, and oh-so light-hearted. Half-joking, whole-earnest, as her mother would say. By the end of the night, they were alone in the box and it was a yes to a church ceremony, small bridal party and a location with guaranteed good food, and a no to nonsense gestures, string quartets or destination weddings. Back in her hotel room, Lydia caught sight of herself in a mirror and saw she was bright with happiness. Glowing, almost. Her certainty startled her. This man, it seemed, was *the* man. Only the asking – and answering, she reminded herself – remained.

In the sterile white of her kitchen, Lydia poured herself a glass of wine. Horses were merely animals. The real gambler got behind the wheel and played with people's lives.

Andrew's phone rang twice before he answered. She pictured him seeing *No Caller ID* and sighing. It was a little early for her call. She typically left it until after 5 p.m., when she could be more certain he wasn't in a meeting. She hadn't the courage to phone in the evening, afraid he might not answer and she would have to worry that he was out with someone else.

'Lydia.'

Lydia said nothing. Just sat as still as she could while still breathing. Like a stalker, she supposed, remembering her mother's words.

He knew better than to ask how she was. 'You had heavy rain yesterday. I bet that was something to see,' he said, then quickly added, 'I have you as one of the locations on my weather app.' He paused as if considering something, then continued. 'When we started doing the renovations first, I used to dream about being down there during a storm. Lying in bed with the radio on low and the rain pelting off the skylight.'

The air warm with our breath, Lydia added silently, *and our bodies safe under the quilt.*

It wouldn't be a sacrifice if it didn't hurt.

But if there was a way to erase herself entirely from her husband's memory and spare him, she would do it in a heartbeat. Ask no questions. Give him the pill. *Give him the pill.*

His chair creaked and she knew he had leaned back and was rolling his shoulders. He had talked for so long about replacing his old desk chair that it had become a joke between them. The creak reverberated in her head. In her chest. An ache that she deserved.

'Do you need anything?'

In the silence that followed, she considered the question. What was it she needed? For him to see that this was who she was now.

When he told her she had changed, she couldn't believe he was so blind as to have to say the words aloud. *What kind of monster wouldn't?* she wanted to ask him, but they were already mired in the Red Sea, Nick the chasm parting them.

What did she need? Really need? She thought again of Dominic's office and her wish for a time machine. For a do-over.

'Other than a time machine,' Andrew muttered.

She laughed, a rusty pale-brown sound.

'Lydia?' She could hear the fumbling as he took off the headset and put the phone to his ear. 'Oh, Lydia, I—'

She disconnected the call, her hand trembling.

No. No. No. No. No. No.

She had always known the day would come when she

would break her resolve and her silence, but she had imagined a more considered event. Enough time having passed that he understood the futility of his solutions. Enough days and nights alone to constitute water under the bridge. To push them from the present to the past tense. *Remember Andrew and Lydia?* their friends would ask. *Not really* would come the answer.

She never thought it would be a joke that would do it. She had been so sure that that Lydia, that joking Lydia, was gone as surely as if she never was.

One little pill and she could float away on her blue sea, calm and able to sleep through the rest of today and wake in a fresh tomorrow. She had one foot on that slippery slope. It wouldn't take much more to sever the last threads of structure in her life and drift through her days suspended between napping and half-waking.

Mary had no such luxury, she reminded herself. Mary set her alarm clock at four-hour intervals in the night to turn Nick to prevent him developing bedsores. In her pyjamas – not for Mary the frivolity of a nightgown – Mary leaned over her sleeping man-child and deftly put into practice the manual handling she had learned in order to bring him home. The careful choreography known to nurses and carers the world over.

The heaviest part of loss is the weight it adds to the days. Do you find that too, Mary? Fridays are hard because it happened on a Friday. The number 11 is off limits, as is its digital companion, 23. Even seeing it on the clock closes your eyes. Time itself is booby-trapped. Either you remember or you have forgotten. There's no in-between.

Eventually, Andrew forgot. He asked me what was wrong, Mary, can you imagine? He forgot and I had to remind him it was a Friday and it happened on a Friday and it took him a second to look inside himself and find sympathy for me. I could see him looking for it. Having to look for it. I wouldn't

expect sympathy from anyone else, but Andrew? I expected
more. Wouldn't you?

[Delete. Delete. Delete.]

Lydia woke on the couch in the early afternoon, her heart racing from a troubled sleep and with a sense of foreboding.

She couldn't – shouldn't – complain. She had no entitlement to sweet dreams.

With the inevitable coffee in her hand, Lydia stood at the living-room window and surveyed the beach. There wasn't a soul in sight. She shivered. If the zombie apocalypse came, how ever would she know?

Overhead, the sky was heavy, the rain a load it was aching to put down. A pregnant sky, she thought and, clear-headed, let the idea pinch her.

The advantage – the *distinct* advantage – to living out here on her own was the certainty that she would never be ambushed by someone else's newborn. Whether pinkly sleeping or wailing for comfort, her peace was never disturbed by the needs of a tiny being.

The car was driven by Ms Lydia O'Gorman, a childless woman in her late thirties... one tabloid had described her.

Childless, it said. As if having no children of her own made her somehow careless with other people's.

She was staring at the column when Andrew went out to work in the morning and was still looking at it when he got home that evening.

'What can I do, Lydia? I'll do anything,' Andrew had said, kneeling beside her chair, but there were no words to tell him that the sole available comfort was in knowing that it was a pain she deserved.

Childless. Such a meaningless term, with its implication that parenting ended when childhood did. As if the two were connected. When Lydia's own mother was barely a parent even when Lydia was a child, and Mary's parenting responsibilities stretched to infinity.

Childless Ms O'Gorman. In black and white, evermore. It was a done deal.

She could never admit to anyone that there were days when she looked at Mary's posts and was relieved it would never be her. But so too were there lonesome days – seagull days, she thought of them – when, if she were to open her mouth, all that would come would be that high-pitched keen. Those were the days she looked at Nick's constant company and envied Mary.

The sky gave up its burden in one fell swoop, tipping its bucket of dirty grey water and letting it splash wherever it liked. From her window, Lydia looked for her sight line but couldn't make it out through the murk. The sea wouldn't rise for rainfall, she reminded herself. If it were to come for her, it would need an almighty push from behind.

The rain was still sheeting down when Sis Cotter appeared, this time pushing her bike. The straight edges of her upright posture had been softened by the rain and she bent over the bike like sodden cardboard.

Did she look forlorn only because Lydia knew she was going into an empty house? Which begged the thought: if things were different, would one of Sis Cotter's children have bought this house from Lydia's parents so they could be near their mother? Strange, wild Doreen, maybe, dancing joyfully in her kitchen and everyone around the place telling each other delightedly she was home for good. And none gladder than Sis Cotter herself. Her child at the perfect distance for privacy and comfort and friendship. Lunch or dinner several times a week. A weekend TV show looked forward to and watched with a glass of wine.

No. Impossible to imagine Sis Cotter's old hands holding a glass of wine.

A hot whiskey. Or an Irish coffee. Just the one. Go on, so, I will. And the silence more companionable than any chat.

Lydia shook her head to clear the image. If Sis Cotter's children wanted to live here, they would. Lydia's choices had no power over their lives. People made their own choices.

Outside, Sis Cotter disappeared into her house. She would be feeling the anticipatory joy of the long hot shower to come. The welcome sting of warm water on cold skin. Almost chemical in its release. Alchemical, even. No one to answer to besides herself.

Perhaps this was intentional. A penance. Perhaps Sis, too, had done something unforgivable. Notoriety wasn't limited to one instance in a family. A pillow over her husband's face while he slept, maybe. A hand holding his face under the tepid water of the bath. A wasp trapped with him inside a locked car, while Sis herself stood outside watching the horizon, an EpiPen snug in the zipped pocket of her handbag.

Tell the truth, Lydia.

Tell the truth and shame the devil (thank you, Mother).

Tell the truth because there is no one here to see or hear you and no reason not to.

'What is it you are hoping to gain from being here?' the friendly psychiatrist had asked when Lydia, dazed in the weeks after the accident, after listening to Andrew read aloud profiles of wellness practices as if they were restaurant reviews and agreeing that, yes, this woman sounded like the best.

'What is it I hope to gain here?' Lydia repeated. She was mystified by the question. Surely it was clear that the reason she had come was to provide a degree of second-hand comfort to her husband, who seemed to believe that spending time in a room with a stranger would somehow bring back the woman he married. As if this tired-looking middle-aged woman would read from a list of passwords until she hit on the one that rebooted Lydia.

'I want Andrew to feel… better about things,' she said.

'Not for Andrew. For you. What is it you want for you?' the woman asked.

Why did everyone persist in forcing her to talk and then refusing to hear what she said?

To her credit, the psychiatrist was the purveyor of the blessed little tablets. Her doves, she thought of them, bearing her off to a vast emptiness where not only were there no consequences, there were in fact no actions. With them, she could join Andrew on the couch in the evenings, her jaw slack, while current affairs or comedies or game shows droned in the background. She needed to do nothing except try to remember not to smack her dry lips together and to refocus her eyes when he spoke to her.

Her doves let her ignore the fact that she and Andrew were in two different worlds. Or, rather, in two different times – he in the past, she in the unendurable present.

A shared future was no longer negotiable.

If she were to take one step outside – to simply be on the other side of this glass – Lydia would be soaked to the skin in minutes. Then a shower. The blessed, unmatched relief of it.

Should she?

Could she?

The colour rose in her cheeks and she placed her cold hand flat on the glass. Counted to ten, to thirty, to one hundred, to five hundred. Until her legs were steady enough to carry her to the kitchen, her hands steady enough to take a pill from her bottle, her throat open enough to swallow it down.

'Hang on a minute, Mother. I was chopping shallots – let me just wipe my hands.' Lydia put the phone down and pulled a tissue from the box.

'What are you making?'

'Just a salad.'

'In the winter? Oh, Lydia. You're like something out of Dickens.'

'It's a warm chicken salad, actually,' Lydia lied. The prospect of switching on the oven and messing with tiny tinfoil pouches had seemed unutterably depressing, so she had settled for a tin of tuna. In oil, though, not brine. So there was that.

'You should be glad I'm not slobbing around in yoga pants comfort eating,' she said.

On the other end of the line, her mother shuddered audibly. 'Yoga pants would be preferable to pyjamas. Honestly, Lydia, you should see the parade of them up and down the street in the mornings. Everything hanging out for all to see. Shameless. In their horrible furry boots. And this is not at dawn, mind you, but at eight-thirty and nine o'clock in the morning! I feel like standing outside the front door and showing them what a face ready for the world should look like. Do people go around in their pyjamas there?' She paused, sipped, swallowed. 'I suppose you wouldn't know.'

'I thought you were happy there was some young blood around the area,' Lydia said. It was a polite way of saying that her mother and her friends now had something with which to fill their days. Cataloguing the tiny transgressions, breaches of a long-dead etiquette, and gathering to exchange notes over early-afternoon gin. Such was the pleasing shape of her mother's day since the large family homes that surrounded hers had begun to be felled to make way for apartment complexes.

'Is your cleaning lady coming today?' her mother said.

It was a familiar tactic. Lydia had once had the thought that conversations with her mother were like the famous fencing scene in *The Princess Bride*. All assumptions and shifting ground. 'Not today,' she said. 'Just me, myself and I today.'

'Are you lonely, darling?' her mother asked, wrong-footing her again. 'You sound lonely.'

Lydia pulled out a chair and sat down. Care, even packaged in a careful veneer of bright, shallow chat, was still care.

'I'm sure Andrew would—'

'No, Mother. We've been over this.'

'He's your husband, for heaven's sake. Let him be there for you. That's what family does, Lydia. We show up. That's all there is to it.'

'You said it yourself: he's my husband and it's my decision to make.'

'Meanwhile we worry ourselves sick while you lounge around in your rural retreat—'

'It's hardly a retreat.' Lydia pushed away the thought of the *An Cúlú* sign at the gate, proclaiming that it was, in fact, exactly that.

'It's hiding, Lydia. It's playing at sacrifice while you lick your wounds and wait for it all to go away. What will you do when your redundancy money runs out and Andrew is less keen to forgive and forget?'

'He is not the one who needs to forgive and forget, Mother. I am.'

'What has he done that you need to forgive?'

'Not forgive him, Mother. Forgive myself.'

Night fell and revealed a whiskey evening.

Lydia eschewed her wool-winding and, at some point, went in search of her mother's box of goodies.

The little bottles and potions smelled wonderful when Lydia opened them. It was automatic, almost, the steadying of her hands, the smearing and dabbing, a muscle memory, a hearkening back.

When she was finished, her old face stared back at her in the mirror.

Her work face.

Her Galway Races face.

A little more used-looking, but still unmistakeably, disappointingly hers.

It seemed shocking that she could look like herself with so little time and effort. That if she chose to, she could present herself to the world as the person she used to be and all it would take was a steady hand and some contouring.

Why, when her mother asked if she was lonely, hadn't she answered 'yes'?

Why hadn't she told her mother she was scared and trapped inside her mind and her home? Or if that was too much, why hadn't she simply said, *come, please*, and trusted that her mother would?

Her old face was ill-equipped to handle questions like that.

Her old face belonged to the past.

Lydia dipped a cotton bud in baby oil and began to carefully remove the eye make-up.

Andrew himself was usually a present-tense sort of person. Not in a way that was irritating or smug; it was more that he made the best of things. Or, if no best was available, he tried to salvage whatever good there was.

It should have come as no surprise then to learn that he visited Nick in hospital, having first contacted Mary – 'reached out', as he put it – to make sure that it was all right.

Lydia felt faint when he told her and she had to sit down before her legs failed her. *Why?* she wanted to ask. And *how bad is it?* And *does she hate me?*

'What is she like?' she asked instead.

If she hadn't asked, would Mary have remained somehow removed, unreal?

'Should I visit her?' she asked before she lost her nerve.

He looked at her strangely. 'Visit him, you mean. Nick.' He shook his head. 'I don't think so. The lawyer thinks it might... inflame things.'

It was then that the anger came. The accusations that Andrew had taken Mary's side. Allegations of hypocrisy from Lydia to Andrew and from Andrew to Lydia.

'You've made it clear that you don't want my help,' he told her. 'Mary does.'

'I'm sure she does,' Lydia spat.

And on and on it went.

Eventually, when all the words had been flung and stuck and they were sitting on opposite sides of the living room, Andrew raised his hand and said one final thing. 'Is it so hard to believe that I can see how awful the situation is for everyone? That I could want to relieve the pain in whatever way I can? You are not the only one permitted a degree of complexity, Lydia. You are not the only one suffering.'

That was the last honest conversation they had.

Forbidden to meet Mary, Lydia began to follow her online.

On August 14th, when Mary posted a photo of an older woman holding a baby, accompanied by a series of broken-heart emojis, Lydia guessed that her mother had died of cancer. Mary frequently posted in support of the Irish Cancer Society and in March she had changed her profile picture to include a frame for the national Daffodil Day fundraiser.

Lydia looked closely at the photo of grandmother and grandson. So many new baby photos featured a sleeping infant and a stiff-shouldered adult. But not this one. Mary's mother, Nick's grandmother, held him with the kind of careless certainty of someone used to handling babies. In slacks and cardigan, she was dressed for comfort. For house cleaning or washing or baby sick. She would have shooed Mary up the stairs to bed for a nap and then woken her when dinner was on the hob, baby Nick bathed and watching her wide-eyed.

When Lydia told her mother that she had decided not to have children, that she didn't feel the urge, that it wasn't for her, her mother simply toasted her and said, 'To never having to worry you will turn into one of those boring women who are all baby-baby-baby.' Whether it was Lydia or her mother who had worried was unclear.

Lydia could have told Mary the story of her mother at the lunch table telling guests that she had prayed for a son, that a boy would be like having a knight for life. She would smile around at the silence and take a sip of gin while Lydia's face burned as high as her heart was low.

Not poor Mary, Lydia could have told her, but lucky Mary.

She began to imagine befriending her.

'Lydia means "kindred spirit",' she could tell her. Couldn't you do with one of those?

All those months earlier, Lydia had asked Andrew what Mary was like and waited a lifetime for him to consider the question and find an answer: 'She's just a normal woman. Ordinary. Busy. Tired.'

I am tired, too, Mary. It is the great universal, isn't it, tiredness? The great leveller. Everyone, no matter how rich or thin or unhappy or broken, has to close their eyes at some point in the day. Has to voluntarily shut down their body and let it do its work in peace. You, me, Nick: we all submit to sleep in the end. We are all powerless before it.

[Delete. Delete. Delete.]

The nightmare kicked Lydia out abruptly, sending her gasping into real life, like the water slide on which she had spent an entire childhood holiday. She clutched at the banal calm of the memory: the smell of suntan lotion and salt-and-vinegar crisps, the sound of laughter and splashing, sliding down, climbing back up the ladder, sliding down again, wearing the fabric of her swimsuit thin and shiny, the loose feeling in her legs each time she staggered up out of the water. Her mother in sunglasses on a sun lounger. 'Did you see me, Mother? Were you watching?'

The car. Her hands on the wheel, tapping along to the song on the radio. Knowing what was ahead but unable to turn the wheel. Unable to—

Stop. Lydia reached for her pillbox. Her trembling hand dropped the box and she scrabbled around on the floor, finding a pill and swallowing it.

Night demons were smothered. Day demons drowned.

Her phone lay on the bedside table. Lifting it and pressing the button that connected her to Andrew was like watching someone else.

'Hello? Lydia?' His voice was sleepy, then suddenly alert. He was only skimming the surface of sleep, she guessed. She used to see it happen whenever he worked on a particularly stressful project.

She searched for whatever it was had prompted her to speak earlier but found only a tight ball of tears stoppering her voice.

'Let me just…'

From the change in his breathing, he had sat up in the bed. Left hand holding the edge of the mattress, left knee bent and foot braced against the bed, push until his back met the pillow against the headboard. She stretched her hand across her empty sheets.

'Bad dream?'

She nodded.

'Had to be either that or a booty call,' he said, yawning, and the image of him, tousle-haired and garlic-breathed, raised a giggle in her throat, bringing with it a great surge of fear and panic and sadness, all vomited out into the quivering darkness.

'Do you want me to talk or just sit with you?' he asked when the tears subsided and her ragged breathing was calming. 'Door C, please, Bradley,' he answered himself and, a moment later, she heard the sound of music. Some gentle acoustic guitar and a thin, sincere voice. Lydia closed her eyes and breathed. When it got to the bridge, Andrew hummed along, driving the monsters back, back, back. Back through the bedroom door, back along the hallway, back down the stairs.

'Do you want to tell me what the dream was about?' Andrew asked.

There was only one thing it had been about. Lydia took a shallow breath. 'Tell me about him.'

He didn't make a fuss. Didn't exclaim at finally hearing the shaky croak of her voice. Didn't ask who she meant.

'He likes watching TV. Sports, mostly, or the comedy channel. Mary says...' He cleared his throat, ever his tactic while weighing his words. 'Mary worried at first that watching sports would make him depressed, but she says it has the opposite effect. It absorbs him. Everything from golf to football, Mary says.'

'Not cycling,' Lydia said before she could stop herself.

'We don't talk about that,' Andrew said. 'He likes the comedy channel early in the day, before the sports come on. *Frasier*, *Seinfeld*, *The Simpsons*. Typical young lad stuff. I gave him the *Blackadder* box set, but it went over his head, Mary said.'

Mary said this. Mary said that. As if they were the unit and it was Lydia herself who was the outsider.

'Tell me how you became friends.'

He sighed. 'We've been over this, Lydia.'

He didn't say, *We're not friends, Lydia.*

He didn't say, *I wouldn't call it friendship, Lydia.*

'Tell me,' she insisted. She leaned back against the

pillows and closed her eyes and listened while he told her the story again.

'The day after the accident,' he began.

Once upon a time, thought Lydia.

'The day after the accident, I sat in the hospital car park for an hour trying to decide whether or not to go in. This was before we saw the solicitor. Before we were told it might not be advisable. While I sat there, a woman came out. She didn't seem to be a patient, although she was wearing slippers. She looked... stunned. I knew she was Mary, I just knew it. I got out of the car and told her who I was and asked if she was all right.'

Was that the point where their lives diverged? Where Andrew did the right thing, instinctively, on the heels of her monstrous wrong thing? Or when he did the right thing, *knowingly*, on the heels of her monstrous wrong? Two statements with a marriage's worth of difference separating them.

'When she had to modify the house to bring Nick home, I put her in touch with a reputable architect to do the design and offered to get my lads to do the work for her. There wasn't a lot of time, so it seemed the fairest thing...'

He had the grace to stop and let the word hang there between them.

'If you're thinking it sounds cosy somehow, you're wrong. It's awkward and messy and half the time she lets me help and hates me for it and she's right.' He sighed. 'I'm not looking for sympathy. Jesus. This is coming out all wrong. She didn't want money or she would have taken a civil case but nor could she afford all she needed for Nick. I still help out a bit here and there. That's all. There are no winners here, Lydia.'

He helped out a bit here and there.

That was what it all boiled down to. Here and there.

Lydia *here* listened to him breathe *there* until her thoughts faded to merciful black.

PETER

'Howdy, Sheriff.' Anita tipped an imaginary hat when Peter passed her desk.

In the early days, he had felt like asking her when she thought the joke might grow old, but then he realised she still did it to Lou as well, who had been here years longer than Peter. Today he was grateful for her easy warmth. 'Hi, Anita.'

'Feeling a bit better?'

From the sympathetic tilt of her head, he might have been on his last legs. 'Getting there.' Peter was as glad now that he wasn't a blusher as he was on his first day at every new school of his youth.

'You shouldn't be having coffee on a fragile stomach.' Anita took the cup from him. 'I'll make you a ginger tea and drop it in to you.'

'Drop it in to me?'

'Team meeting this morning. Remember?'

'I hadn't forgotten,' Peter said.

'Liar,' Anita said cheerfully and disappeared in the direction of the staff kitchen.

It was an unwritten rule of meetings that once the first whinger started, the floodgates would open and people would try to outdo each other for effort and/or exhaustion. Tales of impossible hours worked, obstacles overcome.

Everyone convinced that they alone had their finger in the dam, holding back the flood.

For a while there, it had indeed felt like a flood.

Peter was brought in to help Lou when, in the backwash of the recession, one sheriff alone couldn't cover all the house repossessions. When he was invited to apply for the job, he went to talk to Lou, to find out what the job entailed, see if he would be up to it.

'We cover Munster,' she told him. 'Ten thousand square miles, give or take. In reality, you'll be on the road one or two days a week and likely no more than three hours' drive in any direction.'

Peter nodded, as if those practicalities were what he had come to hear.

Lou eyed him across the desk. 'I'll tell you the same two things I tell everyone. One: I sleep fine, thanks. All night long. Two: they're real people. Knowing that is how you make a shitty situation better. I'm a lot nicer than most people expect.'

That was Lou.

Peter let the others' talk go over his head, looking instead at the activity tracker Lou had projected onto the wall to go through the work plan for the remainder of the month. There was an unspoken slackening once December hit. Nobody wanted to stand on a doorstep with their hand out for keys within a donkey's roar of Christmas. Nicer than people expect, indeed.

Court judgements pending were in red and cases closed were in green. Their job, his and Lou's and the team's, was to turn the amber cases – the ones who had lost their final appeal – green.

Not for the first time, Peter wondered at the morality of representing people's lives in colour in this way. What did it say about the people around this table that each green was welcomed, never mind that it represented the worst day of someone else's life?

Most repossessions are developers, he reminded himself, and it was true. But those weren't the ones that stuck.

This wasn't what he pictured in school, when he decided he wanted to study law. All the hours watching *Columbo* (Noel's favourite, he chuckled 'Oho now' when Columbo turned back with his just-one-more-thing) or *Matlock* (Sheila's choice, she liked the twinkle in his eye) left him with more of an interest in the law itself than in arguing points to a jury.

This wasn't what he pictured at university, either.

Or when he specialised in tax law.

Or applied to the legal graduate programme with the county council.

Or. Or. Or.

At what point would he own his decisions?

When he looked ahead in those days, all he pictured, if he was honest, was a front door of his own that he would paint a rich dark blue and do everything in his power to protect.

If it wasn't for Fintan, he mightn't ever have got to university.

'They literally tell you what you need to know,' was Fintan's take on secondary school. 'Really, it's as easy to do well as to do badly.'

So they spent a couple of hours studying on Saturdays and Sundays before heading off to town or for a cycle or to a hurling match.

It was fine for Fintan. He was always going to be an engineer, no two ways about it. 'Rebuilding the world,' he used to say. 'Only better.' And Peter would be mortified and thrilled and proud at the sheer scale of his friend's vision.

Although Fintan talked sometimes about wishing he had done theoretical physics, that was after he'd had a few drinks, when Peter himself was a breath away from admitting that ever since he had seen Sheila's shelves of encyclopaedias, he had half-thought he might quite like to work in a library.

It was fine for Fintan. Imagine coming out with that clanger in front of him!

'Remember, if you refuse to execute a removal order, you yourself can become liable to the creditor,' Lou finished, as she did every meeting. 'Peter, can you hang on a minute?'

When everyone had left, Lou came and sat in the empty seat beside Peter. 'You all right? You look like the lights are on but no one's home.'

'I'm fine.'

'Dolly-bird trouble?'

'If I said "dolly bird", you'd have me straight over to HR,' Peter objected.

'And rightly so,' Lou said, nudging him gently. 'Everything okay with your friend Fintan? You were out yesterday.'

'Dodgy tummy,' Peter said without looking at her.

'Dodgy tummy, my hole,' she said.

'They moved him to the hospice Tuesday night,' Peter said. He said nothing about the few days. He didn't think the words would come out even if he tried.

'Ah, shit, I'm sorry. Go if you need to. Take the day, take the week, whatever you need. I can hold the fort here.'

Peter shook his head.

'Is this one of those situations where I have to talk you into it? *You only get one shot and it's better to have no regrets* kind of thing?'

'Actually, he's not really able for visitors, so I'm as well off working.'

Where did that lie come from? He didn't want Lou to think badly of him, and she would. *He'd love to see you.* He would see him. He would. Just as soon as he could be sure of making things better rather than worse. *It was fine for Fintan.*

'Okay,' Lou said. 'But if that changes, just shout.' She was quiet for a moment, scratching the back of her ear. 'Will you come for dinner at the weekend?'

'I don't know, Lou. Food poisoning twice in one week might fell even a mighty oak like myself.'

'Smart arse. Ollie's cooking. He said something about a lamb tagine?'

'Thanks, Lou. Can I let you know?'

'Your name will be in the pot either way. No notice required.'

Peter nodded and gathered his files. 'I'd better hit the road.'

'Peter?' Lou said when he had his hand on the door handle. 'I wish it was dolly-bird trouble.'

He nodded. He did too.

Overhead, bright white clouds clustered together in groups, one piled in behind the other like the receiving line at a wedding, their heads pressed together in whispered commentary. 'A mackerel sky,' Noel called it. 'A buttermilk sky,' Sheila would correct him, and a look would pass between them as if sharing an old, fond joke.

Peter's spirits lifted as the grey buildings of the city gave way to fields and ditches. Without ever knowing the science of it, a person would know that the green of grass and trees was somehow connected to breathing. He stopped at a garage and bought himself a bar of chocolate, then ate it in the car while tapping along to the radio. He didn't know the song, but it did that thing that certain songs do, where they reach inside and drag your heart upwards to the light.

There was dinner with Lou and Ollie to look forward to. Their house was a restful place to be – warm and tidy and welcoming. The teenagers seemed to do their own thing. They might put their heads around the door to say hello or to snag a slice of whatever was going for dessert but otherwise left their parents unbothered. They were a good team, Lou and

Ollie. Years of practice, Lou said. They had drifted together at school and never really parted since. There was no backstory that wasn't well known between them.

When did it become near-mythical to go home to the same person every day? To the spaghetti bolognese or chicken dippers or fish supper, the box sets and comfortable silences?

Caroline went through a phase of trying to set him up with this friend or that. He had something in common with almost everyone, according to her. Throw a stick and he couldn't fail to hit the perfect woman. It terrified him, the implication that she was describing him in such loose terms. That she was describing him at all.

Over dinner one Friday night, he told them he was thinking of joining a dating agency. It was sort of true. He had heard one advertised on the radio – an old-fashioned-sounding agency, with interviews and profile matching done by people rather than algorithms. He had listened to the ad all the way through. That counted as considering it, didn't it?

Caroline looked at him for a moment, then counted off on her fingers. 'Forty-something. Thinker. Non-drinker.'

'Jesus, I sound like a right killjoy.'

'Clean-living?' Caroline suggested. 'Or is that too puritanical-sounding? You need three.'

'Why three?'

But none of them knew.

'I have it,' Fintan announced. 'Joker, smoker, midnight toker.'

And the evening collapsed in laughter.

Over the next few weeks, Caroline kept checking in with him about his progress with the dating agency. Texting him a description here, a phrase there. Later, Peter realised she must have already been shouldering Fintan's worry by then.

The initial interview with the dating agency was surprisingly detailed, although he came away with the distinct sense that he had disappointed Patricia, the agency owner.

'A sheriff is nothing like a detective then?' she asked.

'More like a civil servant,' he explained.

'How would you describe your work?'

'I wouldn't.' Peter's attempt at humour fell flat. He gathered himself and tried again, conscious of Patricia's expectations. He found himself listening out for the click of her nails on the keyboard that suggested he had said something worth noting. They were a bit sparse, he thought, on balance.

When it came to describing his job to people, he had two options, as he saw it. He could emphasise the rule-following nature of the thing – himself as the sheriff, maintaining law and order against the hard chaws out to game the system – or he could focus on the surprising humanity of the job, the gentle easing of good people out of a system that had outrun them and into the next phase of their lives. He sometimes found himself claiming that the repossessed houses were taken on by the local authority and used for social housing. He never looked into it too closely. If he wasn't certain, he couldn't be said to be lying, exactly.

The town was that distance from the city that was called commutable, though the prospect of forty-five minutes twice a day was not one that appealed to Peter. As a consequence of selling itself well, it was medium-sized and well-heeled and its clean streets attested to there being nobody around by day to mess it up. A foreshortened town centre yielded to housing estates with their arms stretched wide, ready to suffocate everyone within their comfortable grasp. Modern quicksand, Peter thought them. Once they sucked you in, it was just a slow capitulation to whatever were the dearly held norms of the upwardly mobile.

The address was in one of those housing estates. Big identical houses, whose different coloured doors were the height of rebellion. Everywhere Peter looked were pristine

SUVs and clean wellingtons. Noel would be puzzled by the artifice of the place.

'Mr Derek Roche? I'm Sheriff Peter Nyhan,' he said when the presumptive man of the house answered the door. 'As of October 2nd, 2018, the courts found in favour of—'

The man closed the door.

Inside, Peter could hear him shouting, 'Get the last of your things, Yvonne. Time to go.'

Peter leaned against the bonnet of his car and waited. His personal rule was not to get back into the car. Even if it was bucketing rain, he would put up his umbrella and wait it out. No phone either. That was another of his rules. It looked – and felt – disrespectful. People were people.

He was happy for people to take their time, within reason. For the most part, they did it to make a point and it wasn't worth the hassle of taking that from them, too. He was similarly happy for them to take whatever the hell they wanted from inside. What was it to him if they loaded their washing machine or treadmill into the car? More fool them to leave it until the day of the eviction itself was more his line of thinking, but hope died hard in people.

As long as they didn't do any damage. He couldn't abide people who wrecked the place for the sake of it. Radiators pulled off the walls. A toilet disconnected and pulled out onto the landing, then used, and badly. Things written on the walls in indelible ink. Awful things. Wishing all sorts of evil and lack of peace on him. The joke was on them. He had left more places than they could imagine.

He used to get home from school or the park or wherever he had spent the day and see Karen the social worker's car parked outside his mam's flat.

'Your mam is feeling a bit under the weather, so you're going to go and stay with some very nice friends of mine until she's feeling better,' Karen would say. Then she would produce a backpack and tell him to put in his pyjamas and a change of clothes and his favourite toys. As he got older, she dispensed with the fake cheer, instead asking him how he was doing. Telling him it wasn't his fault, like he didn't already know that.

He saw Karen arriving once. He was just on his way home, walking slowly so as to pretend to himself that his heart wasn't both sinking and racing at the idea of opening the front door and finding... what? Well, he never quite knew these last few months, did he?

Karen had parked directly opposite the flat and had the boot of her car open. Inside, Peter saw three big plastic storage boxes lined up neatly inside. Backpacks in one, sweatshirts in another, and stuffed toys in a third. She rooted around for a minute, then pulled a plain dark-blue backpack from the box and gauged its size. As Peter watched, her shoulders slumped. It was unbearable. Like when his mother's dressing gown gaped a little at the front and he had to look away.

'Hey, Karen!' he called loudly. His words had a galvanising effect and her shoulders squared right back to their capable right angles.

'Peter!' Her hug was warm. 'Look at you! You're nearly as tall as I am. How are you?'

'Mam's not doing too well,' he said.

'I know, pet. I have a lovely family for you to stay with. A couple of hours away, but that can't be helped, I'm afraid. And it's out in the countryside, all fresh air and good food. Noel and Sheila, they're called, and they are very excited to meet you.'

It was a different family each time. After a while, there was no point in asking why. Karen would just say that someone he had stayed with before was busy with another foster kid now or had stopped fostering or they thought this family would be a better fit for him. All of which were just polite ways to say the last people had moved on to someone new.

'Here is not there, Peter. Now is not then,' Karen said every time, which he took to mean that he should give everything and everyone a chance. He tried not to think about what would happen if the chances ever ran out.

His mam always wanted him back. Karen would bring him home and he would walk into the flat to the smell of bleach and lemon furniture polish and his mother nervously offering him a Diet Coke, making sure to open the fridge door wide so he could see it was full of fruit and vegetables.

'You can call me,' Karen would tell him quietly as she hugged him goodbye. 'You can call me any time, you know, even just to say hello.'

It would be great for a while, him and his mam. Then there would be a day when the flat smelled of cigarettes. Then the smoky sweetness of weed, which meant his mam had stayed up late and wouldn't be getting up before lunchtime. Then she would start going out and not coming home until late. Then she would come home and bring some man with her, who treated the place and everything in it as if it was his own. Eventually, Peter would get home from school and find Karen's car outside the door and be relieved to see it and relieved that he hadn't given in to the urge to call her. That he hadn't been the one to tell on his mam.

Leaving a place was no different to anything else, Peter thought. You just put one foot in front of the other until you were gone.

The door of the house opened and a child emerged with a dog on a lead. He walked it over to the grass verge and ordered it to go. It ignored him and began to bark at a crow on a nearby roof. The child jerked the lead and the dog stopped. Child and dog looked at one another. Bark. Jerk. Bark. Jerk.

Peter walked over. 'Nice dog,' he said, bending down to pet its head.

'S'useless,' the boy grumbled. 'I wanted a husky, but instead my mother got her.'

'Good to have a dog,' Peter said.

The boy looked at the dog speculatively. 'My dad said if we have to get rid of it, I can get a PlayStation instead,' he said. 'To stop me being sad.'

The little feck. Peter judged the chances of sorrow to be minimal, but it was none of his business. If he took a dog every time the thought occurred to him, he'd end up on one of those Channel 4 documentaries.

The front door opened again and the man emerged with a laptop bag under each arm. 'Finn,' he called sharply. 'Get away from there.'

Peter looked at the bags, making sure the man saw him.

'Tools of my trade,' the man said. 'I know the law, too, you know.'

'The cap is nineteen euro,' Peter said under his breath to satisfy himself he had said it. What did he care if the man took his laptops or left them? He could have ten more loaded into the boot. He could have a fucking warehouse full of them. All Peter needed were the house keys and he could go home at the end of the day with a clear conscience.

'Did Thor go?' the man asked the child as the door closed behind them again.

Thor. For a spaniel. Jesus wept.

Years before, Peter was meandering home from school one afternoon. He wasn't long with Noel and Sheila and he was enjoying the feeling of not having to race home to do jobs. Once he kept his room tidy and helped with the dishes, that seemed to be all they expected. It was nice to feel he didn't have to avoid the place either. He was just taking his time. 'Taking his ease,' Noel called it and it was just as fine as it sounded. 'Cock of the walk,' his mother would say, but he didn't want to think about her right now. He used to pretend that he had a secret brother who came to mind his mother while Peter was away, but he was too old to believe that anymore. He should be glad he didn't have one really. Karen had told him a long time ago that it was difficult to place siblings together. He hadn't heard the word before and had to ask her what it meant.

Peter kicked a stone along the ground in front of him and was pleased to find the sense of peace return to him.

Jaunty, he thought. It was a word he had come across in *The Joy of Knowledge* and was storing up for the right moment. He was half-afraid that he would say it in school by accident. That it would squirt out in response to some bit of new wonder in English or History class and mark him out as weird. But the worry didn't take away from the pleasure of the word. If anything, it gave it an importance. The weight of a secret. A good one. One he had chosen himself.

When he got to the gate, he leaned on it to look into the field. He had seen Noel do this on days when he was taking his ease. It seemed somehow part of the process of relaxation. Peter didn't know how exactly, but he was willing to give it a go and see if it took.

The road was quiet. It usually was. It wasn't on the way to anywhere much and the local children all walked or cycled to school. If he was still here at Christmas, Peter thought, he might ask Noel and Sheila if he could have the use of the rusty old bike in the shed. He had been keeping a casual eye on it the past few weeks and it didn't appear to belong to anyone in particular. With a bit of work, he thought he might be able to get it up and going. Alex, the dad from – Peter counted back – three foster homes ago, had a bike and he sometimes let Peter help him tighten the brakes or sand away rust patches or mend a puncture. That was Peter's favourite job – putting the wheel into a basin of water and watching for the little bubble of air that told you exactly where the defect was. Then all you had to do was patch over it. It was like magic.

What wouldn't he give for a bike of his own! The thought of the distance and speed and freedom of it was enough to make his legs tremble. What would he do? Where would he go? Not home, it was too far. He was glad. The thought came fast and guilty and he climbed the first two rungs of the gate to give his hands and feet something to do. In comics, when people were angry, lightning came out their fingertips and Peter knew that whoever drew them must have loved and hated their mam, too.

He didn't notice the whimpering at first. Eventually it caught his attention and he climbed another rung on the gate, feeling it wobble slightly under him, to see if he might see what it was. It was coming from his side of the gate, which meant he didn't have to venture into the field and risk making the owner angry if they came along and found him there. He climbed back down and walked slowly along the verge of the road, looking into the long grass to find the source of the noise.

It wasn't long until he saw it: a pup with its neck caught in barbed wire, crying and shaking as if its world was ending. He supposed it would have been if he hadn't come along. Freeing the pup was another matter entirely. It resisted all efforts to get near it, biting down on his hand with teeth that were surprisingly sharp. In the end he had to take off his jacket – newly bought by Sheila the same day as the shoes – and use it as a shield around his hand while he tried to work the barbed wire free of the pup's neck. Eventually, Peter lifted out the pup in the shredded sleeve of his jacket and held it against him while he tried to figure out what to do next.

'What have you got there?'

Peter turned and found the pyramid boy – Fintan, he reminded himself – in the road behind him, pushing a bike.

'Pup. It was caught in barbed wire.'

'Lucky a fox didn't get him,' Fintan said cheerfully. 'What are you going to do with him?'

Peter looked at the pup lying limp in his arms and considered his options. Noel would know what to do, he thought. 'I'll take him back to No... back to the house,' he said.

Fintan walked back with him without asking, pushing

the bike and talking about constellations and about the Dog Star, in particular. 'The brightest star in the sky,' he said. It didn't seem to bother him that Peter had nothing to add; he had plenty of detail to cover both sides of the conversation. It was something Peter would come to recognise, Fintan's random passions that changed daily or weekly, depending on what caught his fancy. There was little that wasn't worthy of Fintan's interest and enthusiasm.

Peter half-listened and half-worried what Sheila would say when she saw his jacket. He could offer to work it off. He had taught himself to cook the basics and iron his school clothes. Surely there would be something useful he could do to make it up to her.

When he got home, Noel was in the back kitchen, washing cement from his hands and scraping under his fingernails, while Sheila pottered over and back between table and stove. The smell of apple tart was so thick and sweet that Peter felt he could nearly take a bite out of the air.

'Who have we here?' Noel asked.

'Fintan Molloy,' Fintan said cheerfully and Noel laughed. 'I know who you are, young Molloy.'

'It's a puppy,' Peter said. 'I found him in the ditch. He was stuck on barbed wire.'

'Where's his mother, I wonder?' Noel said.

'His mother will have tried her best,' Sheila said, stopping her rolling. 'Dogs can't get each other out of traps. Poor creatures can only work with what they're given.'

Peter looked at Noel, who gave him a ghost of a wink. 'Put him up here on the draining board till we have a look and see what can we do for him.'

Noel turned the shivering pup this way and that. 'Some kind of collie cross, I'd say. A few months old. He's very thin, poor fella. And with a bad leg, too.'

'What's wrong with his leg?' Fintan asked with interest and the two boys crowded in close for a look.

'I'd say it broke and didn't fix right,' Noel explained, pointing to where it curled awkwardly inwards.

'Could we splint it, do you think?' Fintan asked.

'Too late for that, I'd say. He'll just have to get along as best he can.'

'What will you do with him?' Peter asked. He was afraid to look at either Noel or Sheila.

'I'll ask around and see if anyone is missing him,' Noel said, patting his pockets for his keys. 'Ted Roche will know if anyone had a collie pup or is missing one. No better man than the postman for knowing every dog in the parish.'

'He looks to me like he could do with a good meal for a start,' Sheila said when Noel was gone. 'And we can put a box here by the range for him to have a bit of a sleep until Noel gets back.'

Fintan sat at the table eating buttered scones and telling Sheila everything he had already told Peter about the Dog Star.

'Is that so?' she would say now and then.

Peter couldn't find any words. His whole body was taken up with waiting, tense with listening out for Noel's car turning into the yard. He hardly dared look at the puppy, conked out by the heat of the fire, with his belly full of Sheila's home-cooked ham, shredded finely so he wouldn't choke.

'Ted says Hennessy over behind the creamery had two collie pups got for the sheep, so I went over and sure enough it was one of his.' Noel's voice tightened. 'Turns out he hit him a slap of the car reversing out of the drive and he decided he was no more good to him so he let him go.'

'He let him go? Does that mean he doesn't belong to anyone?'

'I wouldn't say that, exactly,' Noel said. He bent down and patted the dog's head. 'He looks like he belongs here. What do you think, Sheila? I reckon Shadow is a good collie name. Or Rover—'

'Get away out of that,' Sheila said. 'It's not the 1950s. Peter will want his dog to have a more modern name. Something from a book or film you like, maybe?' She patted his shoulder as she passed by with a bowl of water for the dog. His dog. He didn't trust his voice in front of Fintan.

'How about Jupiter? Or Pluto, like the Disney dog?' Fintan suggested. And he was off. A dozen suggestions, each more outlandish than the next. 'No! Sirius, after the Dog Star!'

Peter listened to him, but around and around in his head was the question of what would happen to the dog when he went home to Mam. He pictured the small flat, the days when beans on toast was all they had for dinner, and knew it was impossible.

'Don't worry,' Sheila said as if she could read his mind. 'We can mind him for you any time you need us to. For as long as you want,' she added. 'He isn't something you have to worry about.'

Peter nodded and turned back to Fintan, who was still listing possible names.

'Solo,' he said, at last, glad that his voice came out right.

'*Star Wars*. Cool,' Fintan said.

Peter busied himself with stroking the dog's soft fur and pretending not to see the tears standing in Sheila's eyes.

'They're decent, your aul' pair,' Fintan said when Peter walked him to the end of the yard, Solo tucked into a blanket in his arms.

His aul' pair. Peter turned the phrase over in his mind and liked it. An image of his mother on one of her good days came to mind.

'They're all right,' he said.

'See you tomorrow for a walk, Solo.' Fintan scratched the dog under its chin.

'He won't be up to a walk,' Peter felt obliged to point out, hating himself for it.

But Fintan just shrugged and climbed on his bike. 'We can carry him. Show him around the place. See ya.'

The door to the house opened and the boy emerged again, dragging Thor on his lead. Not cruelty, exactly. Just the lack of awareness that the dog might have feelings of its own. Peter sighed. There was no good pretending he might get a dog again. It wouldn't be fair. Not when he was out at work all day.

The boy's parents followed him out and tucked themselves into their car, slamming the doors. The man reversed out of the drive at unnecessary, ostentatious speed. He stopped beside Peter, rolled down his window and threw the house keys onto the front lawn of the house opposite.

'You needn't think I'll fucking hand them to you,' he said.

Peter reminded himself that moral judgement wasn't his job. As gestures went, he'd had worse. Assuming they hadn't left worse inside for him to find.

They hadn't, as it happened. Although he had to open fifteen microaggressively closed doors to find that out. If anything, they made it look easy. Transactional, almost. A blip in their lives rather than a defining moment.

He should be grateful, he knew. These weren't the people that kept him awake at night, retracing his steps to see how he got here. How he turned into the man on the other side of the door. He was looking for his mother, the self-help books would tell him. To save her or to punish her, he supposed. It didn't much matter why, he told himself. It was his job and he was doing it.

Coming back down the stairs from a second, full-breath recce, Peter's phone vibrated in his pocket. It was a chirpy reminder from Patricia – dating-agency Patricia, as he thought of her – of his 'meetup' with Helen that night.

Thirty-something. Independent. Cheerful. No bullshit.

Although Patricia didn't say bullshit, she paused for just long enough before saying 'nonsense' that Peter could hear it in the air.

Peter didn't think he could face it. Helen would likely fall into one of two camps, either a wistful believer in the power of happy-ever-after or a busy working woman who expected Patricia to manage her romantic business in much the same way her office Nuala or Frances or Anita managed her administrative affairs.

For fuck sake. Who was he to judge anyone for not wanting to be alone, for believing in romance or practicality or whatever it was they believed in? Hadn't he signed up for the same reasons himself? If he never took a risk, then he was accepting that it would be himself and the television from 6 p.m. to bedtime, until his options closed themselves down to nothing more than a dog when he retired at sixty-five.

Just because his mother took the wrong risks with the wrong people and chased the wrong kind of happiness didn't mean he would. Didn't they say now that nature and nurture together made up one half of a person, with the other half determined by all the small randomnesses in life? That was another bit of Fintan trivia.

What it boiled down to was that one tiny thing could change everything.

If it was a belief good enough for Fintan, it was good enough for him.

Peter dropped the house keys in the bank deposit box and found the steering wheel turning as if of its own volition towards the hospice.

By the time he parked, the interior of the car was stuffy from the heating and he opened the window a few inches before switching off the engine. He could sit and let himself believe he was going to go in, at least.

Maybe on some level Fintan might know he was there.

Shite, yes, but comforting shite all the same.

The building could have been formed of the grey gloom

in which it stood. Few lights shone from the windows despite the muddy afternoon light, and Peter wondered if it was deliberate. The low natural light might help people on their way, he supposed, in the way that bright sunlight might make it harder for them to let go.

On the radio, the talk had turned to Christmas and the number of shopping days left. It was a puzzle that people needed to count these things. Or to know them at all. You made your list ahead of time and, come Christmas week, in you went. Noel. Sheila. Lou. Fintan and Caroline. Decent chocolates for the office. Collecting one item from each place. Like a computer game. All method, no need for madness.

The day itself always took the same format: down to Noel and Sheila on Christmas Eve for fish pie, a dinner that was resolutely un-Christmassy. It was a point of pride with Sheila, the better to emphasise the turkey-and-trimmings feast the following day. So fish pie, followed by an apple tart or something equally everyday. Then up to the church for Midnight Mass at 9 p.m. It was the one day in the year he went. Sheila – no fool – said nothing about his stumbling over prayers whose words had finally changed after years of stasis, or his standing when he should kneel or kneeling when he should sit.

The hymns were what he went for. All of them together vibrating out their sorrow and hope. Another year behind them and the next one stretching ahead of them if they were lucky and everyone lifting their voices to whatever they believed in. At Midnight Mass, belting out 'Silent Night', there was neither doubt nor a dry eye in the house.

Caroline was a sucker for the Christmas hymns too. That was one reason she wanted to get married at Christmas, Fintan told Peter. That and the fact that all her old school friends would be home for the holidays.

'No point getting married on your own doorstep without having the mother of all hooleys,' she said. 'Might as well start the rest of our lives as we mean to go on.'

They booked out the whole hotel and had themselves a

hooley all right, but the rest of their lives, as it turned out, fell a long way short of expectations. This Christmas would be their fourth anniversary, if Fintan saw it.

That was all life was in the finish. Forever hoping for the best and lacking the foresight to know how precisely the whole thing would let you down.

Where had Fintan's fucking optimism got him?

In our last year in school, you refused to worry about the future, do you remember that? 'We could be anywhere this time next year, lads,' you'd say in that way you had. Including right here, if we want. Smiling as if being right here was every bit as good as everywhere else. The waves of sincerity and Lynx Africa pouring off you.

Peter had wanted a future. Of course he had. But if he left, could he return? It was a savage misery to lie awake at night hating himself for fantasising that his mother had died, opening the way for him to stay here permanently. In the dark of 4 a.m., it was easy to imagine that Noel and Sheila didn't really love him, they just didn't know how to let him go, having never done it before. Easy to imagine that one day they would realise they could simply pick up the phone to Karen and explain that since Peter would be an adult shortly, they had better think about a new foster child.

In the morning, there was porridge and tea and warm questions about how he slept and how his day was looking and he would eat and answer and feel a thudding guilt for the imaginings of the night. But the night always came and he was always powerless against it.

Shortly before the October midterm of his last year in school, Sheila met him at the door on his way in from school. 'Come into the kitchen for a chat, Peter, will you?'

All he could think as he followed her was that he didn't see Karen's car outside.

Noel was already at the table, his hand hovering over the

teapot in its dark-green cosy. In the centre was a plate of biscuits, but there was no smell of baking. Shop-bought biscuits. In Peter's experience, Sheila's disdain for biscuits out of a packet was overcome by only two circumstances: a dental appointment or a death. Peter's stomach felt like it was trying to escape down his school pants and out through his shoes.

He sat while they poured the tea and offered him a biscuit, feeling miserably like a guest.

'I spoke to your career guidance teacher,' Sheila said. 'He was talking about university for you, maybe, so myself and Noel have been having a bit of a talk here ourselves.'

Peter didn't know what to say. Were they asking if he wanted to leave?

'If things were different, you know we would have already…' Sheila began, and Peter stared at a point on the wall behind her so he could fool himself into hearing without feeling.

'If things were different—' Sheila said again.

'Your mother is your mother,' Noel cut in. 'We'd never try to say otherwise—'

'Your loyalty to her is a credit to you,' Sheila interrupted. 'And a comfort to her, I'm sure—'

'So it isn't that we expect you to think of yourself as ours—'

'It's more that we think of ourselves as yours—'

'And everything that goes with that,' Noel finished.

The two of them took a breath. Sheila smiled at him. Noel took a drink of tea. Peter continued to look at his spot on the wall.

Sheila tapped the table. 'We're doing this all wrong,' she said cheerfully. 'Mr Healy was saying you might have a head for law, if you wanted. At university.'

Her face glowed over the word and Peter wished the ground would open up and swallow him. He had assumed that he was talking to Mr Healy hypothetically. The careers office with its poky little window and dusty shelves had an air of the confession box about it. So much for that.

'I thought I might stay.' Peter returned to looking at his spot on the wall. 'Learn a trade, maybe. Help Noel out.'

'There's nothing wrong with a trade,' Noel began and Sheila shot him a look.

'If university is what you want, we wanted to tell you we have a bit put by. To help out with your books and digs and that,' Sheila said.

'That's... that's what you meant?'

'It won't cover weekends in the city, mind you, so you'll have to come home to us on Fridays. That'll cramp your style, I'm sure, but you'll have to make do. You could get a job, I suppose, but that might interfere with your studies and—'

'Young Fintan Molloy will be doing the same, his dad says. Away Monday to Friday and home on the bus at the weekend.'

Peter nodded, afraid to say anything. Solo padded into the kitchen and all three of them gave him the kind of welcome reserved for returning Antarctic heroes. He took it as no more than his due, taking his shop biscuit and flopping down on his belly by the range.

'Sure haven't we the finest hostage in the land?' Noel said and threw Solo another half of a biscuit.

Peter got out of the car, needing to feel the ground under his feet. 'Here is not there. Now is not then,' he said, under his breath, but their magic was long gone.

I wrote to my mother the night of my eighteenth birthday. I told you that before. Told her I was doing fine, better than fine, starting university, even. I didn't tell her that it all turned out for the best, but I wanted her to know it all the same. She was no fool – she would have read between the lines. Assuming she read it at all. I told her I hoped she was doing well and that if she ever wanted to see me, all she had to do was ask. The same thing I'd written twice a year for the past four years: once on her birthday, once on mine. Then I tore it up and started over.

Peter looked up at the hospice windows, where lights were now being switched on here and there. The nurses needing light to work by, probably. To do their work of turning and measuring and easing. He hoped Fintan's was one of the lit windows.

Shower. Shave. Iron a shirt from the right-hand side of the wardrobe. The side with the pinks and greens. The Florence Cathedral side, he thought of it. Close one eye and all he could see were the workaday blue, white and grey shirts. A pessimist's wardrobe. Close the other eye and it was all pale pastels, the shirts of a man that wouldn't let a woman down on a weekend away in a nice hotel.

He opened both eyes and sighed. Doubtless the same wardrobe was repeated up and down the country and he was fooling himself he was any better than the rest.

He left the shirt (pale pink, not too shiny) draped carefully over the back of a kitchen chair while he made himself something to eat. They were going to the Italian for dinner, but he didn't want to arrive hungry and unable to pay attention to the situation at hand. Salvi's was Peter's go-to for first dates. It catered for both common and uncommon allergies and the Italians took all disasters and emotions in their stride. For a situation like this, two cuts of buttery toast was the job. Took the edge off so that he could order drinks before the food if Helen wanted to take her time over the menu.

'Make sure you order a starter on a first date,' Caroline

advised him before the first agency date. 'Anything else feels rushed. It should feel like you have all the time in the world. Let her get to know you.'

'That's a nice way of saying I don't make a great first impression,' Peter said.

Caroline laughed. 'It means you're our man of hidden depths, Peter.'

While the bread was in the toaster, Peter tidied the living room. He liked it neat generally and it wasn't much of a job to straighten the cushions and put the newspapers in the recycling. He lit the candle on the mantelpiece. *Fresh linen* it was called and it made the house smell nice and homey. Not that he was counting his chickens, but it never hurt to be prepared. More of these first dates ended in sex than he had imagined. People hadn't time to waste, he supposed.

He left the living-room light on to remind him to blow out the candle before leaving.

He scrolled the news on his phone while he ate his toast, filing away bits and pieces that might be good for sparking chat. Helen's profile said she was interested in travel and current affairs and while that meant she was likely well able to keep things moving, it was better if they had equal share of the conversational heavy lifting. Take out politics, religion and anything controversial and there wasn't a whole lot left. It had been that kind of year.

Saudi Arabia giving women the right to drive. That might do, maybe. The Thailand cave rescue, for certain. The Canadian zookeepers arrested for putting a bear into their car and taking him out for ice cream. They were coming into the winter, so if all else failed, talk could turn easily to the prospect of record cold and storms like last year. Nothing objectionable there.

No, but was it interesting, Peter? Did it say *here's someone who could brighten an evening or a weekend or a life*? Fintan and Caroline had a sort of constant low-level chat going on and it all looked very easy and companionable.

Peter's job would come up, of course. He could be euphemistic about it, say he worked in the legal affairs department of the council, but that was risky when a cursory search of his name told the world who he was and what he did. He would hate to start off with her thinking he was the sort of man to prefer an easy lie to a difficult truth.

He blew out the candle, turned off the light and put on his coat. While he was waiting in the hall for the taxi, the phone in his pocket vibrated and he thought it might be Patricia calling to say Helen had cancelled.

But it was Noel's name on the screen. Peter's finger hovered over the green button until it stopped ringing. Chances were Noel had heard that Fintan had moved to the hospice and was ringing to check in. But the taxi was due any minute and if he answered and gave Noel the bum's rush, it would leave both of them feeling bad.

If it rang again, it would mean something was wrong and he would answer. When it didn't, Peter tapped out a quick text. *Out for dinner. Call tomorrow.*

Noel sent back three thumbs-up emojis, a rocket, and a high-heeled shoe.

The mind boggled.

Sheila was disappointed when he told them it was all over with Lynn. As much because she wanted to see him settled as out of any great love for Lynn herself, Peter suspected.

'There's no chance this break-up is temporary?' she asked him.

'You can't talk a person into love, Sheila,' Noel said out of nowhere and the very air around them blushed.

Last Christmas, Noel had left the *Ireland's Own* magazine folded to the classifieds. '*Young-at-heart lady 46, seeks soulmate (35+). Must have own home.*' '*Tired of single life? Let's be each other's plus-one.*' Noel stopped short of circling them. That might be his move this year.

Peter looked at his reflection in the mirror and heard Sheila's voice.

Shoulders back. Meet the world like you mean it.

'Peter. Aren't you thoughtful to wait outside and spare us both the awkwardness of pretending we're not trying to figure out who's who.'

Peter liked her immediately for saying awkwardness instead of shame. 'Shall we?' He held the door open for her.

They followed the manager to their table. Helen in front, Peter behind. She had black trousers on, not jeans, and he was glad he had made an effort with the good shirt.

They kept the conversation light over the menu and ordering. A bottle of wine and antipasto to share. He had a bit of a ropy moment when she ordered vegetarian tagliatelle – a brave move, he thought – just as he was deciding between the osso buco and the veal piccata, but he managed to switch to sea bream in time.

'Have you been on many of these?' Helen asked, spearing an olive with a toothpick.

He wondered what answer she was looking for. It seemed like the kind of question to which there was a right and wrong answer. Too many and he would look flighty. Too few and she might think she was only a warm-up. His gut didn't see them flying off into the sunset together but, as Patricia said – somewhat severely – if his gut was that reliable, he'd have been paired off long ago.

'I suppose it takes them a few goes to figure out what might suit and what wouldn't.' He groaned inwardly. What had possessed him to say 'goes'? As if he thought women were a fairground ride. Whatever you do, he told himself, don't explain. And don't – for the love of all that's holy – use the word *ride*.

She smiled and held up her hand, as if she had been asked to take a vow. 'Helen. Forty. Never married but two significant exes. Eleventh date with Patricia.' She made a face. 'Through Patricia. You know what I mean.'

Peter smiled and held up his hand in the same way. 'Peter. Forty-five. One significant ex, one less so. Four Patricia interventions.'

'Broken heart?' she asked.

'I don't think so,' he said. 'We weren't right for each other. It just took us a while to see it. We didn't make each other better, I suppose.'

'A philosophy of love, Peter? I like it.' And she leaned across to clink her glass to his.

'What's your safety move?' Peter asked and liked that she didn't pretend not to know what he meant.

'Oh, I've sent three texts already to my flatmate. She could nearly pick you out of a line-up at this stage. How about you?'

Peter gestured around him at the restaurant. 'Not my first time here.'

'Aha. Your escape route through the kitchen awaits if things go horribly wrong?'

'Chopper on the roof, actually.' He tapped the side of his nose. 'I know people.'

She graced the poor joke with a laugh and they were off.

Conversation continued lively and pleasant through their main course. Being similar in age, they spent some time trying to figure out if they knew anyone in common but couldn't come up with any possible names.

'We're fake Irish, evidently,' Helen said cheerfully, and Peter had a brief moment of panic wondering if he should tell her he didn't know his father. But the moment passed and they were on to other things.

When dessert was placed in front of them – two affogatos – Helen cleared her throat. 'So,' she began.

Whatever she was going to say, she had planned it beforehand. Sitting on the bus on the way here, or earlier perhaps, practising in the mirror while putting on her make-up, or earlier still, over breakfast with her room-mate. It was endearing, Peter thought, even if nothing good was coming.

'This is a little bit awkward,' she said. 'All right, it's a big bit awkward. The thing is, a good friend of mine is getting married next month and I would like a date for the wedding. I could go alone, obviously,' she added quickly, 'but the truth is that there is too much dead time at a wedding when you're on your own. All that initiating small talk or feeling you are intruding on someone else's romantic day. Plus all the questions. It leaves women… vulnerable. I could take a woman friend, I know, but I'm not braving those questions either.'

She was right, it was an awkward one, but he admired her directness.

'I'm not asking for a yes now,' she said. 'It's just… we're having a grand chat and you seem like you can handle yourself socially and I'm fairly confident you wouldn't let me go around with spinach in my teeth or my dress tucked into my tights—'

'That's a high bar you have there,' Peter said to ease her discomfort.

'Don't knock it.' She wagged a finger at him. 'On such things are successful weddings built.' Realising what she had said, she blushed all the way up the neck of her blouse and as far as her ears. 'That wedding. My friend's wedding, I mean. I didn't mean… oh, fuck it, I'm going to escape to the bathroom and hope you forget I said that while I'm there.' She turned after a couple of steps. 'It's on the 23rd of December, in case you want to check your diary or come up with an excuse while I'm gone. Either would be understandable.'

The date cut through his wondering how he felt about the invite. December 23rd was the day Fintan and Caroline got married. It was a popular time of year evidently.

Over their Monday night pint a few months out from the big day, Fintan had said casually, 'You'll be the best man, won't you?'

Peter didn't know what to say. 'The speech and the stag and the whole lot?'

Fintan took a gulp of his pint. 'No stag. For the love of God. One of the lads from work suggested a table quiz and a few drinks and that'll be enough fuss.'

'I can sort that out. A Fintan-themed table quiz.' Peter began to count on his fingers. 'Round one: Fintan's dodgy haircuts – your mother will sort me out with photos there. Round two: Fintan's dodgy music taste. Round three: girlfriends past. Hang on, that won't make a full round, although, no, wait, that headbanger from first year in college should be good for several questions.'

'Fuck off,' Fintan said. 'Or I'll demote you.'

'Just the speech, so?'

'Just the speech. Nothing big. Short is fine. No one listens to them anyway.'

'Take all the good out of my big moment in the spotlight, why don't you?'

'And I'll have you know my music taste was never less than impeccable,' Fintan said, laughing.

'You were dadrock before your time,' Peter reminded him.

'Classic rock,' Fintan corrected him. 'You wouldn't know a classic if it bit you in your easy-listening Top-40 hole.'

Best man. It was an easy, warm thing that Peter carried around with him. Right up until the night before the wedding, when his mind was as blank as the speech cards Noel had given him. Short was all well and good, but it had to be the right kind of short.

No matter where he started or what he said, he would get no more than a few lines in and be too overcome to go on. Lord, but if he carried on like that on the day itself, Fintan – and everyone else – would take the unmerciful piss out of him until kingdom come. He knew if he didn't get hold of himself, he would let them both down the day of the wedding.

He rang Sheila.

As ever, she was unequivocal. 'Get it out of your system.

Say it all out now and it won't bother you a bit tomorrow. You never step in the same river twice. Then sleep, that'll give your brain a good rinse overnight. And mind you remember to say nice things about Lynn as well.'

'Caroline,' Peter corrected her.

'That's what I said,' Sheila said irritably. 'Caroline. Give your ears a good clean while you're at it. Don't let the side down.'

Right, Peter decided. If he was going to do it, he would lean into it. He got a pillow off the bed and dressed it in a hoodie Fintan left after him one evening. He put it on a chair, with a baseball hat on top, and turned the chair slightly sideways. It didn't look anything like Fintan, but with a beer for ballast and looked at out of the corner of his eye, it did the job.

He recorded the whole thing on his phone. All the sentimental guff that would have no business being discussed on his friend's big day. Himself and Fintan. The past. The present. He welled up, then listened back and welled up again. Thanks Sheila. Before going to the church the following morning, he revised and tightened it so that when he delivered it later in the day, it hit the right note. Heartfelt without making anyone cringe.

Caroline's father stood up from the table and caught Peter's hand in his own two powerful hands. Butcher's hands, Peter thought, giddy with the speech done and the pressure lessening.

Caroline herself was particularly touched. 'You did a lovely job,' she told him. 'Fintan was lucky to have you to stand up for him.' She hugged him. 'I have you now, too, you know. That's how it works.'

'Are you all right?' Helen asked gently.

He hadn't noticed her coming back towards the table and hadn't a chance to wipe his eyes. For a minute he thought about blaming allergies or the wine, but the first glass was still half-full in front of him.

She gestured for two more coffees. 'Tell me,' she said. 'If you want to.'

He found he did.

To her credit, when he finished, she just squeezed his hand on the table. Didn't offer him the story of the friend who had it and beat it, or the friend who had it and didn't. He was grateful for her ease.

When their taxis arrived outside, she kissed him on the cheek. 'Think about the wedding,' she told him. 'If you feel like letting off a bit of steam where nobody knows you.'

'You'll know me,' he pointed out.

'I'll pretend you followed me in from the street,' she said, and they parted smiling.

The lingering smell of the fresh linen candle met him at the front door and for a split second he thought *someone is home before me.*

He had no reason to feel sorry for himself. Hadn't he a home of his own to go to and people who cared whether he was there?

As ever, his pep talks rang of Sheila. Their cadence and vocabulary hers entirely.

He should phone Noel back. He looked at his watch – it was early yet. Better, on balance, to wait until he was feeling a bit more like himself. If Noel asked him anything now, he would only have questions for him instead of answers.

Peter made himself a cup of tea. Well, he called it tea, but it wasn't. It was one of those chamomile and marshmallow root infusions that were meant to help you sleep. 'Fancy grass,' Noel called it when Peter tried to give him a box for Sheila.

He wondered if Helen was doing the same thing. At home, cup of tea in hand, thinking about things. Talking to her sister on the phone (younger, married, two teenage children. A bit of a sore point, Peter felt. There was something wistful in the way Helen talked about her) and saying… what? That he was too sad, that she regretted her offer and would have to find a way of getting out of it? Or that it had been pleasant, a worthwhile evening?

Maybe she was sitting with her flatmate. One at either end of a pale fabric sofa – pea green, he imagined, or a soft turquoise, with proper cushions – their feet tucked under them, having one last glass of wine. Women were good at that sort of thing. He wasn't sure what sort of thing he meant, exactly. The glass of wine with dinner had filed away the edges of his thoughts so that where they should fit together, there were cracks and crevices that would trap him were he to fall in.

Better at making friends and keeping them. Better at being on their own, too. Better at being in the world.

Such crap. It wasn't about men and women at all. Fintan had that same sense of ease in himself that drew people to him.

Peter's mother had the opposite, whatever that was. Some ineffable thing that drove people away.

Her funeral, when it came, was attended by a handful of people, most of them his – Noel, Sheila, Fintan and a couple of the lads from college. Karen. Retired by then, she said. His old school principal. One of the Christian Brothers. Peter watched him during the Mass and remembered how the other pupils used to laugh at the Brothers for their habit of patrolling the school grounds with their hands behind their backs. For the smallness of their lives. Peter thought it sounded kind of nice, knowing where you would be in a year's time, five years, ten. Where you would be buried. He was wise enough to keep that thought to himself.

There was a woman whose hands shook as she held his sleeve and told him that his mother was proud of him. That she told everyone who would listen about her son at university. He let her shake his hand and hug him, all the while thinking how weird it was that her grief for his mother outstripped his own. Thinking about how grateful he was for Noel and Sheila, for Fintan.

Fintan, whose funeral was surely next. Where the same people that stood up at his wedding a few short years ago would do the same for his coffin. They would listen to the words, to the mournful wail of the violins, and cry and kneel and remember and then go about their daily business because it was that or give up on themselves.

Humans and sharks. Keep moving or die.

It was only at his mother's graveside, when she was being lowered into the ground, that Peter looked his feelings in the eye and let his gratitude encompass his mother, too. For dying when he was too old for it to be formative, yet too young to feel responsible for her last days, unimaginable as they were.

'Heaven,' the priest said, again, and Peter wondered what heaven would look like for his mother. Whether it would be a syringe that was always full, or no syringe at all. Heaven and hell were so close together for her that they squeezed her out of her own life.

'What do you think it'll be like?' Peter could ask Fintan, if he had the courage.

It'll be an endless hurling match, but everyone is winning and there's no need for a ref or a whistle.

It'll be like being at a music festival, but the music is the very air itself and you breathe it in and become part of the joy of it all.

It'll be a comfortable chair, with a bottomless mini-fridge in arm's reach and a spyhole down onto what everyone is doing here so I can watch over you on all those awful dates and it'll be better than any TV show.

It'll be pitch-black, the kind you collapse into – weightless, relieved – when you've finished your final exam and everything you studied came up. Even Yeats.

No matter what he described, Peter would listen and nod and ask the right questions. The ones that would gather in the fear from Fintan's very heart and soul and take them into his own. *Let me carry that for you*, his questions would say and in his answers Fintan would relinquish some of his burden.

If the moment was right. If he covered Fintan's hand with his own and they sat quietly like that, in perfect accord or as close as it was possible to get, he might have the courage to ask his friend for help.

'Will you look out for Sheila when she gets there?'

Fintan would nod peaceably. 'I'll do better than that. I'll let her mind me.' And there would be the ghost of a smile between them.

What would he do without them? His two anchors. Each with an arm around him. Until now. He put his hands on his own two shoulders and took them away again so he could feel what it would be like. The slipping of their lives from his. Leaving him to stagger forward alone.

If Peter was being honest, he didn't think they would let him in at ten o'clock at night. That was the main reason he braved the front door at all. So he could say he tried.

The rules were different in this pale in-between place it seemed and when he gave his name, they checked a list and told him he could go right in.

'I don't want to disturb him if he's sleeping,' he said.

'You won't disturb him,' the woman at the desk said. 'Caroline said you could go in any time, day or night. That Fintan would want to see you.'

Was there any greater death knell than that of normal rules being suspended, Peter wondered as he walked down one corridor and then another.

The door to Fintan's room was open and Peter walked straight in before he could second-guess himself.

The room was quiet. Should he sit down by the bed? Talk? Pray? Trapped in indecision, he stood at the foot of the bed with his hands behind his back, like a county council worker overseeing the digging of a hole.

Fuck it.

'Did you ever notice…' he began, then had to clear his throat and start over. It took him a few words to get the level of his voice right – audible without being strident. 'Did you ever notice that the skirting boards in hospitals are always black?' Without Fintan to supply the other half of the conversation, he continued on by himself. 'To avoid scuff marks, I suppose. Sheila would say that must have been decided by a man. That every woman knows that grey is easier to clean than black.' He stopped.

Fintan didn't look like himself. He was thinner. No, it was a more thorough, more fundamental lessening: he was looser, slighter. There was less substance to him. His colour was different, too, shiny somehow, and his hair was wispy. Baby-like. As if he was letting go of his physical self.

Caroline was right – seeing Fintan made it easier to accept the idea of death as a taking-away of pain, rather than solely a taking-away. To expect Fintan to continue like this, stripped of everything that made him *him*, was to be unimaginably selfish.

Peter used to wonder what made people who they were. Oh, not out of any grand thoughts about the world, but from a selfish fear that he himself was unfixed, somehow. Hadn't he changed his accent, his interests, his life, after arriving at Noel and Sheila's? If personality was the story we told about ourselves, Peter worried that his was written lightly, or in pencil.

'Do you ever agree completely with something and then, not long after, find yourself agreeing with the entirely opposite thing?' he asked Fintan one night.

Fintan considered for a long moment. 'I read somewhere once,' he began, as he often did, 'that our minds are flat rather than deep. So we're not the product of our "deepest thoughts" at all. In fact, we don't have any deep thoughts. Rather, we're a million different possible things, with the lightest little touch needed to nudge us into who we are at any one time.'

'Do you think that's true?' Peter asked.

Fintan saw the question behind the question and parked the theorising for a minute. 'I think that people are generally either fixed or adaptable. Fixed doesn't mean stubborn and adaptable doesn't mean fickle. Of the two, I'd say adaptability has the stronger chance of social survival.'

Peter pulled the chair closer to the bed, wincing a little as it scraped on the floor.

'Sorry I was late. I had a dinner date. Helen, her name is. You'd like her, I'd say. No bullshit about her.'

What was he here for, if not to say what he needed to say?

'Sorry I'm late,' he said again. 'Really. I was putting it off. You know me.'

It was true, he did. Fintan had seen his fear all the years and never turned away nor thought any less of him for it.

Before starting university, Fintan's parents gave him his mother's old Ford Fiesta so he wouldn't be dependent on the buses for getting home at weekends. Their new gang of friends nicknamed it 'The Pimple' for its dirty-white colour, but Fintan didn't care. The lads in engineering – mostly country lads like themselves – didn't mean anything by it.

Not in the way Peter's law classmates would have. Around them, Peter said little, just got on with his work and let the references to schools and holidays and parties float past him. Instead, he spent his free time over in the engineering building with Fintan and the lads, reading his textbooks while they fooled around sketching and talking of inventing this or that and telling Peter he'd be representing all their business interests yet.

'You heading to the match tomorrow?' Fintan asked as they walked out of Mass on New Year's Day. Peter was fairly certain by then he didn't believe a word the church had to say, but it was easier to keep going than to disappoint Sheila. It wasn't the worst hour. He could sit and parse landmark cases there as easily as anywhere else.

'Not tomorrow.' Peter kicked a stone along the ground in front of him. 'I thought I might take a train, head east for a few hours.'

Fintan knew, of course. However he knew, he knew. 'I'll drive you, if you like,' he offered. 'I could do with picking up some library books on the way.'

That was what Peter told Noel and Sheila, that they were going up to the library for the day. With exams in a couple of weeks, it was an easy sell. It wasn't that it would bother them if he said he was going to visit his mother, it was more that their sympathy for her might take the wind out of his sails. He wasn't sure yet if he was intending to get angry with her, but if he did, then he could do without hearing Sheila's kindness in his ear. Her soft voice telling him to go easy, that his mother had it far harder than a human being should.

They didn't talk much in the car. Fintan chatted for a while about the Rialto Bridge – bridges were his thing that year – how the fact that it was the only fixed structure across the canal gave it a social and political role, but when Peter managed no more than a grunt in response, he turned on the radio and drove wordlessly.

At the junction where they should turn for the university library, Fintan just shook his head and continued east out of one city and towards another.

Peter had a map to get to his mother's apartment but found that once he was in the city proper, he remembered the way perfectly. Down towards the water, past the hotel on the right, then left up the hill, straight as far as the supermarket, then a series of little lefts and rights until they reached his mother's street. His old street.

'I won't be long,' he told Fintan, although in truth he had no idea whether he would or not.

'I'll be here,' Fintan said easily, taking his A4 pad and pencil from the pocket in the door of the car.

Peter climbed out and walked to the front door, wondering if his mother was looking down at him from four floors up. If she would recognise him. Hello was all he needed to say, he told himself. He wasn't looking for anything. He didn't need anything. All he wanted was to say hello. After all this time. After all the years. He straightened his shoulders and rang the buzzer as if he meant it.

Once. Twice. Nothing. Maybe the buzzer was broken. Beside him, a seagull picked at a cigarette butt – his mother's? – and he shooed it away.

On a whim, he buzzed the flat next door and, after a minute, the intercom crackled into life. 'Hello. Yes?'

'Hello. It's Peter Nyhan. I'm looking for Eileen Nyhan, in 4B?'

'This is 4A you're ringing.'

'I know. I thought… I wondered if maybe… is she still living here?'

'She's still in 4B, if that's what you mean. But she's not around much at the moment. In and out.'

'Okay. Thank you.'

Not around much. In and out. A phase he remembered. It was a miracle she still had the flat at all.

When he got back into the car, Fintan offered him an apple drop from a bag and they sat in silence for a minute or two.

'Do you want to look for her?'

'I wouldn't know where to start anymore.'

'Start anywhere,' Fintan said, but Peter shook his head. 'No.'

'Anywhere else you'd like to go? To see a friend or a school or a playground or something?'

Peter looked out the window. The seagull had returned to the cigarette butt and was pecking it along the ground. 'To be honest, it all feels like another lifetime. I think I'd just like to go home.'

'Home it is so.'

A few minutes later they were back on the road west. Back home.

Peter woke when a nurse slipped into the room. He went to stand, but she shushed him back into his chair. 'You're grand – stay where you are. I was just checking on him.'

'Is he… will he…' Peter didn't know how to ask the question.

She smiled gently. 'It's hard to be certain. We're keeping him comfortable and you're keeping him loved, isn't that it?'

The easy way she said it straight out.

'I am.'

'Well then.' She patted his shoulder and left as quietly as she had entered.

Her bravery lingered and Peter found himself taking Fintan's hand. 'I read somewhere once,' he said, but that was as far as he got. He wondered if he would ever again hear the expression without it piercing him. Maybe that was the way it should be.

He squeezed Fintan's hand and waited to feel an answering pressure. He yawned. He needed home and sleep and time.

Sharks and people, he thought.

He settled back into the chair. 'You sleep easy, Fintan. I'll stay put a while yet.'

SKY

SIS

When Sis woke, she was as stiff as poor dead Laddy in her lap. Every ounce of the bike's weight and every stone in the road announced itself up and down the length of her body. She had to knead her fingers deep into her collarbones before she could rise up from the floor. It was a longer matter to roll Laddy into the blanket and get him out into the front garden.

It was her own fault for putting off this day. For wanting the comfort of Laddy with her for as long as possible.

She stretched and creaked and heaved. At the home, she supposed, there would be someone to massage her shoulders for her. Whether she wanted them to or not.

The ground was rain-softened and for that she was grateful. If Frank were here, he would have called on one of the neighbours to take the body to the quarry lake, like all the dogs of the parish before him.

Maybe he wouldn't. Laddy was different. Frank might have been as glad as she was to think of him buried where the wild flowers would burst over him in spring, gathering together the bees that used to fascinate and torment him in equal measure. Bless him, he never copped that it was better to chase them than to catch them.

She stopped from time to time and leaned on her spade, looking at the Blue House lights winking in the predawn. The kind of lights that suggested a night-waking, a need for comfort. God love the woman. Comfort could be hard found when you lived alone.

When she finished, the sweat was fairly pouring down between her shoulder blades and the sky was lightening and she was sorely in need of a breath of sea. She had too much to do still and little time to do it. She could take her writing pad with her, she decided. Trust to the sea for the words.

At the top of the concrete steps, the fingers of her right hand opened reflexively towards the ground, dropping the lead she wasn't holding. She had coiled it in with Laddy, the nylon already saturated and softening. She slipped the stone into her pocket and continued down the steps.

It was slow going. One foot onto the step, test it under her, second foot onto the step. Slide her hand a couple of inches forward on the handrail. One foot down onto the next step. And so on until the safety of the sand, wet and firm in the wake of the outgoing tide. The waves were hushed, nearly, in the pearly grey light, their fierce power quietened.

In the days after Bunty's death, she used to come down at night and sleep tucked in against the rocks, her sorrow and fear so huge that the sea was the only container with the capacity to hold it.

'Make of that what you will,' she told the seagulls and they screeched their laughter at her foolish earthbound body.

She turned to look at the house, at the fine big double-glazed windows that were fitted after Radio Flyer came home in the 2.15 at Fairyhouse. At the time she thought them a foolishness. Why look out at something when you could step outside your own front door and be part of it? But a person took the good with the bad and if that made parts of their story less attractive, well… what else was it to be human?

Of her children, Mike was the one that loved the beach. Maybe because she used to bring him here as a baby, tucked inside her coat like trying to turn the clock back. She walked and walked with him and, as she walked, she talked to him about Bunty and sometimes she talked to Bunty, too.

The girls were frightened by her restlessness. She heard them with Frank: Cathy asking if Mammy was crazy, and Doreen back sucking her thumb as if they had money to burn on braces.

'She's not crazy,' he told them gently. 'She's just making space for it all in her head.'

'Does Mike coming mean she has to push Aunty Bunty out of her mind?' Cathy wanted to know.

To his credit, Frank didn't laugh. 'No, pet. She's just juggling it all around to make it fit. The same way you shake the dominoes until they settle and you can close the box.'

'And will the box close?' This from Doreen.

'It will, pet. It'll close perfectly in its own time.'

He was right. Time passed and she began to feel better and to sleep again in her own bed at night.

Mike left school when he turned sixteen, saying simply that it wasn't for him. They didn't argue with him. The girls were gone by then. Cathy to Dublin and then promoted to Canada. Doreen to Dublin behind her sister, then on to London.

They waited to see what he would do next. An apprenticeship, Sis supposed, or work of some kind. On a boat, maybe. Mike loved the water. But the weeks passed and Mike did nothing much of anything. Too young to sign on the dole, he took to collecting the children's allowance for her on a Tuesday and she let him keep it. A person needed money in their pocket if they were to keep their head up and look the world in the eye.

Frank didn't like Mike hanging around doing nothing. He was harder on him than on the girls. When Mike was small, and bold, Frank would send him in to Sis to be slapped for his transgressions.

'Sit on your hands hard until they're red, then tell Daddy I gave you three slaps on each,' Sis would say, tapping the side of her nose.

Who knew whether it was Frank's hardness or her softness that let their son down?

I think of you when I'm walking the beach, Mike, so you're the one with me the most. Not in an angry way. I don't mean it like that. More that I wonder how it could all have gone differently. If you and your father got on better. If you could have confided in me. If the girls had still been at home, watching you and picking at you and teasing you into living your life. If I had kept one eye turned to home instead of out towards the horizon.

Did I ever tell you that your dad stopped gambling for a while? It was never that serious for him – I know when I say that, you all think I'm codding myself, but indulge me for all the years I knew him and loved him, good and bad. When Cathy was born, he stopped entirely and it made him irritable. He would haunt the house on Saturdays or on the afternoons he wasn't working, breaking Cathy's routine, letting her sleep for hours in his arms. Oh, he had her ruined. Would things have been different if I weathered it out? But with one small baby and another on the way, to be truthful, I felt I was weathering enough.

I started giving him the job of lighting the range in early mornings, telling him that leaning my face down over it was bad for the child I was growing. At night I would prepare the twists of newspaper to use as firelighters and I started twisting them so that the horse racing showed. That's it. That's my great confession. It didn't take much, but I did it all the same.

What I want to say, I suppose, is that I don't want you to think it was all you. You have to take responsibility for your actions and I for mine.

A seagull landed on the sign for Bunty's Cove and looked at her. 'I had a dream last night,' she told the bird. 'Frank on one side and Bunty on the other and me in the middle not knowing which way to go.'

Bunty was suspended in time, in the dream, waiting for Sis. The way she used to sit in her chair just inside the open kitchen door, looking down the road for Sis returning from school. Bunty spent her life waiting. It seemed both entirely reasonable and entirely unreasonable to suppose that her death would be the same.

Sis ached to talk to her. She had so much to tell her. Low-cost flights and mobile phones. Velcro shoes and leather trousers. Love and sex and childbirth. Indian food. Vegans. The internet and rap music. Kitesurfers on their doorstep. The Blue House. The beach. So much to say always.

Frank, on his side, only stood looking at her. Steadily, the way he did. A whole lifetime they had had together, the good and the bad and the ordinary everyday.

The bird cocked its head to one side, waiting. 'What would you have chosen?' Sis asked, but the bird flew away, uninterested in her flightless nonsense. 'Yerra, what would you know?' Sis called after it.

What did she herself know? 'I carry no religion,' she said of herself and was satisfied with the truth of it. The reverse was also true: no religion carried her.

She had the sea itself to believe in. The sea in all its grandeur, its glory and gladness.

Overhead, the sun's fingers were curling around the sky's edges and time was getting away from her as quickly and surely as the tide. She started back the way she had come.

The steps loomed and she began to climb, the stiffness in her hip and knee after the night on the floor such that she had to swing her left leg in a wide arc to get it up on the step above. The handrail was cold, colder each time she slid it along to haul herself up another few inches. On the second or third step, she thanked her stars there was nobody to see and comment on her ungainly progress. By halfway up, she was grateful there was nobody to pity her or wonder who had let her out alone at her age and with her difficulty. But by the time she crested the final step, she was fiercely glad that her whole life had seen her able to come and go from the beach under her own steam. It wasn't everyone could say the same.

She took the stone from her pocket and held it in her hand, looking around her. In front of her, the hotel lay quietly, biding its time until the people returned and gave it purpose.

For years, she had worked the late shift, cleaning the spa and the meeting rooms, then later the restaurant, and later still, the bar. When she finished at 2 a.m., she gave herself half an hour to walk the beach before going home. To clear the noise before she could sleep, she told Frank, and he simply nodded and told her to mind herself. They were different times. Different fears.

From the beach at night, the hotel was its own skeleton. She couldn't help but look at it differently then. The way washing a person's naked body changed them for you.

She was glad it was closed now and she was spared the goodbye-ing that would be expected. The high talk she would have to endure about how she was the heart and soul of the place and there was a permanent welcome for her.

She had been in there once since retiring. Walked into the lobby and let them fuss around her and sit her by the fire and bring her a coffee. Endured their parade of well-meaning remarks.

'Sure you can't stay away from us, Sis!'

'Don't be rating us too harshly now, Sis!'

'I hope you didn't bring your white gloves, Sis!'

She smiled and nodded as they tried their hardest to make her feel she was still part of the team, when all she wanted was to feel like a guest and not the cleaner.

The sound of a car in the distance brought her back to herself. It must be close on nine o'clock, which meant it could be the bailiffs.

It could well be.

She wasn't ready. What kind of a streel would they think

her and she fairly sleeved in sand and with last night's water still in the bath? She didn't realise she was holding her breath until the car turned in the gate of the Blue House.

Enough wool-gathering, she told herself, or the reprieve would be gone itself and she would still be standing in the middle of the road. In the middle of the past.

The stone was warm in her hand and she bent awkwardly to place it in its usual spot at the bottom of the newel post before changing her mind and placing it back in her pocket. As she straightened up, she pressed the fingers of her free hand to her lips and then to the metal of the post. She snorted at her own carry-on. Imagine if anyone saw her! They would say she was no better than a tourist kissing the Blarney Stone.

She was really against the clock now. Should she eat or clean? If Cathy were here, she would know the right thing. Still dithering, Sis went into the bathroom and let the water out of the bath, wiping the scummy ring with a facecloth. There. That was one thing done.

She looked at herself in the mirror, the jagged crack down the middle. Her two faces.

Time is a great healer for grief, they say, but what they don't tell you is that time doesn't simply pass through you like standing in a stream. You have to wade through it, Cathy, uphill, like a salmon through a waterfall, with nothing but the raw belief that you can.

'You were never my mother,' you told me once. Oh, you may say it was during an argument and anything said in anger doesn't count, but you and I both know that's the one time a

person can be relied on to tell the truth. A heated-up version,
maybe, but the truth nevertheless. 'You weren't my mother,'
you said, 'I was theirs.' You had one arm around Mike and
one around Doreen and you believed it, heart and soul. That
much was clear.

When Mike left on that awful day, it was to Cathy he went.
And like any good parent, it was Cathy who continued to
support him and encourage him and provide news of him.

'Mike is doing well,' Cathy pronounced on that one ill-
fated visit to show her children her home place.

She had waited until the children were in bed, the better to
savour her small power, Sis suspected.

'Although he doesn't feel he can visit, he wants Dad to
know that he is all right and that he is grateful for… what he
did for him,' Cathy continued.

'Just Frank?'

'You're hardly in a position to demand more, as the person
who threw him out of his home. Did you even stop to think
about what it took for him to start over?'

Sis made an effort to keep her voice low and even. Frank's
sleep was fitful enough these days without a shouting match
in the kitchen disturbing him.

'Where do you think he would be now if he had stayed here
in the same town with the same so-called friends? How long
would it have taken for all the hard lessons to be unlearned?'

Cathy tossed her head and refused to hear it, herself robust
enough to imagine that anything could be withstood.

We are alike, Cathy, you and I. More than the others. You
won't want to hear it, but that doesn't change the truth of it.

I can admit to you that I envy you your certainty, your
ability to make a life for yourself where before there was
nothing but blank space. I will follow your example now
and make a fresh start and believe that I, too, can make the

unfamiliar familiar. Who knows but I might surprise us all and make new friends and a new life for myself.

Imagine! You meeting my friends when you come to visit, before taking me out for a spin to the town or to the beach or somewhere we can sit and talk the gentle talk of people who have made their peace with each other. When I think about joy, that is what I think about.

She sealed and stamped the three envelopes and put them in her coat pocket. That was one thing done, even if all else had failed and around her was a silent kitchen with its presses still full of mismatched crockery and glassware.

No matter. The bailiffs would be here shortly and that was all right too. She was ready. She had her memories and that was all she would carry with her. Everything else belonged to the house. To the past.

LYDIA

Lydia woke to the delicate insistent fingers of a hangover. *There are no winners here*, it whispered, petting her dry eye sockets with its dirty fingernail.

She swung her feet out of bed and was met by a scatter of tablets on the floor. She bent to pick them up to flush them away, her head spinning as she straightened.

She bent again, straightened again, spun again.

It was heady, knowing precisely what caused the world to tip and right and tip again.

In the spare room, she got on her exercise bike and pedalled slowly into another day. *There are no winners here.*

Did Andrew think she was engaged in some kind of misery-off with Mary? Was that what he thought this was about? That it was some kind of monstrous selfishness that saw her seek to centre herself in Nick and Mary's story? Did he think it was all for show, something she hoped he would mention to Mary?

And was it, Lydia?

She pedalled harder, away from the answer.

'She can't cope with the accident,' Andrew told the counsellor, his hands tap-tap-tapping his knees.

'*The accident*,' Lydia repeated. 'He can't even say it.'

'What would you like him to say?' The counsellor was unflappable.

'I hit a cyclist with my car and destroyed his life and destroyed his mother's life. I had a glass of wine and I chose to get in the car and drive home, so *stop calling it a fucking accident!*'

'Lydia. He—'

'Don't.' Lydia found herself shaking. 'Don't you repeat that tabloid muck. I can't bear it.'

The papers had made much of Nick's blood-alcohol limit. 'It was a one-off,' Mary told reporters. 'A few drinks at a leaving do for a friend. He isn't – wasn't – a big drinker.'

But even that shift in tense didn't stop the sideways headlines. The descriptions of *Nick's ill-fated boozy evening*, complete with vacuous testimony from the barman as to what was ordered and how often and for whom.

Lydia read on, waiting for Mary to snarl that he was on a bike and had done nothing wrong, but Mary made the mistake of answering only the questions she was asked.

'I'm just trying to help,' Andrew said to the counsellor, with a desperation that was unattractive. 'To balance things out. To be fair.'

'Not fair,' Lydia said. 'Nothing can ever be fair.'

She stopped short of saying the rest of it. That if that outcome seemed fair to him, then he wasn't the man she thought he was.

It wasn't goodness or kindness that held her tongue, but the fear of his inevitable reply: that she, too, was not the woman he thought she was.

She might be the next best thing to a murderer, but she was no fool.

Andrew just sighed. 'Don't twist my words. All I want is for us to find some way to get past this.'

'For me, you mean. For *me* to get past it. You are already over it. You opened your wallet and bought yourself your night's sleep,' Lydia said with a cruelty even she found remarkable.

'Is it not enough that two lives are ruined?' Andrew asked her later that evening.

'I won't survive if I stay here,' she told him. 'Make it happen, please. Please.'

Her hands shook as she showered. Shook as she made the coffee. Shook as she opened the blinds. Shook as she took her sight line against the predawn grey uniform of sea and sky. Shook as she watched Sis Cotter walk slowly past her gate with no sign of the dog at her heels.

Lydia made a mental note of the time in case a phone call needed to be made later to the guards. 'It was three minutes past eight, Garda. I made sure to check. I thought she looked a little uncertain. A little flushed, maybe. Mrs Cotter is usually well wrapped up, but she had no coat on and no dog with her, which seemed unusual.'

How kind and civic-minded she would sound. How very neighbourly. Dressed in her grown-up clothes and reasonable words, she would appear entirely functional.

That was all it took to fool the world. Everyone more than happy to hear 'I'm okay' and move on.

The sky over Sis Cotter was heavy. With her bent back in her thick jumper, she looked like she was shouldering it for the world.

Lydia watched her walk. If we stopped pretending, she wondered, would the sky fall?

The GP's receptionist was severe, her words at odds with the sing-song of her accent. New Zealand, Lydia guessed. Or South African. Something southern hemisphere in it anyway. The sun. Or optimism.

'We require forty-eight hours to issue a repeat prescription,' she told Lydia. 'I can do it today for you, but you'll have to come in.'

'Do you make house calls?'

'In certain circumstances. Can you give me a reason you might need the doctor to come to you?'

Lydia looked out at the heavy sky. 'I hit someone with my car.'

'Right. It's the ambulance you need. I'll—'

Lydia continued. 'It's nearly two years ago now. Nick, his name was. Is. He's still alive, although it doesn't look anything like a life anyone would want. His mother might disagree. My husband, too. Ex-husband. They're friends now. Which is nice for them, don't you think?'

'It sounds like you're having a tough time, Lydia. Can I ask if you're on your own there?' The receptionist's voice was slow and careful, as if trying not to startle her.

'I'm not going to hurt myself if that's what you're thinking. That's not part of the deal.'

'What deal is that, Lydia?'

'They live, I live.'

'Lydia, I'm going to put you on hold for just one second and check if the doctor can speak to you straight away. Can you wait on the line for me?'

At least there was no music. Lydia felt that music might just be the last straw.

'The doctor is just going to have a quick word with you, Lydia. Putting you through now.'

Convincing someone of the soundness of your reasons for being afraid of everything outside your own front door was a puzzling argument for sanity, Lydia thought, but the doctor didn't remark on it.

'I'll do you a script for a week at a time,' the doctor told her. 'And I'm going to make you an appointment to speak to a counsellor locally.'

'I can't—'

'It can be by phone or online. Whatever suits you.'

'I didn't know I could—'

'Not a bother, Lydia. Sure haven't we plenty of remote people and places that need help as much as those in towns?'

The relief was powerful. The practicality of it. Small-town doctors had seen everything, Lydia supposed. Nothing surprised them.

'We'll do a phone check-in three times a week and if anything changes, I'll be out to you straight away,' the doctor added. 'In the meantime, take it easy on the drink while you're taking the tablets. It's easy to forget what you've taken, so very little to drink, okay?'

'I have a box,' Lydia told her. 'You know, a days-of-the-week one.'

'That's good, Lydia. It's good to be organised. Even so, next to no alcohol. All right?'

Outside the window, a tiny stripe of horizon was appearing between the sea and sky. The sky lifting its head, looking forward.

'All right.'

Lydia took the last tablet from the box in the kitchen and returned to the window to wait.

For the magic to kick in. For the miracle delivery from the pharmacy. For Sis Cotter to return safely home. There was no end to the waiting Lydia was capable of.

She rocked back and forth on her heels. Whoever said waiting was passive had never stood in a window and watched the clock. Every cell in her body was braced in the action of waiting.

When I was a reader, Mary, I read stories of the wives of the polar explorers. I was fascinated by them. The way their lives, too, were given over to endurance and perseverance. One foot in front of the other, around and around their own small enclosures, while the men navigated the world and all its spaces and praises. I think of them often, Mary. All those virtuous women, waiting.

[Delete. Delete. Delete.]

A flash of headlights announced Sofia, cheerful in her little car with the ubiquitous phone clamped to her ear. Lydia moved away from the window, not wanting to exert pressure on the young woman. Still, she willed her to hurry up and come indoors.

'Sorry, sorry!' Sofia called as she closed the front door behind her.

As if she was entering her own home, Lydia thought. Emphatic in her right to be there. Her right to be startling and noisy and cheerfully apologetic. Unlike Lydia herself, who paced silently, afraid to disturb the very air around her.

'How are you today?' Sofia called over her shoulder, already on her way to the kitchen with her bucket and her caddy of cleaning products.

She would assume that Lydia's answer was lost in the clattering and splashing from the sink, Lydia told herself. Nobody sane would imagine that she simply didn't know how to reply.

'I know it is not December yet,' Sofia said, pausing on her way through the living room, bucket in hand. 'But if you need extra work before Christmas, tell me and I will make a note.' She smiled and continued on her way.

Christmas. The thought was enormous.

Last year, Andrew had done everything: the decorations, the turkey, the cake, presents under the tree. Aftershave for him, perfume for her. *Presents of least resistance*, she used to call them, back when she laughed at people whose imaginations stretched only as far as the nearest chemist. When really they were simply sad or tired or trying their hardest to hold on to hope.

That Christmas evening, while Andrew dozed off the effects of the wine with dinner, the brandy after, she scrolled to Mary's feed. Photo after photo of the day, a colourful montage of celebration. Nick in front of the tree, football merchandise piled high beside him and a crested blanket draped over his shoulders. Nick at the end of a laden dinner table, a paper crown slipping sideways on his head. Mary and Nick together, their faces squeezed into the frame, Mary clinking her can of Fanta to the one on the arm of Nick's wheelchair.

Happy Birthday to my favourite person! And Happy Christmas to everyone else! With love to you and yours from us and ours! Mary & Nick #gratitude #holidays #family

Her favourite person. Who was Lydia's favourite person? she wondered. Did she even have one?

Was she anyone's?

If she needed extra work done before Christmas, Sofia had said.

Lydia could refuse to entertain the idea of Christmas at all. It wouldn't be abnormal. It wouldn't even be remarkable. Plenty of people didn't. Whole cultures, even. She could be just one more person for whom December 25th was simply another day.

Take Sis Cotter, for example, who was now walking slowly homeward on her own, still no sign of the dog. What kind of Christmas would she have? Midnight Mass, perhaps. Candles and carols and a good wool coat. On the television, maybe, if the roads were bad or it was too cold to risk her health. Then a day surrounded by her children and grandchildren. Not allowed to lift a finger. Spoiled and centred and fussed over. One of the children put out of their bed so Granny Sis could sleep over. So everyone could have a drink and nobody had to die for their enjoyment.

Sis Cotter would want for nothing.

While Lydia was putting on another pot of coffee, Sofia appeared beside her in the kitchen.

Seeing Lydia, she pulled out her earbuds. 'True crime podcast,' she explained. She shook her head. 'The things people do. It would blow your mind.' She popped them back in again and continued her work.

Sofia thought that exposure to the worst of people's nature would blow her mind. She looked at Lydia and saw someone whose concern was the upcoming Christmas holidays rather than her immortal soul.

She looked at her and saw normal, instead of someone whose name was stamped in police records and news bulletins and the daily papers. The details in black and white, complementing the technicolour memories in her head.

Herself driving with the radio on loud. One hand firm on the wheel, the other tapping along to a pop song from her youth, as if she was still as entitled to be carefree. A teeny-bopper, her mother used to call her. That was the thought in her head at the time, imagine! Of it all, somehow that seemed the worst thing. The sheer casualness of her thoughts. As if, driving, she could afford to let her attention wander where it would.

She didn't see him. Not in her peripheral vision. Not in a vague 'what's that?' kind of way. Not unconsciously. Not subconsciously. Not according to the counsellor, or – shamefully – the hypnotist she went to when she couldn't eat for the effort of swallowing down the hours and days.

The truth was that the first she knew of him was when he hit her windscreen.

The first she knew of herself was when he hit her windscreen.

Now there is a permanent statement of her character. Should she be tempted to forget, to forgive, it is all there, waiting to remind her.

It rains a lot here, Mary. When it is dry, I stand in my window and I wait for the rain to start again so that I can feel, briefly, like everyone else, in my wanting to be indoors.

That's the truth and it is also a lie, Mary.

The whole truth is that rain is clean. It is like looking at your own feelings, your insides pulled out and painted on the windows for the whole world to see and understand.

How pitiful you would find me, Mary, if you didn't find me monstrous.

[Delete. Delete. Delete.]

When Sofia was finished and gathering her things together, Lydia joined her in the hall. 'Do people still give neighbour gifts at Christmas? I was thinking of getting a little something for Mrs Cotter. Just a token. Biscuits. Some nice cheese. You know the kind of thing.'

'Oh, but she is leaving today, I think,' Sofia said.

'Her daughter must be coming to pick her up.'

'I don't think so. Someone said her family is not coming.' She flushed, as if she had said something she shouldn't. 'I couldn't help overhearing.'

Not all families were close, Lydia reminded herself, stemming the rising panic. The absence of Sis Cotter's family did not mean that a person could succeed in pushing them away.

It did not mean that, repeatedly told to leave her alone, they finally took her at her word.

'Someone will buy it for a holiday home, I imagine. Summer people.' Sofia brightened. 'Hopefully they will need a cleaner. If they ask, will you recommend me?'

'Of course,' she said, and Sofia smiled as though Lydia's word was worth a damn.

Without the sound of someone else moving about the house, the silence gathered in the hallway until Lydia felt cloaked in it. If it was true that Sis Cotter was indeed leaving today, then

Lydia would be left alone here at the edge of the world. She sat on the bottom step of the stairs and put her head between her knees to stop the roaring in her ears. She might be on the shore, the waves crashing about her and the seagulls shrieking, pitiless, high overhead.

'Get a fucking grip,' Mary might tell her.

Mary used bad language rarely, Lydia had noticed. But always when it was called for.

'If anyone is having a pity party around here, it shouldn't be you. Don't cod yourself that your sacrifice is for my son. It isn't your place to do anything for him. To build your life around him. Who do you think you are?'

Live your own damn life.

Just because no words can express how sorry I am doesn't mean I shouldn't try.

The doorbell, when it rang, reverberated through her body and frightened the breath out of her. Sofia, she thought. Having forgotten something. Or the taxi, with her prescription. Hopefully not Danny Creed again. She felt like the merest hint of philosophising might pierce and shatter her, vampire-like, on the tiles.

It was a long moment before she processed that it was Andrew on the doorstep.

Seeing her, he held up both hands, in fear or in surrender.

'I know you said not to come,' he began, 'and I've tried to give you space, but I was listening to the radio and I heard…' He took out his phone and scrolled through his notes. 'Hang on. I want to get this right.'

He was the wrong generation for voice notes. She could imagine him, repeating whatever it was over and over until he could safely pull the car over and type it out.

He cleared his throat. 'If all you see is the dark, the light will blind you,' he read.

The unexpectedness of it froze her in the doorway.

'Someone said it. On the radio. And I thought of you,' he said. 'I wondered if that was what it's like for you.'

She could drive him away with words.

She could ask, rudely, 'What *what* was like?' Then list the options. Waking every day to the lives she had ruined. Knowing that if she lived a hundred years' worth of days, each more miserable than the last, it would still be more freedom than she deserved. More than she left Mary and Nick with.

She could let him in, even knowing that to do so would invite it all in with him. All the pain and the expectation and the failure and the disappointment. But who was to say it wasn't already in here, inside herself?

Over his shoulder, she saw the silver flash of a car as it navigated the last of the bends before the end of the road. The car stopped at Sis Cotter's gate, but nobody got out. Maybe they never would, she thought, and Sis Cotter could continue in her house as if nothing had changed.

Yet what good would there be, what joy or lightness or relief would be found, knowing that the car was idling out on the road? The axe always falling, falling, and Sis Cotter never able to take a step for fear of where it might land.

Lydia looked at the phone in her hand, the open message, the blinking cursor.

Just because no words can express how sorry I am doesn't mean I shouldn't try.

'Does she hate me?'

'You're not a bad person,' he told her. 'We're not bad people.'

'Does she hate me?' she asked again, and it seemed as if everything hung in the balance.

Say it, she willed him.

Say it and be in this thing with me.

'Yes,' he said simply.

Lydia looked at him in his unsuitable suit and his shiny shoes, every inch the tourist, the summer man.

Send.

'Will you come in?' she said.

PETER

How was it, Peter wondered, that a person could go to bed suffused with peace and goodwill yet wake up full of fury at the level of death and disease and needless pain in the world? As if goblins had spent the night ploughing the calm of his mind into furrows of monstrous anger.

He looked at the address on the file. West. Of course it was. West was him and Noel and Sheila and Fintan and Caroline and every bit of the past and the pain.

He was in a fouler before he ever got to the house. If the little baby Jesus himself had crawled off the footpath and out onto the road, Peter would have hit him a wallop of the car and lost no sleep over it. It was that kind of a morning. Some days it was hard to pin down the whys of a mood, but other times, like today, there was no mystery to it. He'd felt it circling him in the office earlier as he looked at the single name on the list, black rage settling like a crow on his shoulder. Everything in him tightened as he headed west. The hedges with their height and their wild disorder stealing his breath bit by bit until he was nearly dizzy behind the steering wheel.

Parked outside the gate, he looked again at the file while he gathered himself. *Sis Cotter* it said still, not having had the decency to change itself while he was driving. Sis Cotter. An old-lady name, he'd lay odds, the kind nobody went in for anymore. God but he hated the old ones. Arguing the sentimentality of every scrap of paper, their eyes milky with beseeching and blame. To say nothing of the children – grandchildren, too, sometimes, just to add to the commotion – waiting to rip into him for reflecting their own shortcomings back to them.

The doorbell was broken. Of course it was. More blackguarding. More likely the bell never worked at all and was only there for show, like one of those empty alarm boxes cute hoors fixed to the fronts of their houses to guard whatever few bits they had. He gave the door a couple of thumps with the side of his hand, the gesture reminding him of those long-ago hurling matches. Noel in his hand-knit jumper. Himself decked out in a shiny tracksuit top and shinier faceful of acne. The two teams in the appropriate colours of the day. The terms of endearment for the game masked in tried-and-tested terms of abuse for the match officials. Fingers greasy with cheese-and-onion crisp debris curled into fists and making that side-to-side motion. *The referee's a wanker.* Noel frowning, upset at the encroaching of football hooliganism into this traditional space. Noel wasn't a man for change. Peter sighed and thumped the door a third time. Lucky number three.

Finally, there was a noise from inside the house. The dull thump of slippers on carpet. Mid to late-seventies, he guessed, from the shuffle of the footsteps. Anyone under thirty ran to the door nearly, eager to eff and blind, to curse him and the sky over him and all related to him. The over-forties came at a measured speed that gave them time to marshal their arguments. To call to mind their days of suit-wearing, throat-clearing corporate speak in glass-walled meeting rooms on the top floors of now-empty buildings that echoed with nonsense and regret. They were the beggars and the pleaders, the ones who still believed their tunnel of debt was open at both ends.

The door opened a crack and for a moment he thought she was one of the tinfoil-hat brigade, the ones that barricade the door as if the law can be left outside on the doorstep. But no, she kept going, pulling and tugging and swearing under her breath at the wood and the warping ways of the rain. He itched to add his weight and speed her up, but the rules said he couldn't touch a thing until his name and purpose were stated and acknowledged.

'Mrs Sis Cotter? I'm Sheriff Peter—' he began, once the door was opened fully and she could meet his words squarely. His fairness in that regard was a point of pride with him. But he got no further.

'Hold on!' She raised a finger and let it sit in mid-air, as if trying to remember a song lyric. Or a particularly obscure European capital. One of the former Soviet states, maybe. 'The front door hasn't been used in years. Why didn't you come around the back?'

'Mrs Sis Cotter? I'm Sheriff Peter Nyhan.' He stammered a little, foolish in the intimacy of her name. 'As of November 12th, the courts found in favour of—'

She waved away the words. 'I know all that. Didn't the solicitor woman phone and tell me.'

'Bank of—'

'Shites,' she finished. 'Save your breath and say no more. She read it all out over the phone. Nothing to be done, she said. The house was in Frank's name alive and in Frank's name dead and it's gone with him. That's the holy all of it.' She nodded as if the symmetry was somehow satisfying. 'You're the bailiff, I suppose. Is there just the one of you?' She looked beyond him, left and then right, as if expecting to see reinforcements lining the road.

'The sheriff, actually,' he corrected her, as if it made a jot of difference. 'I'm afraid I have to read it all—'

'What kind of a title is that at all?' She shook her head, then half-sang, *'There's twenty-one young men I have put bullets through and Sheriff Pat Garrett must make twenty-two.'*

Peter stood on the doorstep, his clipboard a poor defence against singing.

'Sheriff Pat Garrett. Boys oh boys. You'd better come in so.'

She turned and moved down the hallway without checking to see if he was following. By the time he opened his mouth to refuse, she had disappeared into the gloom. He took his time following, not wanting to crowd in behind her. His presence was threat enough. Her wispy-haired head put him in mind of a dandelion clock, the way it bobbed, as if a good-sized cough would blow her away. Or one of those push-out exhales they taught Sheila to do to keep her calm when she couldn't remember if she was today or yesterday. He lifted each boot up behind him and craned over his shoulder to check the sole was clean – the first thing Sheila ever taught him – before stepping over the threshold and closing the door.

'You'll have tea.' Sis Cotter was fussing around with a kettle, opening the hatch on the range and poking at the small bit of fire with a stick evidently kept there for the purpose. Flesh-coloured tights and other old-lady things were drying on the rail over the range, like a skin that had been shed. He averted his eyes, feeling like a peeping Tom for having caught sight of them.

'I'm all right, thanks.'

She ignored him and put out two cups. 'Sure I have it on now.'

It wasn't unusual to be offered tea. Some people when they saw Peter were glad the sheriff himself had come. Some puffed up a little bit, as if his presence made them somehow more important than the wheeling drunks or the misfortunes who had melted their lives into syringes or the would-be high-flyers suckered into the myth of the economy almighty. The sheriff, he could see them thinking, gave a touch of class to the repossession debacle.

Even so, Peter was uncomfortably aware that the last person to make him tea had done it just so she would have something to throw at him. That particular lady had flung it too low, hitting him square in the breast pocket of his overcoat, before heaving out dry, monstrous sobs, half-wild at her own helplessness. He had ignored the unpleasant seeping warmth and told her it was all right; he was after putting in a good drop of milk and the tea was half-cold. Grateful for that small kindness, she was as good as gold after that and handed the keys over as meek as a kitten.

'You weren't above in the court yourself?' he asked Sis Cotter now.

Sociability was a fine line to walk here. Small talk in these kinds of situations was fairly fraught. Chat about the weather and he seemed flippant. Start straight in with asking which of the court-allowed necessary clothes and bedding they wanted to keep and he was callous. Stick to the material facts; that was his credo since the tea-throwing incident. Announce himself and his business, then wait by the car until they were gone. Keep the emotion out of it. Under no circumstances go inside.

'I was, in my eye. Who'd sit above in the dock like a pig at a fair? Not Sis Cotter, I can tell you that much!' She banged the lid of the teapot for emphasis.

'Sis isn't a nickname you hear much anymore,' he said.

'It isn't a nickname at all. My mother's sister, the baby and the pet of the family, passed on just before my mother had me. My mother was determined I'd be called Sis after her.'

'Is that right?'

'There was all kinds of holy hell with the parish priest, of course. Nothing would do him, only that I'd be Bernadette, and Sis then for a nickname. But my mother stuck to her guns. She refused to be churched, said she'd rather die with the stain of my birth on her soul unless the priest agreed. And he did, faith. Sis and Bunty the two of us were christened, not four miles down the road from here.' There was an odd sort of pride in her voice.

Peter cast around for an appropriate comment. 'That took some courage in those days, I'd say.'

'It's on my baptismal cert if you don't believe me. On Bunty's death cert, too.' She eyed him with suspicion over the rim of the teacup.

'I wasn't questioning it,' he said hurriedly. 'God knows—'

She snorted. 'God doesn't know very much at all,' she said. 'I think you'll find that fella is misinformed about a lot of things. Drink up your tea there or it'll be gone stone cold.'

She seemed disappointed in him and he found himself wondering why he had even mentioned God. It wasn't as if he was religious. Mass on Christmas Eve and a handful of funerals hardly counted. It was just the way he spoke to old people: a heavy emphasis on God and the weather, often together – fine day, thank God – and with a touch of an accent he must have accidentally contracted during his fortnight in Irish college the Easter before the Leaving Cert. And there he was thinking all he brought home to Sheila was a bag of dirty washing and a few new spots.

He put his cup down on the table. 'No family around today?'

By now they would have been in on top of him if they were here, he knew, unless they were busy in the bowels of the house, stuffing bags and pillowcases with whatever came to hand. He didn't give a continental damn what they took with them. The house itself was his business. The big ticket item.

'They're long grown and gone. Since Frank passed, it's just myself now.'

Nobody to give her a hand, imagine. Having disliked her family earlier for their assumed presence, he was surprised to find he despised them as much – or more – for their absence.

'Are they living around locally?' he tried again.

Not that it was his business where a person went when he closed their front door behind them. But still and all, let her have family nearby.

Not for the first time he thought the judges should have

to accompany him and see their dirty work in action. Maybe then they'd be slower to find in favour of the banks. He knew it wasn't their money, but every time he met a bank manager, he had the urge to follow them home and peg stones through their front window.

'Scattered to the four winds, the lot of them. Cathy in Canada. Doreen in London. Mike in Spain.' She ticked them off on her fingers. 'I wouldn't leave Ireland if you paid me,' she said, as if it were entirely natural to stay forever in the one place, as rooted and immutable as regret.

Peter had seen the same blinkers come over Noel in recent years. His insistence on seeing choice where there was only circumstance. His intransigence about caring for Sheila himself at home was the tip of the iceberg. No matter how many times the public health nurse sat him down for a sensible chat, Noel resisted all offers of outside help, stubbornly insisting that Sheila would have no truck with strangers.

'Is there someone you can call?' Peter asked Sis. 'To help you get your things together.'

'What things do I have to get together, sure? I thought it was all belonging to the bank now, every last bit of it. Right down to my dirty drawers.' She gave a quick, decided nod, seemingly pleased at the idea of the bank dealing with her underthings.

'A certain amount is yours by law,' he explained.

'What does that entail?'

'Clothes, bedding, the tools of your trade—'

Another snort. 'They have their own bedding above in the county home.'

He nodded, although in truth he had no idea if they did or not.

'Would you let your parents finish up in the county home?' she asked suddenly.

'I… never really thought about it.'

'Fine for you.'

'No, I mean, they are my foster parents. So it's not something I... It wouldn't be my decision.'

He thought of Sheila's Bible, his name carefully lettered on the family page under hers and Noel's. The way it appeared there one Christmas, as black and white as her favourite old movies, but was never spoken about.

'Foster parents, is it? What was wrong with your own?'

It was years since anyone had asked. Not since the schoolyard. He used to daydream answers – *witness protection* or *spy mission* or *exploring. Dead*, sometimes. Followed by grisly details of car wrecks, fires, failed rescues. He would see Karen's car pull up outside and be overcome with terror that she was coming to tell him his mother was dead and he had wished it on her.

Sis was looking at him, waiting, and he settled for the simplest answer. 'Drugs, mainly.'

'You know the state system so.' She took his empty cup to the range and poured him another.

He was grateful that she offered no apologies. Most people told him how sorry they were, as if they were the ones to fill his mother's veins and lay her out on the floor.

Sis got to her feet, levering herself up and out of the chair with her two elbows. 'I'll gather my few bits and not be keeping you. You'll have other houses to visit, I'm sure.'

She left him at the table with his tea and his thoughts. It was the usual uncomfortable partnership and he didn't last long, but had the phone out of his pocket while her feet were still sliding along the hall carpet. If he were to touch her, he thought, the electricity would jump from one of them to the other like nits in a playground.

He should ring Noel. Sitting in this dim kitchen with its sweet-and-sour old-person smell, he was ashamed of having put it off for so long. For being so quick to accept it when Noel said he was fine, thanks, Sheila was fine, thanks, they were all fine, thanks. It was three months or more since he had stayed a night with them. The truth was it was hard to go there anymore and harder still to stay. Talk was slow and television the only relief. Daily news and farming chit-chat drifted past him and he half-listened, glad he didn't have to retain any of it. Noel refused his help putting Sheila to bed, telling him they had their routine down to a T; it wouldn't take him more than two shakes. He came back to the kitchen a full hour later, a bottle of beer in each hand for them. Smiling away as if Peter hadn't heard the raised voices or what sounded like Sheila crying. They drank in silence and watched a detective show. Afterwards, Noel went to bed and Peter went out into the yard to look at the stars. They were a thing he missed in the city. Out here he could see them grand and bright, but Jesus the silence could be terrifying. It was hard to know if the one was worth the other. He felt like the last person on Earth and had a child's urge to run into the house and down the hall to Noel and Sheila's bedroom to check they were still breathing.

They never expected him to make the farm his life. There were days he thought it was because it would never be his and days when he thought they, too, had a secret belief that somewhere buried in the murk of his DNA were thinking men, men of words rather than men of earth. They were good that way. Seeing the possibility in him. They were good in every way. He should drop in on them when he finished up here. Their corner of the back of beyond wouldn't be much out of his way. He had nothing to bring them, though. He would have to go in with his hands hanging. He ran a quick inventory of the contents of his car, but there was nothing that would do. Even Noel would baulk at a squashed breakfast bar.

He could make it a quick visit. Just checking in. Arrange to come down and stay a night in a couple of weeks' time. Five or ten minutes was Sheila's limit anyway. She became agitated in company, sending up a musty waft of day-old baby powder with every restless kick of her legs in the bed. He would put on the kettle before going into the back bedroom to her and leave the door open the way she would hear the kettle whistling and tell him to go out and have his tea before it went cold. In the final scrambling of her brain, hospitality would be the last thing to go. In the kitchen, Noel would sit across from him and they would open with the weather. Then, Noel would ask him about work and not listen to the answers and he, in turn, would ask about local doings and not listen to the answers, and then they would revisit the weather until the tea was drunk. Peter would intend to stay longer, to have a second cup, to really ask, really listen, but in the end, he would stand up from the table and stretch and offer to rinse the mugs, knowing that Noel would shoo him away and tell him he had nothing else to be doing for the evening, and all the while he would be wishing himself into the car and east. Into the quiet of the road and the radio and the sun warming his right shoulder through the window.

Sis was taking her time. He gave her another minute or two, washing their cups in the sink and looking around the worktop for a tea towel. There was one hanging above the range, but it was flanked by her underthings, and he didn't like to lean in over them, just in case.

Down the narrow hallway to his right, a thin plastic sheet protected the centre of the carpet from wear and tear. That pride didn't extend to the edges, which were coming away from the skirting boards, their frayed hems lifting like brazen teenage skirts up and down Patrick Street the night the exam results came out. He wondered when he had slipped into the middle-aged habit of frowning slightly at them. Early on, Caroline, seeing him, had rolled her eyes and told him that women could wear what they liked and if he had a problem with that, he could move east or west where they would no doubt welcome him. He protested that he was thinking of the girls' safety, but that, it appeared, was just as bad and backward.

The first door down the hallway was a bathroom and he was relieved to find it empty. It was old-fashioned, with lino on the floor and painted walls instead of tiles. No shower, just a bath faintly ringed with dirt and with a low step-stool beside it. Peter wondered suddenly if Sis would have been better off to slip and fall and die there on her own before he ever darkened her door. Before whatever little future awaited her came calling.

The next set of doors were locked and he moved on. She didn't seem the type to barricade herself in in protest at the turn her life had taken. He found her in the room at the very end, standing in front of an open wardrobe, her arms hanging limp and empty at her sides. Damp bloomed on the wall behind a double bed neatly made up with old-fashioned sheets and blankets. For a minute he thought of Sheila tucked under her duvet twenty hours a day or more. Her 'continental quilt', she called it when she bought it first. She had got one for him, too, as a surprise, and the three of them nearly smothered from the heat until she realised there was no need for the blankets as well.

Sis stood beside the bed, a long-life plastic bag in her hand. On the bed was a small deck of postcards wrapped with a thick orange rubber band, and a set of rosary beads.

'I took Bunty's rosary, of course. I hid them the day they laid her out. My mother was bone-dry with anger. She didn't understand they would be no good to Bunty underground. If she was in heaven, she wouldn't need them. If she wasn't, well…' She patted the beads where they wrapped around the bag. 'But then I got stuck,' she told him, turning away. 'On Frank's pyjamas, of all things. There hasn't been a night since my wedding day that I didn't have his pyjamas next to me, whether he was in them or not. Only I wasn't sure if they counted as my essentials. I thought maybe they'd be taken off me.' Her shoulders trembled slightly and he gripped his phone in his pocket so as not to put his fist through the flimsy wood panelling on the wall.

What kind of useless hoor of a solicitor did this poor woman have at all? Some big company, no doubt, who looked no further than her dead husband's misunderstanding of their mortgage affairs. They probably drew straws to see who'd have to take her on. He had come across their like in his time, back when he was training as a solicitor. They were exactly the kind that drove him out of the law in search of something better. From the frying pan into... not so much the fire as into hell itself. The irony of it could kill a person.

Sheila never remembered his failure, either pride or disappointment wiping it out when he tried to remind her. 'Are you the solicitor?' she would ask, beckoning him in close, while Noel fiddled with biscuit packets and plates and pretended he heard nothing. 'Come here till I ask you...'

For Sheila, there was no such thing as a small grievance anymore. Everything was magnified inside the shrinking circumference of her world. After the diagnosis, Noel took her to New York, fulfilling her bucket list while she still knew what a bucket was. Shortly after returning home, she announced she was going to sue Hollywood. New York was ruined for her, she said crossly, by the feeling of having seen it all before. Worse, she added, than finding out on her wedding night that all the fuss was for very little in the finish. He hadn't known where to put himself. Behind him, Noel broke the silence with a clatter of crockery and some off-key whistling. Even now, Peter worried when he visited that she would tell him something he had no business knowing. Caroline told him that loss of inhibition was part and parcel of the condition. She had seen it in her own mother, she said. It was better not to dwell on it, the way that even that little bit of border was crumbling to nothing.

'You take whatever you want, Mrs Cotter,' he said, his voice coming out as thick as the time he had swollen glands. 'I'll take nothing away from you, sentimental or otherwise.' He moved to the doorway, intending to leave her be. He could wait in the car, the way he should have done in the first place.

'I'm worse than a teenager,' she said. 'You'd swear we hadn't spent the years arguing, Frank and myself. There was nothing we didn't quarrel over. Put two halves of an apple on the table between us and we'd find a way to make a fight of it.'

'I know,' he would have said, except he knew nothing of the sort.

'"An argument stitches you together" my mother told me every time I was in tears on the bed. A lie of good intentions, you know, but it left me certain that stormy meant hidden depths. Frank liked a good set-to, sure of course I thought it was love. I used to wonder what the children made of it.' She gave a little tut. 'They're all with people who wouldn't say boo to a goose, so that put an end to my wondering.'

'That's the way of it, I suppose, for long marriages,' Peter said from the doorway.

'Are you married yourself, Sheriff Pat Garrett?' she demanded.

A handful of times in his life he might have wished he was, but it was fair to say this wasn't one of them. 'I'm not, no.'

'Any romance at all?'

He marvelled at the casual intimacy of her inquiry. They might have been at the wedding of a neighbour, just two fellow parishioners idling at the church door. Lynn was the nearest story he had. Sis seemed like she would appreciate the value of a strong woman. A woman who knew her mind and what she wanted. But if she probed – as well she might – he would have to admit to being exhausted by Lynn's unrelenting views on everything the world held. The state of the nation, foreign policy, the accuracy of the weather forecast, the colour of a neighbour's front door, all of it met with immediate, confident commentary. If he had mentioned his balls, she would have known more about them than he did himself.

There was Helen. Or there might be, if he got his head straight.

'No,' he said. 'No romance at the moment.'

'Much you know about it so.'

She moved hangers from one side of the wardrobe to the other until she came to a dress wrapped in plastic. This she lifted out, peeling back the covering and pressing her fingers to the modest lace collar as if feeling for a pulse.

'My wedding dress,' she told him. 'It still fits me, you know.' Her laugh crossed the room to him. 'I put it in the will that I'm to be buried in it. That'll be one in the eye for Cathy and Doreen. For all their faddy diet nonsense and their I'm-worth-its, neither of them has a figure worth a damn.' She turned to him, her forehead anxious. 'They'll have to honour that, won't they? If I put it in the will, they can't just ignore it, sure they can't?'

'That's a long way off yet—' he began.

Sis snorted.

'But I'm sure it'll be just the way you want,' he tried. A useless nothing wish if ever there was one.

With the dress back in its plastic wrapper and folded into the bag on the bed, her movements became more certain. A hairbrush. The Bible from the bedside locker, a more battered version than Sheila's. Her nightdress, with Frank's pyjamas folded into it, causing Peter to look away and wish himself somewhere else. Someone else.

Last into Sis Cotter's bag was a black canvas notebook tied together with a shoelace, a bookies' pencil tucked inside.

'I could take the tools of my trade, you said. I suppose you were a college boy, were you, Pat Garrett? Here, see can you read that.' She took the notebook out again and thrust it at him.

On each page was a series of lines and squiggles that could have been anything from Ancient Greek to ignorance-exposing modern art, to some kind of coded war artefact. He squinted one eye, then the other, but it made little difference. 'I can't make sense of it. Sorry.'

'Pitman.' She nodded with something like triumph. When he handed the notebook back to her, she caught his hand and held it. 'Shorthand, you know. We learned it, all of us girls. The teacher told us it would open the doors to the world. It was more than that he opened for some of the slower girls, God forgive the dirty bastard. But that was the way of it. We did what we were told.'

Jesus, Mary and Joseph. She had a tight hold of his hand in mid-air, as if he were that long-ago teacher whose smutty intentions needed to be held at bay.

'It's all in here. Every morning I write in it, no matter good or bad. The bright days when there's a lightness to the air. The dark days.' She looked at him closely. 'You've the look of a man who knows the days I mean, Pat Garrett. The days when even the washing hangs crooked on the line...' She let go of his hand. 'No one but myself can read it, but that's no matter. Sure who'd have time to be bothered with an old woman's rawmaishing?'

He massaged the ridge her thumbnail had left in his palm. 'Everyone is entitled to their say,' he said and meant it, although the loan of his two ears seemed a meagre enough offering.

'That's all we're left with these days. Everyone having their say and no one listening. It's worse than nothing. What do you say to that, Sheriff?'

He should say there was all the time in the world to listen. He should say nobody was ever too far away for help. But it sounded hollow even inside his head and he didn't give it much chance of surviving Sis Cotter's social scrutiny. 'I'd say it sounds lonesome,' he said finally, because that was the truth of it.

In the kitchen, she emptied the bin and he opened the back door so that she could drop the little bag in the wheelie bin outside. A solitary chicken scratched around for scraps and Sis moved it casually aside with the instep of her foot. A move he could have done with when he arrived in Sheila's yard, homesick for the noise of the city. The chickens were worse torment than the gangs. They couldn't be bought off with fags nicked from ashtrays on tabletops and open handbags.

He followed her across the cracked concrete yard to a five-bar gate, where they leaned and looked out into the small field beyond. It held nothing but a low mound of rotting beets, shivering here and there from the delicate movements of the rats inside. He wrinkled his nose against the vinegary smell and she laughed a little unkindly.

'Nothing as sour as what used to be sweet,' she said. 'There comes a time when we all know that full well.'

He watched as she caught the chicken and placed its neck between two longish sticks, stepping neatly onto the overlapping edges and, with a practised hand, pulling the chicken's legs straight upwards until they heard the crack of its neck yielding. Into the wheelie bin it went, landing on top of the rubbish bag with a dull thump. Sis straightened up, one hand knuckled in the small of her back.

'That's better,' she said. 'Tidier than all that headless running around.'

He was suddenly desperate to be out of there, away from the smell of rot and other people's business. The place would steal his sleep and his peace from him, he was certain. That night would find him sleeping on the couch in his jocks – he could feel it bearing down on him from hours away – dreaming uneasy dreams of houses that got smaller the closer he got, until he woke, thick-tongued, in the middle of the night and stumbled to his bed.

'Why don't you take your time and just pull the door out behind you when you're ready, Mrs Cotter?' he said. 'You can post the key back in through the letter box. I'll be passing again in the morning.'

He felt a flicker of relief, a loosening of his knees and the Celtic knot in his ribcage where his heart and lungs and stomach looped and leaned on one another. He could call to Noel and Sheila as easily tomorrow. She was sometimes better in the mornings, in fact. More herself. The weight of the day not yet fully felt. He could pick up some fresh bread on the way or a paper bag of the fruit scones Sheila liked. A pecan plait for Noel. He had a fierce sweet tooth. A mouthful of them, as Noel himself said. He could give Noel an hour off, suggest he go into town for the paper or a walk or a pint. Whatever a man that age did to relax. Or they could sit at the table with their talk and their tea, side by side, the way the truth might have a chance to slip in between them.

Sis stood at the gate with her face held up to the fading sun, her bag at her feet. 'I'll do that,' she said. 'If you're sure it's all right. If you say so.'

'Just pull the door out behind you,' he repeated and crossed back to the cold of the kitchen.

'Dereliction of duty. Boys oh boys,' she said.

But when he turned to reply, to absolve himself, she was looking out into the field and might have been talking to herself or to no one at all.

The car was cold and Peter put on the blower to warm it up, his temper rising with the heat. What kind of children had Sis Cotter, to say they wouldn't be here with her? London, she said one of them lived. Hardly the moon, was it? Easier than coming from Dublin, even. What good was family if they didn't stick it out with you? They probably left with hugs and promises that it wouldn't be for long. Probably believed it, too, for as long as they were saying it.

He popped in the cigarette lighter even though it was years since he had smoked. That was Fintan's one regret, he had told him cheerfully at the last table quiz before his test results. 'If cancer's going to get me anyway, I wish I hadn't knocked the fags on the head.' Peter had stared at his shoes as if they might be a question in the next round and then asked if he fancied a bag of crisps instead. He should have gone and bought him a box of Carroll's instead. Shown him there was no judgement. Ever.

Peter missed the quiz team, the routine of it. Sitting around the small table with their mobile phones in plastic bags in the centre of the table to avoid accusations of cheating, talking about football in between the rounds. They might start up again, he supposed, after a decent interval.

This'll give you a laugh, Fintan. I sat through the football matches on a Wednesday night so that I could join in the table-quiz chat. Paid the fucking Sky Sports subscription month after month just to feel part of things. Did you know that? I'll tell you something for nothing, if I knew in school that fifty would be within roaring distance and I'd still be watching sports to fit in, I don't think I'd have made it through.

The car was suddenly too hot. Grabbing his jacket from the passenger seat, Peter got out and headed towards the beach. A little farther along was a big blue house. The kind Sheila would have called handsome. Comfortably big without being ostentatious, with picture windows looking out over the sea. It could be in a magazine, if it had a garden rather than that poor little square of concrete with a handful of skinny shrubs. As he walked, a woman came and stood in the window, a steaming cup in her hand. He raised his hand to wave, but she was looking into the distance, to the left first and then the right, as if tracking a bird. He found himself looking up as well but saw nothing.

A little way further ahead was a set of concrete steps, then the hotel. Shortly after Fintan booked it for the wedding, they had come down for the weekend, Fintan and Caroline, Peter and Fiona Anne. A *covert mission*, Caroline called it, although she had grown up in the shadow of the place, nearly, and everyone from the barman to the cleaners knew her.

Fiona Anne and himself weren't together long and they didn't survive the weekend away. It didn't help that when she suggested a surfing lesson, he agreed, giving Fintan a gentle dig in the ribs to stop him laughing. It seemed easier to pretend to enjoy it than to explain that he wasn't one for physical activity. Women didn't trust a man who didn't like sports, for all they pretended to go for lads who were into cinema and music. He struggled into a rented wetsuit, afraid he looked like he was trying to stuff a sausage back into its casing, as if the beach on an Indian summer day wasn't already hellish.

He got sunburned on his forearms and neck where the sea washed the sunblock off the exposed skin. Not to mention he was crippled after the surfing itself. Internal injuries, it felt like. As if someone had tied a rubber band around his ribcage and was waiting to see how many of his organs they could squeeze out of him. He didn't know how he made it back to the hotel room without vomiting. Fiona Anne got amorous then – of course she did, in the room with the big white bed and the beautiful view – and he had to pretend he had food poisoning rather than let her down. The following morning he had to sit with a black coffee and a piece of toast, trapped in his charade, while she read the paper and all but ignored him, the romance as dead as the half a pig on her plate.

He was as well off. He had spent the weekend half-wondering if he mightn't enjoy the wedding better without her to look after.

Peter went down the steps and onto the wintry beach, where the shades of grey in the sky, sea and sand could rival any Dulux chart. It was a restful, undemanding kind of colour. Maybe he could go for a pale grey in the living room instead of white. Dove grey and ochre. That could work. Unfussy but with a hint of personality.

He was the only person as far as the eye could see, which suited him. The beach in winter had a solidarity to it that you had to be alone to feel.

He set off across the beach, wishing he hadn't left his hat in the car. Thinner hair came with such responsibilities, he thought, and felt his chest burble and lighten.

As he walked, he could see the big blue house on the hill

above him. The woman was still standing in the window, with a man beside her, the two of them looking out over the water, their elbows almost touching. He thought of Sis Cotter sleeping with Frank's pyjamas under her pillow.

Nowhere was lonely if you had the right person with you. Even here, out at the edge of the world. The right person and peace of mind.

Maybe Lou was right and you just did the best you could. Got through the days trying to make life a little easier, a little better. Not everyone could cure cancer, but not everything was cancer, either.

At the end of the beach was a small sheltered area. *Bunty's Cove*, the little wooden sign said, and Peter remembered Sis saying she had a sister called Bunty. This must have been her favourite spot.

To live in a place, to love a place, to leave a place. None of it was easy.

He sat on a rocky outcrop and looked out to sea. A man was swimming, his head seal-black against the pale grey of the waves. A dog paddled along behind him, barking companionably, as if pointing out the sights. Solo used to be the same, all chat, but people didn't really bring their dogs on days out back then.

Once upon a time, Noel and Sheila brought himself and Fintan to the beach.

'I thought the sea would be blue,' Peter said to Fintan as they stood with their feet perishing in the waves, each pretending they were considering going in further once they got used to it.

'Can't be,' Fintan said. 'The sky is grey, so the sea is grey.' He glanced at Peter and added casually, 'Because the sea reflects the sky.' Then he picked up a piece of seaweed and threw it at Peter and they stopped pretending they were going to swim at all and went back to pottering and exploring and messing.

Peter took a deep breath. Even the air smelled of salt.

Noel answered after a couple of rings. 'How's the sheriff?'

'I'm working near the coast today, so I came down to the beach for a walk,' Peter said.

'I can hear the seagulls as clear as if I'm there with you,' Noel said easily.

'I was remembering the time you and Sheila brought us to the beach. Years ago.'

'Yourself and young Molloy,' Noel said. 'He brought a badminton set, wasn't it?'

Peter had forgotten the badminton set. The waves of mortification that rolled over him when Sheila insisted on taking a turn hitting the shuttlecock, the sweat darkening her blouse from her armpit nearly to her elbow.

But Fintan had cheered her on and applauded her efforts. 'Unlucky!' he called when she missed, or 'Nice one!' when her racquet connected, and Peter's waves of embarrassment receded and stayed gone.

Even when Noel rolled his trousers up to his knees while resisting all suggestion that he remove his socks, too.

Even when Sheila undressed down to a faded navy swimsuit that showed her dimpled thighs and got in the sea for a few brisk strokes.

Even when she unpacked the picnic and realised the tomatoes had turned the bread soggy.

Unlucky! Nice one! Nothing tastes as good as a sandwich at the beach! Fintan's easy acceptance was a glow inside Peter's chest.

'He's not doing so well, I hear,' Noel said. 'Fintan.'

'Not well at all. Not much left in it now.' Peter picked up a piece of seaweed at his feet and rubbed it between his fingers, letting his voice settle. 'I thought I'd come down tomorrow. Maybe stay the night, if it's okay. Spend a bit of time with Sheila.'

'Sure you don't have to ask. We'd be delighted to have you. I'll turn on the radiator in your room and have it nice and warm for you,' Noel said, pleased.

'If there's anything you want to do – head out for the evening or whatever—'

'What would I want to go out for? Wouldn't that defeat the purpose of you visiting? Wait till I tell Sheila. She'll be delighted. She'll have me straight into town for the good biscuits.'

'Don't go to any trouble.'

'You were never any trouble,' Noel said. 'I doubt you'll start now.'

When he hung up, Peter stood and walked towards the waves, the soft sand hardening under his feet as he neared the surf.

'I don't know what I'll do,' he said to the sea.

The sea said nothing, just continued to roll in, wave after wave.

Peter bent and picked up a stone, smooth from the sand or the waves. It smelled faintly of brine. *Now is not then. Here is not there.*

He put the stone in his pocket. With any luck, the sea smell would last until he got to Fintan and, even if it didn't, he could remind him of that day on the beach. The badminton and the soggy sandwiches and the sea belonging to them all.

SIS

Sis looked from the keys in her hand to the bike with its buckled wheel and back again. She put the keys in her pocket and touched the three envelopes that rested there. Leaving her bag inside the gate, she pushed the bike to the Blue House, leaning it against the wall where the car in the drive wouldn't hit it. It wasn't the cleaner's Clio, she noticed, but such noticing was no longer her business.

Not here, at least. There would be plenty of noticing to be done where she was going.

She took the three envelopes out of her pocket and placed them on top of the pillar of the Blue House. There was no good getting sentimental, nor was there any point in wishing things were different.

Take care of each other, she had written at the bottom of each letter. *Your Aunty Bunty told me once that it was easy to find joy, you just had to be on the lookout for it. Keep each other alert for joy and once in a while you might write or phone and tell me about it all. It might be modern to talk of the family you make, but spare a little space for the family that made you too. There's love enough to go around if we can look beyond the wrongs of the past and know that we are loved. Whether first or last, we are loved.*

Glancing up at the house, she saw a man standing in the

window, Lydia beside him. Her big eyes and pale face, the same as if all the years had rolled away.

Sis took her beach stone from her pocket and pressed it to her lips before placing it on top of the envelopes.

Lydia watched her all the while, but that was all right, too. She nodded to Lydia, just the once, then turned and walked away. The letters were gone from her now. They were in the lap of the gods. In the hands of Frank and Bunty and the Blue House. They would find their way to them, she was sure of it.

That was the thing with people. They did the right thing, if you let them.

Sis stopped outside her gate. The next time she opened it, it would be someone else's. Overhead, the sky was changing into its evening wear, fire-tipped still where the sun's low bow dipped it below the sand dunes. Sis looked to the beach and saw them all there: Cathy reading, Doreen dreaming, Mike dragging a stick to write his name in the sand. Frank running into the wind with his two arms out like a bird. Bunty with her head tilted to one side like a seagull herself, the rocks soaking up her quiet laugh.

They would be here still, she knew. The sea cradled them all. They were as much part of the landscape as the storms and the sea and the sky.

The sea alone was the present and she would be back again.

They would never be strangers, she and the sea.

THE END

ACKNOWLEDGEMENTS

I spent Christmas 2019 in my favourite place with my favourite people. My then-one-year-old dog, it turned out, did not like being away from home and did not understand the idea of apartments, startling every time someone next door walked around or flushed the loo or opened a packet of crisps. So I spent Christmas night on the sofa with her, trying to get her to sleep or at least to stop barking the place down every second minute. Around 3 a.m., I began to think idly about a character from a short story I had written a couple of years earlier. She had popped into my head from time to time in the intervening years, sometimes butting into something else I was writing, sometimes just muttering and commenting, always exactly and entirely herself. In the quiet of that (very) early morning, I gave her a bit of time and space and a couple of hours later, I knew the shape of Sis Cotter's story. I also got to sit on the balcony, coffee in hand, and see the sun rise over Inchydoney beach, so it turned out to be a pretty good night in the end – thanks, Scout!

Thanks to Legend Press – to Cari, for loving this novel immediately and taking such delight in it, and for her precise and thoughtful edits. To Olivia, for her work in getting it out there. To the Legend team, who have done the best possible job with three of my novels now – thanks Tom, Lauren, Lucy, Sarah, Ditte, Liza and Anthony. Special thanks to Rose Cooper for the tone-perfect cover design.

Thanks to my lovely agent, Hannah Weatherill, for her gentle certainty about the things that worked and the things that didn't and, especially, for making sure I held onto everything I loved about the story and the characters. Thanks, too, to all the Northbank Talent Management team for their support and encouragement.

My writing group, Rachel and Sylvia, are always the first to meet my new characters, and their generous, patient suggestions keep me focused and sane and – above all – excited, especially in the maelstrom of an early draft, when the burning question is always: 'is this even a story?'

Ireland is proudly, brilliantly supportive of its writers and artists. I was very grateful to receive an Arts Council literature bursary in 2020, which allowed me to dedicate regular time to thinking, writing and editing *Winter People*. It was the first time I could give full days to writing, guilt-free, and it did wonders for my focus and my confidence.

Support from bookshops is both fantastic and necessary and I'm really grateful to all the lovely booksellers who stocked, advertised, recommended and invited me to sign my books. Particular thanks to my local-local, Bookstór Kinsale, and to Waterstones Cork, Vibes & Scribes Cork, Dubray Cork and Carrigaline Bookshop for making publishing in a pandemic (twice!) feel magically connected and vibrant. If you love reading, then please continue to #ChooseBookshops and the wonderful people that work in them.

Particular thanks to Bloodaxe Books for allowing me to use some perfect lines from Matthew Sweeney's poem, *Dialogue with an Artist*, from his 2018 collection, *My Life as a Painter*. Matthew encapsulates in three lines what took me a whole novel, and I am grateful to have his words accompanying mine.

Winter People is here because *The Ghostlights* was here because *Where the Edge Is* was here… so heartfelt thanks, as always, to the book reviewers, bloggers and readers who gave those earlier stories their time, energy and expertise. To read is one thing; to read generously and open-heartedly for the writer and for other readers is something special – thank you all so much, *míle buíochas libh go léir*.

Winter People was written during the first Covid-19 lockdown, when the theme of lives lived in parallel was foremost in all of our minds and experiences. For days and weeks, I walked along the beautiful estuary in our village, watching the swans and hearing the seagulls and remembering to breathe. I read poetry. I listened to the Desert Island Disks back catalogue and lived other people's fascinating lives in forty-minute chunks. I spent hours in my own company, alternating agitation and calm. Alongside all that were the phone calls gratefully repeating the same-same-no-news-all-fine-here. Many WhatsApp threads of friends holding each other up, keeping each other grounded, pulling us tightly together, accommodating anxiety and boredom and bursts of giddy joy. Drinks and jokes and short videos and planning things knowing they would likely be cancelled and still trying to make the best of it and find the joy. Thank you, my lovely friends, for all of it.

Thanks to my family, Murphys and O'Connors and Fays, for unconditional support and for celebrating what we can when we can. Special thanks, as always, to Dee – sister, friend and the first person I pick up the phone to, no matter if it's good news or bad or indeed no news at all.

I am lucky enough to have several formidable older women in my life and I held them in mind whenever Sis Cotter came to a crossroads in her story. Thank you to Auntie Kay and Auntie Kathleen, in particular, for always living by your own lights.

To Ali, whose memory keeps me company and who will never be left out.

And finally, my love and thanks to Colm, Oisín and Cara, for letting me be alone when I need to be and bringing me back in when I need that too. I'm sorry I thanked the dog first.

(Le) Grá